ALL THE THINGS WE NEVER KNEW

SOPHIE RANALD

Storm
PUBLISHING

This is a work of fiction. Names, characters, businesses, places, events and incidents are either the products of the author's imagination or used in a fictitious manner. Any resemblance to actual persons, living or dead, or actual events is purely coincidental.

Copyright © Sophie Ranald, 2025

The moral right of the author has been asserted.

All rights reserved. No part of this book may be reproduced or used in any manner without the prior written permission of the copyright owner. This prohibition includes, but is not limited to, any reproduction or use for the purpose of training artificial intelligence technologies or systems.

To request permissions, contact the publisher at rights@stormpublishing.co

Ebook ISBN: 978-1-80508-979-7
Paperback ISBN: 978-1-80508-980-3

Cover design: Rose Cooper
Cover images: Shutterstock

Published by Storm Publishing.
For further information, visit:
www.stormpublishing.co

ALSO BY SOPHIE RANALD

The Love Hack

The Fall-Out

All Our Missing Pieces

The Girlfriends' Club series

P.S. I Hate You

Santa, Please Bring Me a Boyfriend

Not in a Million Years

The Ginger Cat series

Just Saying

Thank You, Next

He's Cancelled

The Daily Grind series

Out With the Ex, In With the New

Sorry Not Sorry

It's Not You, It's Him

No, We Can't Be Friends

Standalone romcoms

It Would be Wrong to Steal My Sister's Boyfriend (Wouldn't It?)

A Groom With a View

Who Wants to Marry a Millionaire?

You Can't Fall in Love With Your Ex (Can You?)

ONE
ANNA

They say the wife is always the last to find out.

I like to think that wasn't true in my case: the shame, the humiliation, the sense of having had the wool pulled over one's eyes, was bad enough without imagining that everyone else had already known. That everyone – our friends, the school mums, Gray's colleagues – would have been whispering behind my back, exchanging messages on WhatsApp groups I didn't know existed.

It's been going on for over a year.

> *Poor Anna, she has no idea.*

Sometimes it's easier to be in denial.

I like to think that Gray was careful enough – discreet enough – that not many people knew before I did. After all, he was good at keeping secrets. Although, of course, back then, as January turned to February, the relentless gloom of winter seeming as if it would never loosen its grip, I didn't know that either.

After eighteen years of marriage, I thought I knew all there was to know about my husband – or at any rate, all I needed to know.

The way he mumbled to himself as he emerged from sleep in the mornings, although he didn't snore any more. The way he'd often stop, distracted, halfway through getting dressed, one sock on and the other concertinaed over his toes. His hatred of bananas and classical music, so the first were banned from our kitchen and the second endured only if I listened on noise-cancelling headphones.

That makes it sound as if he was an intolerant man – one of those domestic dictators you hear about sometimes, cruel to me and impatient with his children. But he wasn't. He was gentle and funny and generous. He always made time for the kids, listening when Lulu came to him with her friendship worries, cheering from the sidelines when Barney played football. He was always laughing.

When I met him, I thought I'd found the perfect foil to my own introversion – a man who'd always be at the centre of things, always cheerful, always looking on the bright side.

Perhaps over the years the laughter and silliness had dwindled, along with the sex. But that was normal, I told myself, it was to be expected from two busy, tired, stressed people with growing children. We were still close. We were still kind to each other.

But over the past year or so, I'd noticed sometimes I had to say something to him two or three times before he heard me. And there'd been his ever-demanding work, his cycling hobby that took him out of the house for hours or often whole days. I'd found myself increasingly snappy and resentful, sometimes engineering rows over minor, stupid things (the garden paving still unjetwashed nine months after I'd first asked him to do it; the cashmere jumper of mine he'd ruined when he put it in the washing machine with his cycling kit; the cat's food left uncovered to gather flies) just so I'd have the chance to vent at him about the big things.

You only think about yourself.

It's like you have no respect for me at all.

I'm not your bloody support human, Gray.

So not so kind after all, then.

I'd even caught myself browsing the internet for little three-bedroom houses outside of London, imagining what life would be like if it was just the children and me.

But then reality would kick in. I could never leave. I loved Gray. I loved our life together. I loved our house – number eight Damask Square. It had been ours for almost as long as we'd been together. We'd poured years of work and money into it, burying ourselves beneath a mountain of debt I'd thought we would never escape, and now it was finished, perfect.

Almost perfect. I glanced up at the crack that had recently appeared on our bedroom wall, where the salvaged Victorian cornicing met the Shadow White-painted plaster – *We'll need to get someone in to look at that* – and then back to the bundle of socks in my hand, which I'd been sorting into pairs prior to putting them away in Gray's drawer.

Then I noticed the jeweller's box. It had fallen open, tilted on its side, and I picked it up without thinking to close it and couldn't help catching sight of what was inside. Earrings. Diamond earrings.

I stood there for what must have been a minute, looking blankly down at the open box in my hand. Low afternoon sunlight falling through the window caught the gemstones and threw a rainbow of colours on to the wall behind the chest of drawers – they would cast similar light on the wearer's face, I knew, lighting it up like only high-quality, well-cut diamonds can.

I'd never owned a piece of jewellery like this. My engagement ring had come from a stall in Spitalfields Market; Gray and I had bought it the afternoon he'd proposed, giddy with cheap Riesling and love after a long lunch on Brick Lane. The ring was vintage, an opal set in silver, and the stone had chipped round its edges over the years. I've since learned that opal isn't generally used for engagement rings for that reason.

These diamonds would never chip. They were the real deal – perfect round solitaires set in what might have been platinum or white gold. My engagement ring was precious and I loved it, but these were in a different league.

They were beautiful. Objectively, breathtaking. But my breath was taken away for a different reason. Gray had bought these, clearly intending them as a gift for someone who wasn't me. The box still resting on my trembling right hand, I raised my left and touched my earlobe, as if I needed to confirm to myself that it was not and never had been pierced. I imagined the earrings there, sparkling against my skin. I imagined telling people, smiling, *Yes, they were a gift from Gray*, and them thinking, *Lucky woman – he must be mad about her, even after all these years.*

But they weren't mine. I was not that lucky woman, and it wasn't me my husband was mad about.

Apparently.

I fought the urge to take an earring out of the box and inspect it. There was no point – I knew what they looked like and, in the midst of my shock, I was aware of the risk of dropping it and losing it between the floorboards. That would take some explaining – explaining I was nowhere close to ready to do. I put the box on top of the chest of drawers, its lid still open, Gray's sock drawer still ajar, and sat down on the bed, suddenly feeling weak and sick.

I took my phone out of my jeans pocket and navigated to the Liberty website, tapping on the Jewellery tab then navigating to Fine Jewellery, Earrings and on to Diamonds. And there they were – the fifth item out of thirty-six listed, just the same in the picture as in real life. The name of their designer was there, along with their carat weight and, of course, their price.

More than four thousand pounds.

My throat made a dry, clicking sound as I swallowed. Four thousand pounds – it was more than I spent on myself in a year. Not because we couldn't afford it, but because over the years I'd become accustomed to thrift – to looking on Vinted for clothes, tinting my roots myself at home, going to the local council leisure centre instead of to the swanky gym a few blocks away that did hot yoga and had an on-site massage therapist. There were more important things to spend our money on, I told myself.

And clearly my husband felt the same.

My mind flashed to our daughter – to Lulu. She'd be sixteen in summer. Perhaps Gray, in a moment of madness, had decided that a piece of fine jewellery was an appropriate way to mark the occasion?

But Lulu couldn't go more than a month without mislaying her school blazer, her phone or her house keys. Her flakiness drove Gray mad sometimes. He'd never splurge on such an expensive gift for her, knowing that she was likely to lose them almost immediately – and certainly not without discussing it with me first.

And Lulu's birthday was months away, anyway. It was February now: February the thirteenth. The day before Valentine's Day.

No, the earrings were not for our daughter. Not for me, either. They were for someone else. Someone Gray wanted to surprise with a beautiful, expensive present that she would treasure for ever.

Someone special.

TWO
LAUREL

As I turned off the motorway, Taylor Swift's 'Everything Has Changed' began playing on the car radio. I turned the volume up and my speed down, but I felt like I was flying. I felt like I'd felt on holiday as a child, the moment I stopped whining, 'Are we there yet?' and caught my first glimpse of the sea through the car window.

I felt impossibly happy, yet at the same time almost sick with excitement.

Taylor's voice was muted by the satnav telling me to turn left in five hundred metres, and I forced myself to focus, think about where I was going, keep my eyes on the road.

Half an hour later, I turned on to a long gravel drive, and saw my destination up ahead, illuminated by the headlights of my beaten-up Toyota and shrouded by the misty drizzle that had been falling ever since I left London.

I followed the signs to the car park and slotted in next to a silver Mercedes coupé, parked at a contemptuous angle across two parking spaces.

'You don't need to be embarrassed,' I told my car. 'You've got as much right to be here as anyone else.'

Pulling my bag out of the boot, I wished it was easier to follow my own advice.

I crunched back around to the front of the building, where stone steps led up to a pillared portico. My foot turned over on the gravel and I tripped and almost fell, bursting in through the door into the warm, rose-scented lobby. I could feel my face flushing and I was sure my hair was frizzing from the rain.

If she noticed my discomfiture, the polished blonde behind the reception desk gave no sign of it.

'Good evening, madam. Did you have a good journey?'

'Yes. Yes, thank you. I'm meeting... We've got a room booked for the night.'

She glanced down at her computer screen. 'Mrs Graham?'

'I... My...' Fuck it. There was no way I could explain or correct her without looking like even more of a twat than I already felt. 'Yes. That's right.'

'Mr Graham arrived a few minutes ago.' Her smile was as carefully neutral as if she applied it in front of a mirror each morning like lipstick. 'If you'd like to leave your luggage here, my colleague will bring it up for you. Come this way.'

Again, it seemed futile to point out that I could manage my four-kilogram overnight bag perfectly well myself and save her colleague the journey.

'The bar and dining room are just there to your left,' she went on. 'Breakfast is served between seven and ten tomorrow morning. If you'd like tea or coffee in your room, or anything from the bar, you can order using our app.'

'Thank you.' I followed her up a wide staircase, carpeted in royal blue, a heavy velvet rope serving as a handrail, then into a corridor lit by wall sconces. The scent of roses was everywhere – it must be some sort of room fragrance or cleaning product, I thought, rather than actual flowers. The corridor was completely silent, but from somewhere below I could hear the clink of glasses and a woman's laughter.

'Room twelve.' She stopped outside a panelled door and tapped gently, then stood aside.

A moment later, he opened it and I stepped in, muttering more words of thanks which felt a lot more heartfelt now. Then the door closed and I was in his arms.

'Hello, beautiful.' He kissed me and held me close, his hands brushing the hair back from my face. 'You made it. Was the drive okay? Are you very tired?'

'I was,' I admitted. 'I had an early shift, so I've been up since five. But I'm not any more. Look at this – my God. It's fabulous. Is it the honeymoon suite or something?'

'All the rooms here are like this.' He grinned, as proud and delighted as a little boy bringing home a straight-A report card. He looked tired himself, I noticed. There were hollows under his eyes I remembered seeing the last time we'd met, two weeks before. 'Do you like it?'

'It's gorgeous.' I kicked off my shoes, dropped my coat on an armchair and threw myself on the bed, bouncing a few times on my back. 'Can we move in?'

Seconds later, he'd joined me on the bed, his knees sinking into the mattress on either side of my waist.

'I could totally get behind that idea.' His voice was muffled by the duvet and my hair. 'Or better still, get behind you.'

I giggled, pushing him away. 'Not until I've showered. I stink of sweat and hospital.'

'No you don't.' He pushed the neck of my jumper down, kissing my collarbone. 'You smell delicious. You smell of Laurel.'

I felt my heartbeat quicken and a thread of desire work its way down from where his lips were to between my legs. But I wriggled out from underneath him, just in time to answer another discreet tap on the door.

'My stuff,' I reported. 'Just as well we didn't start anything.'

'We should've put the Do Not Disturb sign up.' He grinned unrepentantly, propped on his elbows on the bed. 'Except it's probably a setting on the app.'

'I hope the shower works like a normal one.' I unzipped my case and pulled out my washbag. 'Not some fancy remote-controlled thing.'

'Looked pretty analogue to me.' He followed me into the bathroom, waiting expectantly while I looked around, taking in the huge claw-footed tub under the window, the Oriental rug spread over the wooden floor, the glass-screened rainfall shower.

'Wow,' I breathed. 'Fancy.'

'And plenty of room for two,' he said. 'Bath or shower? You pick.'

'Shower, then. Give me a minute to wee then you can join me.'

Half an hour later, we lay on the bed, gasping and smiling. My head was on his shoulder, and I was running my fingers down the taut plane of his stomach, almost automatically tracing the scar that curved from the top of his left hip bone down towards his groin like a smile.

Was it my imagination or was that bone more pronounced than it had been the last time I touched it?

I felt his skin move beneath my hand as he took a deep breath in. 'Laurel?'

'Mmm-hmm?'

'I've got something for you. A present.'

I propped myself up on my elbow, looking down at him. 'You didn't have to do that. You got us – all this.'

'I wanted to, though. So I did.'

He stood up and went to rummage through his leather holdall. I felt embarrassed – I hadn't got him anything, not even a card. I couldn't have got him one if I'd wanted to – it would have caused too many complications. But the glow of pleasure on his face when he handed me the small square box made me feel better – he wanted to give me a gift more than he would have wanted anything I could have given him.

I eased open the box and squeaked with delight. The earrings were stunning – simple, sparkly crystals, twinkling with rainbow brightness in the glow of the bedside lamp.

'They're gorgeous.' I smiled and kissed him. 'Thank you.'

'You can wear them to dinner. I booked us a table at eight – assuming you're hungry?'

'Starving.' I thought of the dining room downstairs. There'd be starched white tablecloths, battalions of knives and forks and probably a sommelier. There'd be abundant opportunities for me to make a fool of myself. There would also, I was sure, be an extensive room-service menu.

But he'd brought me here because it was special – because he thought *I* was special. He wanted to go down for dinner with me in the black dress I'd borrowed off Mel and feel proud of me. He didn't feel the need to hide away, and nor should I.

'Let's get dressed and get some food,' I said.

So we did. He showed me how to eat oysters in such a way that I was sure the waiter hadn't noticed that I didn't already know. He told me what coquilles Saint Jacques were. He passed a forkful of his duck across the table for me to try without embarrassment. He ordered a bottle of delicious red wine even though we knew he'd hardly drink any of it. He didn't eat very much himself, but insisted that I have pudding.

Afterwards, we went back up to our room and had sex again, slowly and gently because we were both so full and sleepy. I cleaned my teeth and took off my make-up in the posh bathroom and then returned to bed, curling up next to him.

But he didn't curl back. He sat up against the pillows, shifting uncomfortably like they had spikes inside instead of goose down or whatever they were.

'You okay?' I asked.

'Not feeling great,' he admitted. 'Indigestion. Shouldn't have made such a pig of myself.'

'You didn't eat that much.' In the glow of the bedside lamp, I could see that his face was pale as putty and sheened with sweat. 'Are you sure you're...?'

But before I could finish, he flung himself out of bed and ran to the bathroom. Through the open door, I heard him throwing up and up, as if he'd never stop. When I went to help – although really, how can you help, until someone who's being sick has finished being? – he told me to go away.

So I returned to bed and sat there, my knees up under the duvet, trying hard not to bite my nails, trying hard not to think of all the possible scenarios that could be causing this, which weren't just rich food or a winter vomiting bug, until at last he came back.

'Has this been happening a lot?' I asked him.

'A few times in the past couple of weeks. Guess I can't stuff my face like I used to be able to. I'm all out of practice.'

I looked at him – his familiar, handsome face, his deep brown eyes. A new hollowness below his cheekbones; a new sallowness to his skin.

'Gray,' I said. 'I think maybe you need to see a doctor.'

THREE
ANNA

I planned my confrontation with my husband as if I was a general preparing for a military operation. It was displacement activity, I suppose – by obsessing over every detail of what was to come, I avoided thinking about what I believed was happening, or had already happened, because when I'd checked Gray's drawer the previous evening, when he was allegedly away with work, filming a commercial in Liverpool, the earrings had no longer been there.

It was the day after Valentine's Day. The children were out – Lulu meeting friends to go bowling and Barney to go and see *Transformers One* and have a sleepover. I evicted all the clutter from the kitchen and buffed the countertops until they sparkled. I tinted my hair and painted my nails and picked up the plum-coloured cashmere dress Gray had always admired from the dry cleaner's, where it had been languishing since Christmas. I bought beef short ribs from the butcher and simmered them in red wine for four hours.

If my husband was going to leave me for another woman, I wanted him to know exactly what he'd be missing.

By six o'clock I was ready. I'd set two places at the dining table, instead of at the kitchen counter where we usually ate. I'd dug out a highlighting and contouring palette and given my face what I hoped was a youthful glow. I'd lit candles and put a bottle of champagne in the fridge to chill.

I felt oddly calm; only my inability to sit still and the prickling of my dress under my arms reminded me how nervous I was feeling. I poured myself a gin and tonic and, as I was draining the potatoes into a colander ready to mash, I heard Gray's key in the lock upstairs.

'Hey, you,' I called. 'You're home.'

From above, I heard the thump of his laptop bag as he put it down on the floor, then a pause which meant he was taking off his coat and hanging it up. Hearing his footsteps on the stairs, I turned, preparing a smile that I hoped looked more welcoming than wary. But as soon as I saw him, I felt it slide off my face as completely as if it had never been there.

He looked terrible. Tired, as he'd been looking more often recently, brushing off my suggestion that he should take a few days off, catch up on rest, maybe see the GP – but more than that. Exhausted. Haunted, almost.

'Hey, Anna.' He walked past the candles and the table settings and the champagne in its ice bucket as if they weren't there, took a glass from the cabinet and poured a hefty belt of whisky from the bottle on the drinks trolley. He added three blocks of ice straight from the fridge dispenser, apparently not noticing that they caused miniature tidal waves when they splashed into the glass.

Then he stood by the kitchen island, resting his forearms on it as if he needed it to support his weight, both hands wrapped around his drink.

'Whisky?' I said. 'It's ages since you've had one of those. Bad day?'

He nodded. 'You could say that.'

I felt a chill of apprehension. This wasn't how it was meant to go. He was meant to be soothed by my charm offensive, lulled into security so that when I asked the tough questions I'd prepared, he'd succumb to my interrogation and come out with the truth.

Instead, it seemed as if he was about to come out with some hard truths of his own.

He's going to tell me he's leaving me for her, I thought. *He's going to be on the attack, not the defence.*

The champagne forgotten, I poured a second gin and tonic, this one stronger than the last.

I said, 'I made a boeuf en daube. Do you want to eat first, or tell me what's up?'

Gray grimaced, and I noticed the pallor on his face grow even more ghostly. 'To be honest, I'm not remotely hungry.'

'Right, okay.' I perched on one of the stools at the counter, half-turning towards him. 'I thought we could have a nice dinner together. You know – catch up. Do the Valentine's Day thing, since we haven't in a while, even though it's a day late. But if you're not feeling up to it...'

He shook his head. 'I'm not feeling up to it. Sorry, Anna.'

An apology – I wondered if it was the last one I was going to get that night.

'That's okay. It'll keep. The kids can have it tomorrow.'

'Where are they?' He glanced around, almost as if he was afraid they might come charging in at any moment, Lulu with her headphones round her neck, Barney carrying a reluctant Augustus.

If he's about to tell me he's leaving his family to shack up with another woman, I bet he'd be afraid of them.

'Out. Barney's gone to the pictures and is staying over at Marcus's. Lulu's bowling and then going on to some dodgy dessert bar. I told her to be home by ten.'

'Right,' he said again. Then he took another gulp of his drink.

I turned now so I was fully facing Gray. One of the spotlights above the kitchen island was casting its light directly down on to his face, and I could see shadows beneath his cheekbones that I was certain hadn't been there just a couple of weeks ago. He'd lost a load of weight over the past three years, but it looked like he'd lost even more quite recently. I wasn't sure when I'd last seen him naked, and it had been at least a year since he'd stopped complacently reporting back to me after his weekly stand on the bathroom scales, but I saw with shock that he didn't look healthily slim now, but gaunt.

'I want to talk to you, Anna,' he said.

'Sure. I mean, I wanted to talk to you too, tonight. About something.' But abruptly, I found I didn't want to talk at all – not about what I'd planned to ask him, and certainly not about whatever it was he wanted to tell me. I felt cold dread rising up from my stomach, and my fingers gripped the sides of my glass so tightly the nails turned white.

I didn't want to talk. I wanted it all to stop.

'Why don't you go first?' he said.

But, looking at him, I found I couldn't do it.

'No, you go,' I managed to say.

Looking down into his glass instead of at me, he said, 'I went to hospital today.'

'What? You never told me you had an appointment.'

'I didn't. I went to A&E.'

'Shit. Why? Are you okay?'

'Doesn't look like it.' Now he raised his head and met my eyes. 'They're going to do some tests, but they think I've got cancer.'

Dumbly, I stared back at him. Cancer. The dreaded diagnosis. The big C. Something that happened to people who were old, or didn't take care of their health. Something that happened to other people.

'Wait, say that again.' I was struggling to make my lips and tongue form the words.

'Cancer.' He said it gently, like he'd been practising making it sound less deadly.

I stood up, walked over to the sink and found a Tupperware container in the adjoining cupboard, tipping the potatoes into it and putting them in the fridge. I turned the flame off under the cast-iron casserole dish, leaving it where it was on the stove because my arms felt too weak to lift it. I put a plate on top of the bowl of salad and put that in the fridge too.

I fetched the bottle of gin and put it on the countertop next to Gray's whisky.

Then I sat back down. He'd been watching me while I cleared up, his eyes steady and his face still.

'So you went to A&E today,' I said slowly. 'Why?'

'I've not been feeling great. Tired, sick, I've lost half a stone, although I'm not trying to any more.'

'But that could be anything,' I objected. 'It could be nothing. Indigestion or something. A bug.'

'That's what the GP said when I saw her two weeks ago.'

'You went to the doctor? You never said.'

'You told me I should go, so I made an appointment. I didn't want to worry you.' He lifted his glass to his lips, sipped and winced, then poured more whisky into it. 'Then last night I vomited. And again this morning, although I hadn't eaten. So we – I thought I should get checked out. And you know what it's like trying to get an appointment at the local surgery.'

We? Who was the other half of that *we*?

'So you went to the hospital? In Liverpool?'

Gray's shoulders lifted in a shrug, then dropped again. 'I wasn't in Liverpool.'

My mouth suddenly felt as dry as paper. I took another gulp of my drink then added more gin to the glass, not bothering with tonic.

'You weren't in Liverpool,' I echoed. 'Where were you?'

'Gloucestershire.' He didn't meet my eyes, and he didn't sound as if he'd practised saying that. 'At a hotel in the country.'

'Then why did you tell me you were somewhere else?' I asked, although I was certain I knew what the answer would be.

Don't lie to me, Gray. Don't make this harder than it already is.

'Because... Because of who I was with.' The words sounded jagged, like they were physically hurting him.

I opened my mouth to say something, but nothing came out. All I could hear was the screaming in my mind.

My husband has cancer. My husband is having an affair.

The silence stretched between us, taut enough that it felt dangerous to break it.

Tentatively, I whispered, 'Tell me what they said at the hospital.'

I heard him breathe out – a long exhale, like he was relieved to be talking about this again, rather than the other thing.

'They took a look at me. Peered at my eyes, poked my stomach. Took some blood. That kind of thing.'

'Right.' I found myself peering at his eyes too. They looked normal to me – the familiar deep, rich brown, unusual for someone with blond hair, although his had gradually been silvering for some years. Just Gray's eyes. Just Gray's face.

'They said I'm jaundiced,' he went on. 'And they could feel something in my abdomen. So they sent me for a CT scan, and they said it looks like there's something there. Some kind of mass.'

'Some kind of mass?' My words came out high and incredulous. 'What does that even mean? Where?'

'On my pancreas.'

'Pancreas. Okay.'

I thought, *What the hell even is that?* If it had been my husband's liver, or obviously his kidney, I'd have had a clearer idea of what was going on. But a pancreas? It was just a word, just a thing that was there, somewhere in the jumble of meat that made up the inside of all of us.

'So they've referred me to gastroenterology. Or rather, they've written to our GP to tell them to. It's complicated because – well, because of the area thing. It's a different NHS trust.'

The area thing. Not East London, where we lived. Not Liverpool, either. Somewhere in Gloucestershire.

'They said I might have to chase them up,' Gray was saying.

'So what are we meant to do in the meantime?' My voice was rising, thin and panicky.

'Dunno. I guess we wait. That's why it's called a two-week wait, right? Clue's in the name.'

'And what if... What if it does turn out to be cancer?' My throat felt raw, as if I'd been screaming. 'I mean, it's probably something else, right? Gallstones or something.'

'They don't think it's gallstones,' Gray replied quietly.

'Yeah, maybe, but they don't know.' The words sounded almost wheedling, like I was trying to strike a bargain with someone who held all the cards. 'That's why we have to wait to find out.'

'Anna.' Gray turned his glass around on the countertop, a full three hundred and sixty degrees, but he didn't pour any more whisky into it or drink any more of what was there. 'If it does turn out to be pancreatic cancer…'

'Then what?'

'I googled, obviously. Just like you're not supposed to do. But it's not good.'

'How not good?'

'Like, really, really not good. Like the worst sort of cancer there is.'

The worst sort of cancer there is. Wasn't that a tautology or something? Like, The Cutest Sort of Baby, or The Most Boring Game of Cricket?

I had some more of my drink. It was just watery gin now, the ice melted and the tonic long gone. I was feeling lightheaded – like I might fall off my stool or simply float away, up to the ceiling and then maybe out of the window, to somewhere where this wasn't happening.

'Anna,' Gray said. 'Are you listening to me?'

I nodded mutely.

'It's often fatal,' he said. 'More than often. Almost always. If it turns out that's what I've got, I'll probably die.'

'Don't be mad.' I stood up, the floor seeming to seesaw beneath my feet, so I had to clutch at the countertop to regain my balance. 'You won't die. Come on. There are treatments for things like that. Drugs and surgery and – you know. Stuff. It'll be okay.'

Slowly, fumblingly, I put my glass in the dishwasher and flicked the kettle on. I didn't want tea or coffee, but it was something to do. I could take a mug of something hot up to bed with me, and when I woke up in the morning I wouldn't have a hangover because this wouldn't have happened.

But Gray didn't let me take refuge in denial.

'Anna, sit down.' It was the same tone he used when he was going to give one of the kids a telling-off for something – firm but patient, gentle but with a touch of steel.

I sat.

'There's something else I need to tell you.'

FOUR

ORLA

12 February 2023 – One year earlier

I do not think of myself as a curtain-twitcher, but after what happened yesterday I am afraid I must count myself officially within their ranks. I have excuses, though – the curtains were not drawn so there was no actual twitching involved; I was in plain view, should anyone have chosen to look up at the second floor. I was, quite genuinely, cleaning the window: the junior cats, successors to my beloved Maud, have taken to perching on the windowsill for hours on end, chattering at the blackbirds in the square, and their little noses leave smudges on the glass that obscure their view. Until they're old enough to be allowed out, this will have to be a regular chore.

I was, typically, distracted from my work by the view. The trees are still bare, but the first snowdrops have emerged in the grass, their fragile heads modestly bowed against the cold. High on a branch, a robin was singing his lungs out – I considered summoning the kittens to see him, but they were both asleep on my bed. And around the corner, a woman appeared on a bicycle, her yellow waterproof jacket a pleasing splash of colour on the grey day.

I watched as she came around the square, not slowly but not particularly fast either, distracted as people often are by the surprising appearance of the three rows of elegant Georgian houses, perfectly preserved in this neighbourhood that is becoming increasingly dominated by high-rise glass-and-steel towers.

She did not see the Grahams' cat, Augustus, returning from his morning prowl among the trees, until it was too late. He saw her, though, and he made the wrong judgement: instead of dodging beneath a parked car for safety, he made a run for home, darting across the road right in front of her approaching front wheel.

It all happened too fast for me to take in the details. She must have braked suddenly, perhaps hitting a cobblestone or skidding on a patch of ice. But in any event, her bicycle went one way and she went the other, tumbling sideways and forwards over the handlebars and falling hard while Augustus dashed unharmed to the safety of his front door.

I heard her shout of alarm and the clatter of her bike hitting the pavement, shortly followed by an outraged yowl from Augustus as he reached the door of number eight and demanded to be let in. I stood there for a moment, waiting for her to pick herself up and go on her way, but she didn't. She sat up, legs akimbo on the cold cobbles, looking down at her right hand as if it was somehow no longer part of her.

I put down my spray bottle of vinegar and cleaning rag, about to turn and hurry downstairs to see if I could help. But before I could, the door of number eight swung open and Gray emerged, alerted either by the sounds of the woman's fall or the cries of his cat. I couldn't see Augustus any more; presumably he had fled inside to lick the wounds he didn't have.

Gray approached the woman, squatting down next to her. I could hear his voice, soothing and concerned, and hers replying, high with shock and perhaps pain, although I couldn't make out their words. As I watched, he stood up again, taking her left arm in his and helping her to her feet. They stood there for a moment before Gray picked up her bicycle, inspecting its wheels and shaking his head before carrying it inside his house. The woman followed, her right arm cradled across her body.

I resumed my window cleaning, wondering whether the brief drama was over.

And it mostly was. After five minutes, they came out again, the woman now with a blanket around her shoulders. Gray guided her to his car, opened the door for her, they both got in and he drove away.

He would be taking her home, I guessed, her bicycle for the time being unrideable. Or perhaps he was giving her a lift to the hospital to get checked out.

Either way, it was a fleeting incident – a small blip in an otherwise uneventful Saturday morning.

So why do I feel the need to describe it here in these pages?

FIVE
LAUREL

When I was six, I stole my brother's bike. I didn't think of it as stealing at the time – I wasn't that shitty a kid. I thought I was borrowing it.

The thing was, I didn't have a bike and Justin did. He was due to get a brand-new one, and his current one would be passed down to me.

But Justin's birthday was still two months away. It was a Saturday afternoon in July and all my friends were out riding around the cul-de-sac. Mum was having a nap. Justin and Dad were out at the football.

I opened the garage door, wheeled out the bike, closed the door and set off to join my friends. It was Saturday, the sun was out, we were having fun. Someone's mum or big sister was probably supervising us, but only half-heartedly.

It was half an hour or so before the sky went suddenly dark, and the heavens opened. Within seconds, my T-shirt was wet through and my hair was dripping. Justin's bike slid alarmingly on the tarmac where a parked car had leaked oil on the road when I braked.

'Girls!' My friend Stacey's mum appeared in the doorway of their house. 'Look at the state of you! Come indoors right now.'

So we went upstairs to Stacey's room and played with her Barbies while we waited for the rain to stop.

When I went to retrieve the bike, it wasn't there. Stacey's lay alone on the wet grass verge, bright pink instead of silver, one bike instead of two. Full of remorse and fear now, I walked home. By the time I reached the kitchen, I was crying.

Somehow, I must have managed to stammer out the whole story. Mum didn't punish me, though she did give me one hell of a telling-off. And the main thing she said, over and over, was, 'You must never take other people's things without asking, Laurel. That's theft and it's wrong.'

For thirty-four years, I didn't. I never so much as shoplifted a mascara from Boots or returned a library book late. I reached the age of forty without having ever had a speeding fine or taken illegal drugs. I tried my hardest to do the right thing, the decent thing, in whatever situation I found myself in.

Then I met Gray, a man who was unquestionably someone else's, and there was no way of asking if I could borrow him for a while.

I never meant to have an affair with a married man. I knew full well that it was against all the laws of the sisterhood. But by the time I realised what was happening, just the same as with my brother's bike, it was too late, and the damage was done.

It wouldn't have happened if I hadn't been at the lowest of low ebbs at the time. Simon and I had been together for ten years, throughout my thirties, while all my contemporaries were getting married and starting families, and I believed – or wouldn't allow myself *not* to believe – that we'd be next. But as it turned out, Simon didn't believe the same, although it took an ultimatum from me for him to admit it.

He wasn't ready; he didn't know if he ever would be ready; he knew it wasn't fair; it wasn't me, it was him.

So I left and moved into my friend Mel's spare room, and a couple of months later I heard through the grapevine that Simon had met someone else and that she was pregnant.

A couple of weeks after that, I turned forty. A week after that, I met Gray.

I was emotionally in tatters, more fragile and bruised than I could recall ever being before; not to mention literally bruised after taking a tumble from – ironically enough – my bike, right outside Gray's house.

At least, I thought I was only bruised. It was Gray who insisted I should go along to the minor injuries unit at the local hospital to get checked out, then insisted on coming with me because I was all shook-up and trying not to cry.

He was right, as it turned out, and I – a healthcare professional who should have known better – was wrong: I had a distal radius fracture and had to wear a splint for six weeks. Gray waited at the hospital while the orthopaedics team patched me up, even though I told him I'd be fine and there was no need for that. Afterwards, he took me to a nearby pub and bought me a Bacardi and Coke.

Then he asked for my number so he could text and check I was okay.

'You'll need to call me anyway,' he said, 'when you're ready to pick up your bike.'

I looked at the wedding ring on his left hand and wished he wasn't so attractive. *All the decent ones are taken*, I'd complained to Mel just the previous night, after a first date with a guy whose Tinder profile said he was forty-two but who would clearly never see fifty again.

Gray was decent. He was handsome, he was kind, he lived in a beautiful house so must have a good job. On the surface, he was everything I'd been looking for.

Except, obviously, he was taken.

Which meant that nothing would come of this. I'd finish my drink and go home and figure out how to make scrambled eggs on toast with one hand, then in a couple of weeks I'd drop him a message and collect my bike and apologise to his wife for the inconvenience of leaving it at their house – maybe even give her some flowers – and that would be that.

I'd never see him again, because I wasn't desperate or a home-wrecker, and my mum had taught me right from wrong.

I shouldn't have let things go any further than the exchange of numbers and the return of my bike. But I found I couldn't stop thinking about him, dwelling on his kindness, the way his hand had felt in mine when he helped me to my feet, the way he'd taken control of the situation and looked after me when I was so used to being the one doing the looking after.

I know I shouldn't have. But I did.

'You're setting yourself up for massive heartbreak, Laurel,' Mel told me, when the relationship had progressed to the point where I could no longer not tell her about it. 'He won't leave his wife for you. They never do – and if he did, he'd only find someone else to cheat on you with. He's not a good man. You're wasting your time like you were with Simon.'

But I didn't want to hear what she had to say about Gray – and I couldn't bring myself to end it.

SIX
ANNA

It was still almost completely dark when my alarm went off the next morning. Gray and I hadn't got around to closing the blinds in our bedroom, and through the window I could see the dark branches of the plane trees that bordered the square silhouetted like skeletal fingers against an almost-as-dark sky. It was raining too – I could hear the occasional dash of drops on the windowpane and the swish of car tyres on the wet tarmac.

Pulling the duvet up to my chin, I turned over in bed, the movement making me realise that my head was banging and I felt sick. Gray was lying next to me, his pyjamaed back motionless. I didn't reach out to touch him; I just looked at his solid, familiar form on the right-hand side of our bed, where it had been almost every morning for twenty years.

Abruptly, the details of the previous night came rushing back. As soon as Gray had said her name – Laurel's name – I'd stood up, fetched a clean glass and splashed some red wine into it from the bottle I had opened earlier. Now, I found I couldn't remember the details of what he'd told me – the wine and the gin I'd drunk earlier had seen to that.

But the gist was there. My husband was sick. He was sick, and he was in love with another woman.

I remembered Lulu coming home from her night out, responsibly letting herself into the house at exactly five to ten. I remembered hearing her clumpy trainers step across the hallway then stop, and I imagined her standing at the top of the stairs, seeing the lights on down in the kitchen, hesitating while she decided whether to come and tell us she was home or go straight up to her bedroom and start texting the friends she'd said goodbye to ten minutes before.

Don't, Lulu, I thought, watching as Gray too turned towards the stairs, his face expectant and wary. Don't come down and see us like this, the candles extinguished, the Marks & Spencer chocolate torte untouched in its packaging, the bottles of wine and whisky almost empty.

But she did.

She came into kitchen a few seconds later, her face glowing with cold, excitement and make-up (*That had better not be my new Hourglass palette*, I thought inconsequentially), her hands deep in the pockets of her oversized khaki jacket, the hems of her jeans grubby and damp from trailing on the wet pavement.

'I'm home,' she announced.

She paused, looking at us warily. I'd noticed this expression on her face more often recently – hers and Barney's, when they walked into a room when Gray and I were alone together. Sometimes, there'd be a moment of hesitation, just a second or two, between the footsteps outside and whichever child it was stepping through the doorway, as if they were assessing what they could expect on the other side.

There had been too many times when they'd overheard us arguing, me accusing Gray of being too absent, too thoughtless, too selfish. Him accusing me of being too cold, too uninterested in his life, too unavailable.

When the kids were smaller, we'd dreaded them walking in on us having sex. Now, I dreaded them walking in on an argument.

If things had been different – if Lulu's fine-tuned radar had detected nothing alarming, just her mum and dad having a chat –

she might have made herself a hot chocolate, hoisted herself up on to the island and sat there for a bit, legs swinging, and allowed us to ask about the details of her evening, although her replies would be monosyllabic. That night, though, she looked at us and straight away the light went out of her face.

'What's up, Mum and Dad?' she asked warily.

'Nothing, darling,' Gray said. 'Did you have fun?'

'We were just talking about the situation in the Middle East,' I lied.

Lulu gave the ghost of an eye roll. 'Oh. Right. Can I have some of that dessert?'

Clearly whatever cream- and sugar-laden waffle or freakshake she'd had with her pals hadn't touched the sides.

'Of course you can,' I said.

We sat in silence while she tore open the box, cut herself a wedge of cake, balanced it on a piece of kitchen roll, licked the knife and put it on the counter.

Then she stood there for a second, looking at us cautiously.

'I'm going to bed,' she said.

'Sleep tight, Lulu bug,' I said. 'Don't forget to clean your teeth.'

'Mum! I'm fifteen, not five.'

But she kissed us both, her hair smelling of coconut conditioner and her breath of strawberry chewing gum, before clomping away again.

Gray and I had sat in silence until we heard her bedroom door slam two floors above.

Then I said, 'I can't do this any more. I'm going to bed.'

He nodded. 'I'll clear up down here. See you in a bit.'

He's going to text her, I thought. *He's going to tell her he's told me.*

But I'd just nodded, picked up my own phone and left him there alone.

Now, staring at the burgundy-and-navy-striped back of Gray's pyjamas but not really seeing anything, I sifted through my scattered memories of what he had told me about her.

Laurel. At first I thought he'd said *Lauren* and he'd had to correct me – Laurel with two Ls. Like the plant. I wondered if that was what she had said to him, the first time she'd told him her name. I wondered if she'd gone through her whole life saying it. It was a pretty name, more unusual by far than Lauren. I wondered if she was as pretty as her name. For a brief moment, I'd thought of asking Gray to show me a photo of her, but I couldn't bear to – just knowing he might have one right there on his phone, to look at whenever he wanted to see her face, was too painful to consider.

They'd met by chance, he'd said. Randomly, in the street outside our house. That was better, I suppose, than him having actively sought her out on some app for cheating husbands. And they'd been seeing each other for a year. Twelve months, and until days ago I'd been oblivious. They saw each other once a week, maybe, he'd said. At hotels they rented for a few hours, or sometimes at her place, when her flatmate was at work.

How old is she? I'd demanded, and his answer had surprised me: she was forty-one, just a year younger than me. I thought, *And still sharing a flat with a friend? Loser.*

Then I thought, *Maybe not such a loser.* Because if she doesn't have youth on her side, if she's not some naive twenty-something stunner nearer Lulu's age than mine, then she must have something else, something even more special.

I couldn't bring myself to ask what that was.

She was a nurse, Gray had told me. That was why she'd noticed things: the yellowing of his eyes that I'd been unaware of, the intensity of his sickness. That was why she'd insisted on driving him to the nearest hospital the morning after the first full night they'd ever spent together.

On Valentine's Day. Lovely. But Gray spending all night puking would have been quite the buzz-killer, I thought spitefully.

That thought snapped my mind away from her – Laurel – as smartly as if it had been pulled by a string.

Gray was sick. Gray might have cancer. If he did, it was the sort that meant he would almost certainly die.

I squeezed my eyes shut, but when I opened them again seconds later, his pyjamas were still there, and so was that fact.

He's forty-seven. That's wild. He can't be going to die. It's no age at all.

That's what people would say if they heard he'd died. *It's no age at all. Poor Anna. Those poor children.*

Except now there'd be some people – people I didn't know and would probably never know – who'd say, *Poor Laurel.*

And what about me? What about poor Anna and the poor children?

Lulu had her GCSEs coming up. Barney was just entering the turmoil of his teenage years. They needed their father.

Just this afternoon, Barney had a football match. Taking him to football had always been Gray's job – the few times he hadn't been able to make it, I'd spent ninety miserable minutes shivering on the sidelines vowing I would never, ever do it again. If Gray died, I'd have to do it every single Saturday for the next six years.

I turned over. It was lighter now, but the sky was still laden with clouds as heavy as slate, and rain was still falling.

Thinking about those endless football games had focused my mind. Lulu wouldn't be up for hours; Barney's friend's mum would be dropping him off at some point during the morning. I had the next few hours to myself, and I was going to use them. I was going to get out my laptop, make some strong coffee and do some research.

I was going to find out what was what. Because there was no way I was going to allow this to happen. Gray was going to get better. He was going to see his children grow up and graduate and get married and have kids of their own. And he was going to stay married to me.

Laurel was just going to have to suck it up.

SEVEN
LAUREL

After we'd been to the hospital, the morning after Valentine's Day, I drove Gray back to the hotel where he'd parked his car the previous night. How different it felt today, I thought, although the wheels of my car made exactly the same crunching sound on the gravel drive as they had the evening before.

It was daylight now, mid-morning, and I could see the golden stone and elegant proportions of the country house, which had been obscured by darkness last night. There were terraced gardens stretching away down into a valley where presumably a river flowed. There were yew trees pruned to look like peacocks and chess pieces. For all I knew there were actual peacocks.

I'd never find out now. If things had been different, we could have taken a walk in the grounds after stuffing ourselves at breakfast. We could have returned to our room and had a final, hasty, giggling shag before getting dressed and saying goodbye.

But the goodbye would have felt different. It would have been sad, of course, because our Valentine's, our first night together, our special secret treat, was over. But we'd have been able to promise each other that we'd do it again before too long, that this was the first of many times.

We couldn't do that now. We didn't speak at all, from when we got in the car outside the A&E department to when I pulled up in the hotel car park, the crunch of the gravel beneath the wheels audible and familiar over the music on the car radio – 'Same Old Thing' by The Streets, which had me tapping my fingers on the steering wheel without really thinking about it.

'Dvořák's Symphony Number Nine,' Gray said, speaking for the first time.

'What? Is that a request?'

He half-laughed. 'No. That's a sample from the first movement of the New World Symphony.'

'How do you—?' I began, then I stopped and said, 'Cool. I like it.'

I thought, *I used to like it, but I won't like it ever again. I'll never be able to hear it without thinking of this moment.*

I pulled my handbrake up. Gray unclipped his seatbelt.

'Well,' he said. 'Thanks for driving me, Laurel.'

'You were in no state to drive yourself. You probably still aren't. I could take you back to London. We could get someone to pick up your car.'

He shook his head. 'You know that's not possible.'

I knew. The excuse of filming in Liverpool had seemed flimsy when he came up with it, but it wasn't for me to question. It had become an unspoken deal between us: I never asked about his wife, his children, his other life, and he rarely told.

Don't ask, don't tell. We all know how that one worked out.

If he left his car here, he'd have to come up with a whole new cover story: a breakdown on the motorway. A prang that had led him to have to go to A&E (*What do you mean, there's no bump on my head?*). Whatever he did, it would just have complicated things even more.

And we both knew they were about to get quite complicated enough.

'Gray,' I said gently, 'you're going to have to tell Anna.'

'I know. But maybe not yet.'

'When, then? Shit, Gray, she needs to know.'

'About you, or about – the other thing?'

'Both, I guess. But mainly the other thing. You're going to have to have loads more tests. You're not well. You'll need support and she – it's not fair not to tell her.'

'I could wait until I know for sure.'

Frustrated, I unfastened my own seatbelt so I could turn towards him. I stretched out my hands and put them on his knees, feeling the hard muscles of his quadriceps beneath the worn denim.

'Come on. I mean, it's none of my business, but how would that be better?'

'It might turn out to be a false alarm,' he argued. 'Then I'd have worried her for nothing.'

It's not going to turn out to be a false alarm.

'Gray,' I said. 'We could stop seeing each other. We could end this right now, today. Then at least you'd have only one thing to tell her. Or one and a half, if you decided to say you'd been seeing me but you weren't any more.'

'Like hell will I stop seeing you.' He grasped my hands, almost roughly. 'Not through choice, anyway. If you want to tell me to get the fuck out of your car and never contact you again, I'll do it. But that's what it would take.'

I tried. 'Get the fuck out of my car and...'

But I couldn't.

'Contact you when I get back to London?' he suggested.

I nodded.

'Laurel.' He released my hands and, tenderly now, placed his on either side of my face, drawing me towards him. 'You're the best thing that's happened to me in the longest time.'

I felt tears prickling my eyes behind my sunglasses. 'Same.'

'I'm a selfish bastard,' he said, but his smile was tender. 'But no matter what happens after this, I'm glad we had last night. I love you.'

'I love you too,' I said. 'Even though you're a selfish bastard.'

'Thank God for that. Now I should go and get my bag from

inside and settle up. I'm feeling okay. I'll be fine to drive, so don't worry.'

I nodded.

'You drive safely now.'

'You too.'

He kissed me. I felt the roughness of his stubble against my cheeks, the fine fuzz of his hair under my fingertips, the scratchy tweed of his coat against my neck. I felt love more intense and terrifying than anything I could have guessed it was possible to feel.

Then he pulled away and opened the door, a blast of raw winter air replacing the warmth of his body as he swung his legs out and stood up.

We didn't see each other for more than two weeks after that.

We kept in touch by WhatsApp, of course, as we always had. But Gray's text messages had always been brief and factual – I'd never been quite sure whether that was just his way of communicating or whether he wanted to keep the content of our messages neutral enough so that, if his phone fell into the wrong hands, they could be explained away as innocent.

Fell into the wrong hands. For God's sake, Laurel. If his wife snooped, she wouldn't immediately think he was fucking someone else.

There, that's better.

Anyway, he sent me messages saying he was feeling not so great, but not awful either. I told him I'd got back okay and was looking forward to seeing him again.

I didn't say, *I miss you. I'm worried about you. Tell me what's happening. I love you. I'm frightened.*

I had to keep all of those things to myself, save them for when I saw him again, except I knew that when I did happiness would blow them all away, apart from the love bit. I had to wait, as patiently as I could, because that was what I'd signed up for when I started seeing someone who wasn't mine.

The text I'd been longing for came late on a Tuesday evening, the first week of March.

I've got an appointment at the hospital tomorrow afternoon. Meet there for coffee?

Why wasn't Anna going to his appointment with him, I wondered briefly. Probably something to do with the kids.

Of course, I messaged back. He told me which hospital and I replied, *See you there.*

When I arrived at the hospital coffee shop, he was already there, sat on a plastic chair with an empty red paper cup in front of him.

'Hi,' I said.

'Hi.' He didn't stand up. He looked awful, pale and drawn and tired, and, I was sure, even thinner than when I'd last seen him.

'I'll grab a drink.'

I waited impatiently for my tea and then carried it back, sitting on the uncomfortable chair opposite his.

'It's lovely to see you, Laurel.' He smiled, and the smile made him look almost normal again – made me feel almost as if this was normal, just another of our snatched, precious meetings. Except it wasn't. Things would never be normal again, and I didn't know how many of these meetings we would have left.

'You too. I've missed you. So...' I began, taking a sip of my tea. 'How did it go?'

'They saw me quicker than I expected, so that's good. But it was the gastro people again, and they went over pretty much the same stuff they did in Gloucester. But they've referred me for another thing – an ESU, or something.'

'EUS,' I said. 'Endoscopic ultrasound.'

'Where they stick a camera down my gullet? That's the badger. And then we'll know what we're dealing with here.'

I nodded. 'I guess depending what they find, they'll take a biopsy and refer you straight to oncology.'

'Correct.' He picked up his cup and looked inside it, like a fortune teller reading tea leaves. But there were no tea leaves there, just a few spent coffee grounds and the scum left by frothed milk.

'Did you speak to Anna?' I asked.

'Yup.'

'And how's she – is she okay?'

He shook his head. 'About as okay as anyone would be if they found out their husband's maybe terminally ill and definitely cheating on them. But she's bearing up. She's gone all positive. She's decided that whatever it is, I'm going to get better.'

I'd seen that before, in the partners of patients with frightening diagnoses. It was better, in many ways, than the alternative.

'She's been googling like crazy,' he said. 'She keeps going on about something called a Whipple procedure' – I nodded – 'and chemoradiotherapy and all kinds of other stuff.'

'She probably knows more than me already,' I joked feebly. 'It's not my area. But there are lots of treatment options, Gray, if the diagnosis is – what we think it might be. It's not all doom and gloom.'

He went on almost as if I hadn't spoken. 'So I went and did some googling myself. And Dr Google tells me that before you start chemotherapy, you've got to have a kidney function test.'

'That's standard, I believe,' I said, feeling a cold trickle of dread creep down my spine.

He knows, and he knows I know.

'And that could prove problematic in my case,' he said.

I reached across the table and took his hand. 'Yes. Because you've only got the one kidney.'

EIGHT
ORLA

8 March 2024

I have slept badly, a sleep full of troubling dreams, and now that I am awake – the sky still dark, the promise of spring elusive on this icy morning – I remember why, and I feel the need to record what I learned yesterday.

I was returning home from Imran's shop, where I still go almost every day to pick up a copy of the *Guardian* and a pint of milk if I'm running low, as well as to catch up on whatever local gossip he is able to impart, when I saw Anna sitting alone on a bench in the square.

It's strange how – although our houses have their own gardens and ample space indoors – that place, with its regularly spaced benches and iron railings around its perimeter, seems to offer a sense of privacy. I've spent many hours there myself, tending to the roses or simply sitting beneath the trees and thinking, when I feel the need for solitude.

Anna's children would have been at school; her husband, I presumed, was out at work, and yet she had chosen this public space to come and sit alone, hunched against the late-afternoon chill, her coat buttoned and her woolly hat pulled down over her ears.

But I saw that she was crying, and so, after hesitating a moment, I decided I could not bear to leave her to her solitude.

I didn't need to use my key to open the gate; it was standing ajar as she must have left it. I approached her slowly, clearing my throat.

Anna, I said, not sitting down just yet in case my presence was unwelcome. Are you all right?

She looked up at me, her skin bone-white and her eyes red, and she said, No. No, I'm not.

Then I sat next to her, reaching out to touch her gloved hand. She gripped mine fiercely and I waited for her to speak.

Gray is sick, she said at last, with difficulty, as if the cold had numbed her lips or she could barely bring herself to voice the words. Gray is going to die.

Anna! I was appalled. Of all the things for her to tell me, this was the last I had expected. My neighbour, who I've seen almost every day for twenty years – that vital man, so full of life and laughter. It seemed impossible. It was the other thing I had been expecting her to tell me – or one of the other things.

After that, the words came out of her in a rush. She stopped crying, but her voice was as hoarse as if she had been screaming.

He has cancer, she told me. The tests show it is inoperable – it has spread from his pancreas to his liver. The time he has left can be measured in weeks – months at best.

Is there nothing they can do? I asked.

What she told me next surprised me almost more than her original revelation.

He'd only got one kidney, she said. He always has had – she continued – ever since I've known him. But it wasn't congenital – he wasn't born that way, although some people are apparently. He donated it. He gave it to a friend when he was twenty-two, before I met him. He doesn't really talk about it. I always thought it was a good thing – a wonderful thing for him to have done. But now...

Now, it transpired, Gray's body is not strong enough to withstand chemotherapy. That altruistic act as a young man has turned into a death sentence – or so it seems to her. I know very little about medical matters – I have never needed to, thank God – but I suspect the prognosis might be the same even if he had two functioning kidneys. For Anna, though, this feels like the deciding factor, the one thing she is focusing on.

There was something else, too. I could sense it in Anna's utter dejection – the way she tilted her head and looked at me as if she was about to say something else, but didn't. Something equally painful and perhaps even harder for her to come to terms with.

Something she is keeping to herself, at least for now.

I know about secrets. I know how they eat away at the soul in the same way cancer eats at the body – as silent, as invisible and as deadly. I know how it feels to live in fear of them being brought to light.

But I didn't say that, or even ask many questions. I only listened to her, holding her hands as the last of the day faded, and lights began to come on in the surrounding houses.

Poor Anna. Those poor children.

NINE
ANNA

The news from Gray's doctors came in a trio of devastating blows, so powerful that they felt almost physical.

Yes, it's cancer.
It's advanced and inoperable.
Unfortunately chemotherapy won't be possible.

Although the news was delivered with tact, sensitivity and compassion, it left me bludgeoned, almost unable to catch my breath.

We left the oncologist's office together, a sheaf of printed leaflets stuffed into my handbag: advice, information, support, details of people we could contact and people who would contact us. I gripped Gray's hand, feeling the sweat on my palm slippery against his skin.

'Are you okay, Anna?' he asked.

'Yes,' I lied, forcing a smile. 'It's a shock. But I'm okay. I've got to be okay. It's not like there's another option. How are you feeling?'

'I want to get drunk.' I looked at him. His face was pale in the thin March sunlight, his eyes almost feverishly bright. 'Completely arseholed. And then maybe do a couple of lines. And then...'

He didn't finish, but I knew what he was thinking. *Have an absolutely epic shag.* Except the person he wanted to do that with wasn't me.

'You're not going to, are you?' I asked.

'Course not. I'm going to go into the office and talk to Carl.'

His business partner. I knew that Gray had mentioned he wasn't well, was having some tests done. But there was no point in scaring the horses, he'd said. No point in preparing people for the worst until we knew what the worst was.

Now we did. I pictured the bright, edgy converted warehouse in Soho, Gray and Carl's team perching expectantly on their desks with Stanley mugs of coffee, called for an all-staff meeting. *Has someone been promoted?* they'd be wondering. *Will they be making redundancies? Are we moving offices?*

Whatever they expected, it wouldn't be this.

'We'll have to get a timeline in place,' Gray was saying. 'Assuming I've got another month of being able to work. Carl will have to decide whether he wants to recruit another MD, or promote someone – Catriona, maybe – or step into my role himself for the time being. Big decisions.'

In that moment, the question of who was going to be running Flick London in six months' time felt as trivial as who was going to get through to the fourth round of the FA Cup.

'Gray...' I forced air into my lungs, then forced it out again as words. 'We're going to have to tell the children.'

'I know.'

'Tonight?'

I took another step forward and felt a sudden drag on my arm. Gray had stopped walking, although he still had my hand in his. I stopped too, turning to face him. He hadn't cried in the appointment with the specialist, although I had. Right the way through, he'd been controlled and calm.

But he was crying now.

'Do we have to, Anna? Please say we don't have to.'

'I can't say that.' I stepped towards him and took him in my arms, feeling his tears cold against my cheek. 'We've got to, Gray.

It'll be awful, but we can't not. There's no point in waiting. It won't make it any easier.'

He said something, but his words were muffled against my shoulder. I pulled back and looked up at him. His face was bone white.

'All I ever wanted was to protect them.' His voice cracked. 'That's my job. How the hell am I meant to tell them I'm dying?'

I pulled him close again, pressing his body tight against mine. I was overwhelmed with tenderness, love and terrible, terrible sadness for him and for my children and for myself. But alongside all of that came a surge of rage so powerful it scared me.

You wanted to protect our children? How about not risking our whole family for the sake of a bit of fun with some random woman? How about not lying to me about where you were all those nights when I was cooking dinner and helping them with their homework and you were with her? How about protecting them from their mum and dad not going through a horrible, bitter divorce so you could be with someone else?

If I held him tight enough, close enough, he might not guess that I was thinking those things. If I held him for long enough, he might never be able to leave us.

At last I felt the shuddering of his shoulders stop and he pulled away.

'All right. Tonight then. I'll get home by seven.'

'Okay. Good luck in the office. I'll see you later.'

'Bye, Anna. Thanks for – you know. Everything.'

I reached up and touched his cheek, still damp with tears. 'That's my job.'

I watched as he turned and walked away. I wondered if he was going to call Laurel or arrange to meet her, so he could tell her too.

I walked on, my feet and my heart leaden. How would we tell Barney and Lulu? Just a few weeks before, when I'd been contemplating the possibility of our marriage ending, the prospect of telling the children that had been bad enough. But it was nothing in comparison to this.

I thought, *I could make pancakes*. Whenever Barney had had a disappointing end-of-year report or Lulu a falling-out with a friend, we'd make pancakes and talk it out, and by the time the last burned, wonky offering had been consumed, drizzled with lemon juice and caster sugar (Lulu) or maple syrup (Barney), everyone would feel better.

Then I thought, *Yes, Anna – way to tarnish all those happy memories forever with one devastating one.*

We told them after dinner.

I made soup – the vaguely Asian noodle soup I often made to use up the leftovers of a roast chicken, packed with whatever vegetables were going bendy in the fridge, fiery with ginger and chilli – just an ordinary, forgettable weekday meal. When we'd finished eating, the kids stacked their bowls in the dishwasher. Gray wiped the countertop; I decanted the leftovers into Tupperware. Barney poured himself a glass of milk and Lulu took an apple from the fruit bowl, and they both began to edge towards the stairs, the call of their bedrooms and their phones strong.

I heard Gray take a breath, but he didn't say anything, so I said it for him.

'Kids, sit down for a second, please.'

They both looked at me and then at each other, Barney's eyes blue like mine and Lulu's brown like her father's. I could see the silent sibling telepathy passing between them.

What did we do?

Dunno – nothing?

Is this going to be bad?

Looks that way.

The bafflement in their faces was replaced by alarm.

'We need to talk, as a family,' Gray said heavily. 'I'm sorry, it's not going to be easy.'

Barney sat down and took a gulp of his milk, the moustache it left on his top lip making him look like a small boy. Lulu polished her apple on the sleeve of her jumper, then edged on to the stool next to her brother. Augustus came in through his cat flap, meowed plaintively then jumped up on to the counter.

He wasn't normally allowed up there, but I didn't shove him off. This was a family conference, after all.

'You're getting divorced, aren't you?' Lulu's voice broke the silence, high and clear. 'We've heard you fighting, you know. We're not stupid.'

Shit. How could I have planted a seed of fear in my children's hearts that had been growing there secretly, making them afraid of something that wasn't going to happen when something worse was?

'No, darling,' I replied, reaching out to touch her arm. 'We're not getting divorced. It's something else.'

'Has Granny died?' Barney asked anxiously. 'Then I'll be the only one in school with no grandmothers.'

Gray shook his head. 'Please, let me explain.'

He told them about his diagnosis and what it meant. I sat and listened too, my hands clasped in front of me, trying not to cry – trying not to scream and run out of the room. Trying not to betray the anger that was surging inside me again at the cruelty and injustice of it all.

'So, wait, Dad.' Lulu's eyes were wide and brimming with tears. 'You're saying, you're going to, like, die?'

'The doctors don't think there's any way to treat it,' Gray said gently, pulling his chair up closer to her. 'They'll do everything they can. But...'

'What they can do is – well, it's not a lot,' I continued for him, my heart twisting with pain for Lulu and Barney. 'It's all about keeping your dad here, keeping him with us, for as long as they possibly can. That's what we've asked them to do.'

'I don't understand.' Barney put his glass of milk down on the counter. His trembling hand made it rattle against the marble worktop. 'Cancer's something old people get. And it's old people who die. You told me that when I was about four.'

I had, of course. I remembered it clearly – my frightened, crying boy who'd just twigged about the reality of life and death. I'd have told him anything to comfort him, but I thought what I'd said had a pretty decent chance of being true.

'Did your mum have it?' asked Lulu. 'Granny Graham, who we never met? Is that what she died of? Does that mean we'll get it?'

'Of course it doesn't mean you'll get it,' I said. 'It's not a hereditary thing.'

'And Granny... my mother, didn't have cancer,' Gray said gently, but I saw a flicker of something like panic cross his face. 'You know that. She died in a road traffic accident when I was at university.'

I saw Lulu's eyes, wide and terrified in her ashen face, before I scooped her into my arms, feeling her tears begin to flow down my neck. Barney was crying too, held tightly by his father.

'Will Dad still be here for my birthday?' Lulu asked, when eventually she was able to speak again.

'We don't know, sweetheart,' Gray said. 'I can't promise. But if it's humanly possible, I will. Every single second I've had with you has been precious, and however many I've got left are even more important. I can promise that.'

'Dad.' Barney put his thumb in his mouth – a habit he'd broken years before – then realised and bit his nail instead. 'Will it hurt loads?'

'Not if I can help it.' Gray stroked his son's hair. 'I'm going to take all the drugs going. The doctors won't let it hurt.'

At last, when we'd answered all the questions we could, Gray said, 'Come on, you two. Time to hit the sack.'

He stood up, Barney still on his lap, and hoisted him higher to carry him up the stairs. As he reached the landing, I saw his legs buckle and he almost fell before righting himself and struggling on. Barney had shot up recently, and it was a long time since Gray had carried him – but still, his weakness appalled me.

It's happening, I thought. *It's happening already.*

But I couldn't let the children see my terror. I sat on the edge of

Lulu's bed after she'd cleaned her teeth, stroking her hair like I used to when she was small. From the next-door bedroom, I could hear Gray's voice speaking softly to Barney.

'I'll stay for as long as you want,' I told my daughter.

But she said, 'I think I want to be on my own, Mum.'

So I kissed her and left her and went downstairs, my mind already veering to the email I was going to have to compose to their school, the meeting I'd have to arrange to talk through it all with them and discuss how best to support the children.

I poured a glass of wine, took two deep gulps without closing the fridge door, then filled my glass again and sat down. It was done. We'd done our best – but had we got it right? Our children would never forget this night, and nor would I. I replayed everything we had said, everything they had asked.

One moment stuck in my mind.

Barney had asked about his grandmother. Not my mum, who the kids saw a few times a year, who faithfully sent birthday cards and gifts, whose flapjack recipe they considered the best thing in the world, ever.

Gray's mother, who we never spoke of.

She died in a road traffic accident when I was at university.

It was another truth I'd always known about him, always accepted, internalised like I had his missing kidney.

But tonight, when he'd said it, there had been something different in his face and voice. Something unfamiliar.

It was how I'd imagined he'd look when I confronted him about the earrings, except I never got the chance because he'd confessed to me first.

It was guilt.

TEN
LAUREL

It was a Wednesday and my day off work. All week, the sun had been taunting me through the hospital windows as I hurried through the overheated wards and corridors; when I arrived in the mornings, it was still cold enough for my hands to feel frozen on to the handlebars of my bike, and when I left in the evenings it was already dark.

Now, though, it was almost midday and gloriously spring-like. Daffodils were showing their faces in the grass like a host of miniature suns, the sky was a clear, radiant blue and there was barely a breath of wind. I chained my bike to a stand, squeezing it in between a crowd of others and hoping it would still be there when I returned, and hefted my bulging backpack higher on my shoulders.

I found a spot in the park near the lake, half under a tree and half in sunshine, and spread out the blanket I'd brought, unpacking my posh food haul on to it, one eye on my phone.

There in 5, Gray texted. *Got held up in a meeting.*

I smiled. It had been over two weeks since we'd seen each other in the coffee shop. That, by necessity, had been rushed and uncomfortable; this would be special.

It needed to be special.

When I saw him coming towards me along the path in the sunshine, I raised my hand and smiled, then jumped to my feet to greet him. I tried not to let my face betray my feelings – or at least not all of them, only the surge of happiness I felt when I took him in my arms.

He'd got thinner. Even thinner than I'd expected. His cheeks were hollow. There was a scab on his jaw where he must have cut himself shaving, his razor encountering a bone that had been cushioned before. Even the way he walked was different, his usual athletic stride slower, not quite a shuffle but not far off.

'You look beautiful,' he said.

I kissed him. 'So do you. Hungry?'

'I'm trying to be.' He sat down. 'Looks like you raided Fortnum's.'

'Only the best for you. There's bread, pâté, cheese, fruit, chocolates – the lot.'

'But no booze.' He shook his head in mock disapproval.

'You're working, remember?'

'For now. Until the end of the week. But I can't really stomach it now, if I'm honest.'

'So have some sparkling water. It's kiwi flavoured – for all I know it'll taste like wee.'

'Nothing like a drop of wee on a spring afternoon.'

We laughed and I felt my mood lighten. I opened the packages of food, and we ate and drank. Or rather, Gray tried to eat. I watched as he took a bite of bread and butter then put the rest down, bit into a slice of mango and grimaced. I felt a surge of anxiety – almost panic – at how he was deteriorating, dwindling. His appetite for food was leaving him, and eventually his appetite for life would too. I'd been hungry myself when I sat down, but I had to force myself to look enthusiastic as I ate.

We talked about normal things: the long bike ride I'd done on Sunday, in spite of the driving rain. The mouse Gray's family cat had caught and left dismembered on the kitchen floor. The alarming developments in world politics.

When it was clear neither of us could eat any more, I wrapped the food up and tucked everything away in my backpack, and he lay down on the blanket, resting his head on my thighs. I stroked his head the way he liked, smoothing the hair back from his temples, my fingertips exploring the familiar curves and planes of his skull.

'Gray?' I said gently.

'Speaking.'

'What do you think would have happened to us in the end? If this hadn't?'

'Us?' He smiled, his eyes closed against the sun. 'We'd have got married and lived happily ever after.'

I felt a sharp stab of pain – not sadness exactly; I was too used to sadness already for it to give me a sharp stab of anything. But something else, something more like regret.

'You're already married, remember?'

'I could've become a bigamist. Or a polyamorist – isn't that what all the young people are into now?'

'Not sure we're young enough for that sort of carry-on.'

'Laurel.' He opened his eyes, squinting against the sun. 'Here's the thing. I don't know. I met you and I fell head over heels, and I thought that somehow it would all work out. I never really thought about *how*. All I knew was that I didn't want to hurt Anna and the kids.'

'You have hurt her, though,' I went on. 'Now she knows about me.'

'Course. It's been hard for her, finding out about us along with... all the other stuff. But it's not like things were perfect between us before.'

'How weren't they perfect?'

He grimaced, pushing his sunglasses up off his eyes. I could see the yellow tinge in the whites.

'No marriage is. No person is, right? You start out and everything's roses and violins and then you buy a house and suddenly every conversation you have is about money and plastering, and then you have kids and all you talk about is sleepless nights and shitty nappies, and before you know it you've lost your way.'

'Is that what happened with you and Anna? You lost your way?'

He sighed. 'I'm not good with words. I'm a visual guy. But I guess so.'

I thought about me and Simon. The scuffs and chips that had appeared along the way in our relationship, the outworn habits, my awareness that it wasn't right for me any more but my reluctance to change anything because what I had was familiar and comfortable and I thought that was enough – until it wasn't.

'Would that have happened with you and me? If we'd met each other twenty years ago instead of last year? If we'd... you know. Had kids and stuff?'

He reached for my hand and held it. 'You wanted a baby, didn't you, Laurel?'

I hesitated, but there was no point in denying it. 'Yes. I mean, that's why I left Si. He said he wasn't ready yet, but he'd been saying it for ten years and it was pretty darn clear that unless I started poking holes in condoms with a pin it wasn't going to happen.'

'Do you still want one?'

'In theory. I mean, if the stork brought me one right now I wouldn't say no. But when I met you – that kind of felt less important.'

He grinned – that familiar beam of delight that I'd fallen in love with. 'I swept you off your feet so fast you couldn't think of anything else, right?'

I couldn't help returning his smile. 'Well, yeah. You kind of did.'

'And how about now?' As quickly as it had lit up his face, the smile vanished. 'How do you feel about that now?'

'If I'm honest, it's the furthest thing from my mind. I can't even imagine...'

'That in the midst of death, there could be life?' In spite of the grimness of his words, his tone was light.

'I suppose. But mostly, it's still all about you. I can't see past that.'

'Good to know I've still got it.' He grinned, then he went on, suddenly serious. 'Laurel. Promise me something.'

'Of course.'

'If you meet someone else – like, now. Tomorrow. On the Tube home from here. Someone you could fall in love with and have a family with – promise me you'll do it. No matter if I'm still here or not. I wouldn't want you to even tell me. Just do it.'

I shook my head, almost unable to comprehend what he was saying. 'I couldn't.'

He reached out and squeezed my hand fiercely. 'You must. You'd be a fantastic mother.'

'How do you know?'

'Because you're loving and resilient and you're the world's best listener. And I know about mothers, trust me – I had a shit one, and I've seen Anna be a great one. I know which sort you'd be.'

I felt a kind of helplessness wash over me, as if I was drowning, and it was easier to give in to the current than keep swimming. I knew there could be no one else for me now – not while I still had even the small part of Gray that was mine. But I also knew what he needed to hear – that his guilt over Anna was enough for him to have to bear without having to feel guilty about me too.

'Okay,' I said. 'If I happen to get chatting to Chris Hemsworth in the pub tonight and he asks for my number, he's getting it. No ifs or buts.'

'Good girl. So long as you promise to send me a video.'

I laughed. 'But, Gray. There's a thing that's been bothering me.'

'You mean apart from the fact I'm going to cark it? What's that? Boiler playing up? Got a troublesome verruca? You can tell me, Laurel.'

I was laughing hard now, the kind of laughter that felt like it might turn to tears at any moment. I leaned down and kissed him, treasuring the feel of his lips against mine and the warmth of the sun on his skin.

When I could speak again, I said, 'It's just... I've been thinking. There's going to be a time when I see you and it'll be the last time.'

'Well, obviously. I'd have thought you'd have figured that out, what with being a healthcare professional and all.'

He'd stopped laughing now. His eyes were open and looking straight at me, so I could see the golden flecks within the coffee brown.

'I don't mean that. I don't mean when you're not here any more, although of course I've thought about that. I mean before.'

I looked away from him and squinted up at the sun, hoping its warmth would dry the tears I could feel springing to my eyes, but it didn't.

'What are you talking about?' He tried to smile, but I could tell that he was getting what I meant. 'You're not going to wait for me to shuffle off? You're going to dump me first? Even if you don't meet Chris Hemsworth in the pub?'

I shook my head. 'I tried that, remember? You wouldn't let me. I mean when... When you're not going to be able to get up and about so easily. When you can't come and meet me like this any more. And knowing that's going to happen is hard.'

Now he sat up. It looked like it was difficult to do – like he'd stiffened up, lying there, or like the strength in his abdominals wasn't what it was. Or like moving hurt him.

Once he was up, I swung my leg over his so we were sitting facing each other, my thighs either side of his hips, like lovers. He put his hands on my waist.

'Right,' he said. 'I get that. I wish I could plan for us to say goodbye. I wish I knew when it was going to happen. I wish I could have you with me when I go. But I can't promise that. I just want you to know you'll be in my heart right until the end. Right?'

'Right,' I said.

ELEVEN
ORLA

25 March 2024

I am normally an early riser – I have been all my life. But right now I am laid low with a foul cold, so after I had given the cats their breakfast I came back to bed with a cup of lemon-and-ginger tea, and went to sleep without writing my Morning Pages as usual.

While I was asleep – although clearly not deeply, because the sound half-woke me – there was a knock at my front door. It was nothing: perhaps a parcel, and I am expecting nothing urgent. Perhaps a political canvasser, getting an early bid in ahead of the election everyone expects later this year. I ignored it and allowed myself to drift back to sleep.

But that knock awakened something in my sleeping mind – more lucid than a dream and surprisingly vivid given how long ago it took place. Perhaps I recorded it at the time, somewhere in one of my Morning Pages journals, although I can't remember doing so.

It happened on another morning, early summer, perhaps fifteen or sixteen years ago. I had a cold then too, which is perhaps why the memory came back to me so clearly – I'm rarely ill and almost never put myself to bed during the day like this. But on that occasion, I remember, I didn't ignore the summons of the door knocker and go back to sleep. I put on my dressing gown and went downstairs.

A young man was standing outside. Perhaps thirty and strikingly handsome, with the combination of near-black hair and blue eyes I often saw growing up in Ireland but rarely do here.

He seemed as surprised to see me as I was to see him.

I'm sorry to bother you, he said, with a lilt in his voice that was not Irish but Welsh. Does Nigel live here?

I said, No. It's just myself and my daughter, and she's away.

Which I suppose is the last thing a lone woman should say to a strange man on her doorstep, but he seemed unthreatening enough.

In one of the other houses on the square, then, perhaps? He was perfectly polite, but he had the air of someone who wasn't giving up easily. Nigel Graham?

Nigel? Well, that was a surprise – so much so it took me a moment to figure out who he meant.

The Grahams are three doors down, I told him. At number eight.

He thanked me and apologised again for disturbing me and I returned once more to my bed and my self-pity.

But now I found I couldn't sleep. I lay there, upright on my pillows to relieve my stuffy head, listening to the last of the birdsong in the square outside as the sun climbed higher into the sky with the promise of another beautiful day.

I could also hear a knock on the door of number eight, and a few seconds later the strange young man's voice saying, Please don't slam the door in my face, followed by Gray's reluctant reply: I guess you'd better come in.

Then there was silence for perhaps twenty minutes. I was about to attempt sleep again when I heard the click of the Grahams' door opening.

I can remember their conversation so clearly, as if I heard it yesterday rather than all those years ago. Gray telling the other man he bore him no ill will, but telling him – ordering him, almost

– not to contact him again. The stranger saying he understood and agreed.

Then he said something like, We just thought you would want to know. I won't pass on the address if you don't want me to.

And Gray replying, a hint of desperation in his voice, Please don't.

Then there was a moment's silence; some instinct told me they might have been embracing. And then I heard the door close again and the other man's footsteps passing below my open window and fading away as he walked around the square and away towards the main road.

Of course – it must have been almost sixteen years ago: June 2008, because Anna was away visiting her parents with newborn Lulu. How peculiar that I should recall it now, though, and so clearly. Or perhaps it is not so peculiar after all, because now Anna has told me their tragic news, that Gray is terminally ill. And that encounter, with its hints of Gray's past – never mind a first name I'd never have guessed, although I have always half-assumed couldn't actually be Gray – has made me uneasy.

There was something Gray wanted to escape. Something he wanted to hide from. And I find myself wondering – almost fearing – whether his death will bring his secret to light.

TWELVE

ANNA

The day Gray finished at work felt like a particularly grim landmark, but the days that followed were grimmer still.

He came home late on the Friday night, as if it had been just another late one at the pub with his team – someone leaving, someone's birthday, someone having won an award for something. Except in this case it was someone being about to die. I couldn't imagine what Carl and Catriona and the others had been thinking, but presumably it had been something along the lines of giving Flick London's founder a decent send-off, honouring the Gray they'd worked with for a decade and a half, the Gray who'd always been up for a party, the Gray who'd celebrated every engagement, every promotion, every achievement.

I suppose Gray had wanted that too, or at least pretended to want it. But when he arrived home shortly after eleven that evening, he was ghostly pale and exhausted. He threw off his clothes on the bedroom floor and went into the bathroom, and I heard him throwing up, the groans interspersed with retching.

I tapped on the door and went in without waiting for him to answer, wrapped in my dressing gown, trembling with worry.

'Are you okay?' I asked stupidly. 'Do you need anything?'

He was hugging the toilet, naked. I was horrified to see the knobbly rope of his spine, the separate arc of each rib.

'Do I look like I'm fucking okay?' he responded. 'I've got terminal cancer, Anna.'

I flinched, feeling blood rush to my face as if he'd slapped me.

'I'm sorry. That was daft of me. Can I get you a glass of water?'

'You can fuck off and leave me alone.'

I stepped out of the room and closed the door, clinging on to the handle for a moment as if I might fall. In twenty years, he'd never said that to me and I'd never said it to him. Even during our worst rows, there had always been underlying affection and respect, not that cold, dismissive rage.

I got the glass of water anyway and left it by his side of the bed, along with the box of tablets I retrieved from his jeans pocket. There was a fresh indent in the leather of his belt where he'd had to tighten it to a new notch, I noticed, unthreading it and dropping his clothes in the laundry hamper.

I didn't say anything more to him. I knew that if I tried to speak I'd burst into tears, or the hurt and anger that were never far from the surface would erupt, breaking through my sadness and leaving me feeling worse than ever.

Don't talk to me like that, ever again, I imagined myself scolding. But if I said it, I'd have to acknowledge that there'd be a point, not long in the future, when he'd never talk to me at all, ever again.

Then I went to bed in the spare room, dragging mismatched covers on to the duvet and pillows, leaving the door open a crack and listening with dread for further sounds from him. I was trembling with fury and hurt, a pressure cooker of feelings that I couldn't let out. Was that how he felt about me – that cold contempt? Had he felt that way for a long time? Would he feel that way forever, now?

I was relieved to be away from him, on my own in the other room. But I knew that it wouldn't be long until he was no longer there at all, and I hated myself for my relief.

After a while, I heard the toilet flush, water running in the sink and the buzz of his toothbrush, followed by the tread of his feet on the landing. I heard him hesitate when he stepped into our bedroom, but he didn't come and find me, although he must have known where I was.

He got into bed, alone, and that was where he stayed for most of the weekend, emerging only to go to the bathroom. I offered him breakfast on Saturday morning, but he said he wasn't hungry. Desperate to maintain some sort of normality for the children, I took Lulu to meet her friends in the park, where they'd all taken to wobbling around the basketball courts on roller skates. I took Barney to football. I went to the supermarket and bought the ingredients for a lasagne.

While I was there, Gray texted me, just four words.

Can you get jelly?

Jelly? What the hell?
I hurried to the unfamiliar aisle where the instant puddings lived, which I hadn't visited since long-ago preschool birthday parties, and stared blankly at the packs of Angel Delight, Dream Topping and custard powder before picking up half-a-dozen packs of jelly crystals in all the available flavours.

When the lemon jelly had eventually set, I took the bowl up to the bedroom with a spoon.

Gray was asleep, Augustus curled up in the crook of his knees. I stood over him, not knowing what to do. He'd asked for jelly, and I'd provided jelly. But maybe he needed sleep more.

I didn't know, I realised. I didn't have the faintest clue how to do any of this.

I reached out and touched his shoulder. 'Gray?'

He mumbled, then turned over and opened his eyes.

'I brought you jelly,' I said. 'Shall I open the curtains?'

He struggled upright, sending the cat jumping to the floor with an affronted yowl.

'Yes, please,' he said. 'Thanks, Anna.'

I pulled back the curtains, looking out at the sunny square. Vivid green buds were appearing on the chestnut trees and before long the cherries would be flowering. The sun glinted off the black-painted iron railings and I could hear a blackbird singing.

I longed to go outside and sit there, or out in our own garden. But instead I opened a window so Gray could get some fresh air.

The sunlight coming through the window made the surface of the jelly sparkle, turning it gold. I remembered all the times I'd made it before – painstakingly filling scooped-out oranges with it for kids' parties, layering it in trifles at Christmas, never giving it a thought because it was just jelly.

I wondered whether Gray's mother had made it for him when he was a child when he was poorly, and whether that was why he wanted it now.

He took a spoonful, grimaced and put the spoon back in the bowl.

'Is that okay?' I asked. 'I made some of the raspberry flavour as well.'

He shook his head. 'It doesn't taste like I remembered it.'

'They've probably taken out the E numbers or something,' I attempted to joke. 'Where's the fun in it now?'

But Gray didn't laugh. He ate another microscopic spoonful, then handed the bowl back to me.

'I'm sorry, Anna. Maybe custard?'

'Or ice cream?' I suggested.

'Maybe. I'll come downstairs in a bit. But would you mind closing that window? It's freezing.'

It wasn't, but I closed it anyway and then sat down on the bed.

'Gray? Speaking of coming downstairs, I was talking to the district nurse the other day. She called just – you know. Just to see how we're doing.'

'Well, next time you can tell her we're managing splendidly,' he said bitterly.

Ignoring his harshness, I carried on. 'She was saying they could arrange a bed for you downstairs. You might be more comfortable in… you know. A proper one.'

'A hospital bed?'

I nodded. 'And you'd be closer to the kitchen and stuff. You wouldn't need to manage the stairs.'

'And you wouldn't have to run up and down two flights of stairs to bring me my kids' party food.'

'I don't mind doing that.'

'You might not now. But it'll get very old, very quickly.'

'It's fine.' I put my hand on his knee, feeling its boniness through the duvet. 'I mean… you want to stay here, right? Here at home.'

'To die peacefully in my own bed with the cat next to me, like Terry Pratchett?'

'Yes, I suppose so.'

'Living the dream,' he said. 'Or rather, not living it. Here's the thing, Anna…'

'What?'

He shook his head.

I said, 'Gray. This is shit, right? It's shit for everyone, but it's most shit for you. If you want custard, I'll get you custard. If you want me to run up the stairs five times a day, I'll do that. If you want…'

I shrugged helplessly, unable to imagine what else he might want that I could give him.

But he told me. 'If I want Laurel to come here and see me, you'll be okay with that?'

I closed my eyes, staring towards the window, the brightness of the spring day creating scarlet patterns on my eyelids. Seeing red – I was literally doing that. I clenched my fists, digging my nails into my palms.

'I see,' Gray said. 'You'd do anything for me, but you won't do that.'

'It's my home.' I opened my eyes again and looked at him. His face was set in the stubborn lines I knew so well, from so many arguments.

'And my home,' he said.

'And the children's.'

'The children will be at school.'

That was true – Gray and I, together with Barney and Lulu and the school's head of pastoral care, had agreed that it was best for them to continue with their normal routine for as long as possible.

'You don't have to talk to her, Anna,' Gray went on. 'I'm not asking you to offer her coffee and cake.'

'Gray. You can't ask me to do that. Seriously. What are you thinking? It's not—'

'Not fair? None of this is fair, Anna. You think it's all beer and skittles for me? Or for her?'

Maybe she should have thought of that before she started fucking a married man. As soon as the words formed in my mind, I hated myself for them.

'I can go out and meet her, for now. But I won't always be able to. Only until... you know.' His voice trailed off, and he took a breath before continuing, his tone becoming less harsh and more pleading. 'I want to see her, and she wants to see me. Please, Anna. I know it's hard for you. Please do this one thing for me.'

I felt my shoulders slump in defeat. I couldn't deny his request. Gray was dying and therefore he got to have what he wanted. Whatever he wanted.

I picked up the bowl of jelly from the bedside table.

'Custard, maybe?' I said. 'I can go out and get some.'

He said, 'I don't think so. I'm going to sleep.'

'Okay.'

'Anna?'

In the doorway, I turned back to him.

'Thank you. Thank you for everything.'

As I turned again to leave the room, I saw his hand reaching out for his phone.

THIRTEEN
LAUREL

Damask Square. The last time I'd seen it – the only time – I'd expected to just be passing through. It had been a detour, a random decision I took when I got slightly lost cycling through East London to the Docklands, where I was planning on taking the foot tunnel across to Greenwich to do some hill sprint training.

And look how that worked out.

Today I was an official visitor, coming on foot, and that wasn't all that was different. Then, I'd been enjoying the freedom of a Saturday on my own, the pleasure of pushing my bike and my body to their limits, taking for granted that here was my life, my time, and I was using it in a way that would make me happy.

Now, life, time and happiness all seemed like the most fragile things imaginable.

I turned off the main road at the corner by the newsagent – a shabby relic that must have stood there long before the market got upgraded with designer shops around its perimeter and the Square Mile extended its borders beyond Bishopsgate like an invading army.

I felt a bit like an invader too.

The square was just as I remembered it. The iron railings, the tall, graceful houses, the silence that surrounded me as soon as I left the main road behind. *Posh*, I'd thought then, and I thought it again now. Perhaps I should have worn something different, to fit in. A taupe trench coat and over-the-knee boots, or something like that. Only I didn't own anything like that, so I was wearing jeans and trainers.

Gray wouldn't care, but it wasn't only Gray I was going to see.

The smell of compost reached me, and inside the railed square I could see a middle-aged woman on her knees, doing something to the beds of rosebushes that were planted in its centre. She lifted her head as I passed and watched as I approached the door of number eight, raising a gloved hand in greeting before returning to her work.

I didn't wave back. I felt too out of place, too alien, too nervous.

I raised my hand towards the brushed-steel knocker on the door, which was painted an even slate grey. But just as my fingertips reached its cool surface, the door opened.

A woman stood there, looking at me with wariness bordering on hostility. She was tall – statuesque, I suppose you might say if you liked flowery words. Her hair was blonde and shiny, and her eyes were blue. She was wearing jeans too, but hers were perfectly fitting, not baggy at the knees like mine. Her jumper was rose pink and looked like cashmere. Her skin was clear and glowing, the skin of a woman who'd always toned and moisturised and worn SPF 50 even in winter.

Anna. Gray's wife.

'Hello,' I said.

'Laurel.' She pronounced my name like it left a bad taste in her mouth. 'Gray's sleeping, but you may as well come in.'

I stepped into the hallway. The first time I'd seen it, I was too shocked and, let's face it, too embarrassed (because who wants to be peeled off the pavement by a handsome man after somehow fracturing their wrist falling off a bike while travelling at less than twenty miles an hour? Plus, I'd almost killed his cat) to take much in.

Now, though, I noticed the details. The industrial-style

pendant light. The stairs stretching upwards, carpeted in a monochrome geometric pattern. The jewel-coloured paint and peony-printed wallpaper in the front room, which I glimpsed through a half-open door as we walked past.

'We'll go downstairs,' Anna said. It was more a command than an invitation, so I followed her obediently.

Downstairs was equally swanky. At one end was what I presumed was a family room – shelves groaning with books, squashy teal sofas, a television with a picture of the cat on its sleeping screen. In the centre was a huge wooden dining table, one side suspended from the ceiling and the other supported by a single leg, like a letter L on its side. The far end was taken up by a vast kitchen with a marble-topped island, a wine cooler, a space-age coffee machine and shelves stacked with cookbooks. Beyond, glass doors and a flight of flagstone steps led up to the garden.

It was a gorgeous house. The kind of place I might have dreamed of living in if I'd ever seen anything like it for real before.

'Your home is lovely,' I said, pausing to take it all in.

Anna looked back at me, her face still. 'Coffee?'

Clearly, we were not going to be new BFFs – not that I'd expected that. Still, I felt myself tightening with embarrassment, not knowing whether I would offend her more by accepting or declining, or if it would make no difference because I had offended her so much already just by existing.

And sleeping with her husband, of course.

'I was going to make some anyway,' she said, as if relenting slightly.

'Thanks.' I smiled cautiously. 'That would be great.'

She flew into action, as if she was relieved to have something to do, offering me milk and sugar ('Frothed or flat? Brown or white?') and putting homemade shortbread on a plate. I wondered if she always had baked goods on hand in case of unexpected guests or whether she'd made it especially, not as a gesture of welcome but as a way of saying, *See? This is the life he's had with me.*

Or maybe, having teenage children, she simply kept her kitchen full of calorie-dense treats as a matter of course.

We sat together at the kitchen counter and drank our coffee, talking first about the weather and then, formally, as if he was just some mutual acquaintance, about Gray's health.

'He gets very tired,' she said, 'and his appetite's not great.'

'That'll be the pain medication, I expect. Have they given him anything to help his appetite?'

'Yes, but...' She shrugged, then glanced at her phone. 'He's awake now. I've put a baby monitor up there. It seems ridiculous, but it was the best thing I could think of.'

'That's a really good idea,' I said. 'In a house this size...'

I was interrupted by a click and a rattle, and the cat came strolling in through his flap from the garden. Again, I remembered seeing him that first time, unsure if it was a feline or canine trying to commit hara-kiri beneath my bike wheels. Now I could see that he was, in fact, an exceptionally large animal, black and white and fluffy, with a magnificent set of whiskers.

I got off my stool and squatted down to fuss him. 'Hello, Augustus.'

It was as if the temperature in the room had suddenly dropped ten degrees. I heard the rattle of crockery as Anna put our coffee things in the dishwasher, then felt her standing over me.

'You may as well go up,' she said.

'Okay. Thank you. Is it...?'

'I'll show you. And, Laurel...'

I looked at her. Her blue eyes were as cold as marbles.

'You've fucked my husband. You can befriend my cat if you like. But stay the hell away from my children.'

By the time we'd climbed two storeys' worth of stairs to reach the bedroom, I'd managed to compose myself. Anna's words – or not so much her words but the venom with which she'd spoken – had thrown me. Of course she was angry with me. I would be too. Anyone would be. But seeing it like that, seeing that poised, smooth face twisting with rage, hearing her middle-class London voice turn into a hiss of fury, was frightening.

So frightening I wanted to let myself straight out of the Farrow & Ball painted front door and leg it home.

Except I wanted to see Gray more.

The room was at the front of the house at the end of a landing with three other doors leading off it – a guest bedroom and study, maybe, and a bathroom; I couldn't imagine the kids not having a floor to themselves in a house like this.

Anna tapped on the door, opened it and said, 'She's here.'

Then she turned and walked away.

I stepped in. The bed was below the window, the open curtains letting sunlight flood in, falling on the white sheets and Gray's pale face and hands. Was it my imagination, or had his hair got whiter too, since the last time I saw him?

But his smile was the same as always. 'Come to take my blood pressure, nurse?'

It was a running joke between us. The first time I told him what I did for a living, he'd said, 'A nurse? Every red-blooded man's fantasy,' and I – having heard comments like that too often before – had pointed out that, after a day in a polyester uniform running around an overheated hospital, I was no one's fantasy except an anosmiac's.

'Shut it, pervert,' I said.

Gray burst out laughing, and so did I. I ran the few steps across the room and threw myself down on the bed next to him, feeling his arms enfold me. For a few minutes we just lay there, holding each other. I felt our chests rising and falling in unison as my breath steadied. I could smell his familiar aftershave overlaying the other smells that were familiar too, but not *his* smells. I could hear birdsong outside, the distant hum of traffic and a faint crackling from the headphones on the bedside table, which he must have removed without pausing whatever he'd been listening to.

After a bit, I kissed him and sat up. 'I brought you a present.'

'You didn't have to. I'm graped up to the max.'

'Just as well I didn't bring grapes, then.' I stuck my tongue out at him. 'I brought a game. It's called *Oh My Pigeons*.'

I took the box out of my bag and laid it on his lap.

'It says, "Suitable for ages eight and up." Glad you've got such a high opinion of me.'

'I figured it was about the level of your taste in dirty jokes.'

He laughed. 'Seriously, Laurel. This is great. You know, the kids... they come up and see how I'm doing and then they sort of drift off again. It's like they don't...'

'I know,' I said. 'Maybe this'll help. Shall we have a go first though? So you can teach them how it works?'

We unpacked the game and I lay on the pillow next to him so we could study the instructions.

'It says the person who saw a pigeon most recently gets to start,' he complained. 'That's not fair.'

'What's not fair? You're lying here right by an open window and I'm inside a hospital all day. Come on.'

'Next time you'd better bring me a bird feeder, then I'll always get to start.'

'My God, and I thought you public school boys were all about fair play.'

'All's fair in love and *Oh My Pigeons*.'

We laughed, and by the time we got the game under way we were laughing even harder. I won the first, he won the second and I won the third. He tried to insist on playing the best of five, but I could see he was tiring, and I felt I was outstaying my welcome.

So I said, 'Come on, give me a cuddle instead.'

I packed away the cards and pieces and lay down with my head on his shoulder, my hand inside his pyjama top. The skin down the side of his body was as soft as an expensive leather handbag; I stroked it, just firmly enough that he wouldn't get ticklish.

Then my thumb found the end of the nephrectomy scar, and I paused there.

'Do you ever think about him?' I asked.

'Who? Joel? Not really,' he murmured. His voice was muffled, and his eyes were closing.

'You don't see him any more?'

'Haven't done in years. We lost touch. Water under the bridge. I'd paid my debt.'

I didn't ask any more. I just lay there with him, feeling his breathing slow until at last it came out in a snore. Then I eased myself away from him, picked up my bag and shoes and tiptoed out.

Anna was waiting by the front door. It was only when I saw her that I wondered whether she'd been watching us the whole time, via the baby monitor app on her phone.

FOURTEEN

ANNA

I only used the baby monitor the once to spy on Laurel and Gray. When I'd first suggested buying one, he'd reacted with fury, but once I pointed out that if I could see when he was awake, I could come up and ask him if he needed anything, rather than him having to summon me with a text, he saw the sense in the idea and reluctantly agreed.

Laurel seemed to think it was nothing out of the ordinary, either, nor even realise that I'd made her aware of its existence as a kind of warning. Although, to be fair, the first time she came to see Gray she looked as wide-eyed and frightened as Bambi in the thunderstorm, like I was going to kick her out of the house or spit in her coffee. I couldn't help spending a second taking in her appearance – seeing what I was up against. She was shorter than me and petite. She had dark brown hair with a few threads of grey in it. She was wearing faded jeans, a baggy sweatshirt and no make-up. Her hazel eyes were wide and wary, and the freckles were standing out on her pale skin, and I felt almost sorry for her.

Not too sorry to listen outside the door, though. After I let her in, I'd turned to go back downstairs when I heard that shout of laughter, and it stopped me in my tracks. I hadn't heard Gray laugh like that in ages. So I stepped silently back towards the bedroom, avoiding the one floorboard that creaked, and waited. I couldn't hear anything more at all. It was like they were doing silent breathing exercises in there or something.

It was that thought that made me wonder whether I'd been expecting to hear sex sounds. I felt my face flame and turned and hurried quietly away, feeling grubby and ashamed.

The second time she came, I left them to it. I didn't offer her coffee again; I didn't even show her up to the bedroom. I just said hello, gestured towards the stairs and told her to call me if he needed anything. She stayed for about an hour and a half, then appeared in the kitchen.

'He's asleep,' she said, 'so I'll be off. Thank you, Anna.'

I nodded and said goodbye. There was no point in asking when she would come again; she'd arrange that with Gray, and Gray would inform me. That, it seemed, was the way it was going to work.

Then, on her third visit, something snapped inside me. Again, I could hear no sounds from upstairs. Gray hadn't sent her down to fetch him a glass of iced water or the banana ice cream he was currently craving, although he never ate much of it. They were just there, in that bedroom – doing what?

Hating myself, I picked up my phone and tapped through to the app. The sound was turned down, but I could see them both, lying fully clothed on the bed in the sunshine that streamed through the window, Laurel's back against the pillows where mine used to rest before I moved out to the spare room.

Gray was doing something with his hands, twisting them into an unfamiliar shape. Were they communicating in sign language, I wondered, conscious that I might be listening in? But Gray didn't know sign language, and Laurel wasn't looking at his hands. As I watched, she turned to him and said something. They both laughed and his hands dropped. Then Laurel raised her hands, and there was more of the twisting, more of the staring.

Suddenly I got it. They were making shadow animals on the opposite wall. With a fresh surge of self-loathing, I turned the sound up, just in time to hear Gray say, 'It's a cock and balls,' and their laughter ringing out.

I could barely bring myself to say goodbye to her after that. I just opened the front door and let her out, ignoring her thanks. I stood and waited while she walked away, her stride swinging and athletic, across the square and towards the main road, where I presumed she would be getting a bus or the Tube to wherever she lived or worked.

But I didn't go back into the house. I picked up my keys, called up to Gray that I was going out and he should text me if he needed me, and walked the short distance to Imran's newsagent shop. I wanted a cigarette. And not just one – lots of them. I hadn't smoked for almost seventeen years, not since I'd found out I was unexpectedly pregnant with Lulu. I'd knocked the habit on the head right then – surprisingly easily, thanks to being as sick as a dog – and had never been tempted to take it up again.

I wanted to smoke now. I wanted to feel that first harsh hit of nicotine make my head swim, to exhale the smoke in a long ribbon and watch it furl in sunlight before disappearing. I wanted to light a second fag as soon as the first was finished. I wanted to...

Then it struck me. *That shit gives you cancer, Anna. The thing your husband's busy dying of. Do you want your children to have no parents, when as it is they're going to have just one?*

So I bought a disposable vape instead, pointing randomly at the display behind the counter, ignoring Imran's curious gaze. Then I walked back to Damask Square, but instead of letting myself in through my own front door, I knocked on Orla's, three doors away at number five.

She took a while to answer, but just as I was about to give up I heard her hurrying feet and the door opened.

'Anna. My dear. Is everything all right?' She was wearing an apron over a cream silk shirt and turned-up jeans, and there was flour on her hands and a smudge of it on her cheek.

'Everything's fine. Well – fine-ish. I'm sorry – I've interrupted you. I just wanted to...'

'You're interrupting nothing,' she assured me. 'I've just put the bread on to prove. Come in and I'll wash my hands.'

I followed her through to her kitchen, which was at the back of the house as mine was, only on the ground floor rather than the excavated basement. The doors were open to the garden, and the scent of damp grass mixed with the yeasty smell of bread dough. In the patch of sun that fell through the skylight, her two cats, one tabby and one tortoiseshell, were dozing.

'Would you like a cup of tea?' she asked, scrubbing her hands at the sink. 'Or something to eat, as it's almost lunchtime?'

'I... Please don't go to any trouble. I guess I just wanted someone to talk to.'

'In that case I shall open a bottle of wine,' she said. 'The sun's over the yardarm, as they say. Unless you're driving anywhere?'

I shook my head. 'The kids are making their own way home from school. It's Thursday – the one day they've got nothing on.'

'Then that's settled.' She opened the fridge and took out a bottle of rosé, following it with a block of cheddar. She took glasses from a cupboard, bread from the bread bin and a bowl of tomatoes from the countertop, and put everything out on the table. 'This is the best I can do, I'm afraid.'

'It's wonderful.' I sat down and she poured wine into our glasses. 'Thank you. I feel – it's a lot. You know.'

'I know.' She raised her glass and took a sip. 'How are you, Anna?'

It was typical of Orla to ask that instead of what everyone else asked: *How's Gray?*

I said, 'I feel like I'm drowning.'

She didn't say anything in response, just tilted her head and waited for me to carry on.

I gulped my wine and sucked furiously on my vape pen, coughing at the first puff before getting the hang of it. Then I started talking and found I couldn't stop. I told her about Laurel – about Gray's affair. She was the first person I'd told; to everyone else – my sisters, my friends, the mothers of my children's friends –

I'd spoken about Gray's illness, his terminal diagnosis and all that went with that, but not about the other thing.

I couldn't put into words why not, but as I spoke to Orla I realised.

'It's like it's all my fault,' I said. 'He cheated on me and now he's sick. He's going to die. It's like I failed him twice. Failed at everything. I couldn't keep my husband faithful, and now I can't keep him alive.'

'You know that's not how it works, Anna. Of course you do. Marriages are complicated. Men do things they shouldn't. Women too, but...'

'But mostly men. And now I feel – I feel like I wasn't enough. Not only me but the kids too. How could he have risked it all for that? For her?'

'Because he didn't feel like there was a risk,' Orla said gently. 'Or he didn't think at all.'

'I guess.' I could hear my daughter in my voice – an almost teenage petulance. 'But that's how it feels.'

'I understand that,' Orla said.

'And there's another thing. She's coming here. Coming to our house to see Gray. He insisted. He said he'd move into a hospice otherwise. So there was nothing I could do.'

'That sounds unimaginably hard.' Carefully, Orla poured more wine for us.

'And the worst thing... The worst thing is, she makes him so fucking happy. I can't bear to see him like that with her.'

The tabby cat stood up from the floor, stretched luxuriously, then hopped up on to Orla's lap, butting his head against her hand. She stroked him, her fingers almost disappearing into the plush coat.

'You know,' she said slowly, 'this isn't the same at all. But I think perhaps in a way it is. Do you remember my Maud?'

I did, of course. For the first fifteen years Gray and I had lived at Damask Square, Orla's black cat had been a permanent presence, stalking along the garden fences on the hunt for squirrels, terrorising Augustus and occasionally letting out blood-curdling howls in the street at night as she told an invading fox where to go.

'Who could forget her?' I said.

Orla smiled. 'She was a character. One of the things she used to do was wake me up in the morning for her breakfast by pricking my face with her claws. I'd be asleep and I'd feel her paw on my skin, cool and gentle at first. Then she'd extend a claw and I'd feel red-hot pain. Often there'd be blood on the pillow when I eventually got up.'

'Ouch.' I grimaced in sympathy. 'But you still loved her.'

'With all my heart. And after she was gone, for quite a long time, at least until I got these two, I'd find myself waking up with the sense that something was missing. Even though at the time, if you'd asked me, I'd have said I hated her clawing my face.'

'Love hurts, right?'

'Sometimes it does. But the other thing is, if I could have her back for just one day, I'd be jumping out of bed first thing to feed her. I'd do anything she wanted.'

I sighed and gulped some wine. 'Okay. I get what you're saying.'

'I'm saying it clumsily,' she admitted. 'But, Anna – what's coming in the months ahead will be hard. If you give yourself cause to feel guilt as well as all the sadness and… everything else, it'll only be harder for you. It'll only make things worse.'

'You're right. I know you are. It's just – I feel so angry.'

'Of course you do. You can't always control your feelings. But you can't control Gray's either. And, Anna…'

'What?' I asked when she stopped, leaving a silence for me to fill.

'Gray's a complex man. You know that better than I do, of course. There will be reasons why he's acted the way he has. That's not to say it's excusable, but it might be understandable.'

'What reasons could there possibly be?' I demanded. 'Okay, our marriage wasn't perfect. But whose is? I've put the effort in. I gave up work to sort out our house renovation and raise our family.

I put up with him working crazy hours and then going out and getting plastered afterwards. I supported him when he went on that massive health kick and lived on chicken breasts and fizzy water for months. I encouraged him when he took up cycling, even though it meant him swanning off for hours every weekend and leaving me with the kids. I never...'

I trailed off. I'd been going to say, *I never resented it.* But I had, and I knew that Orla would be able to hear that in my voice. And Gray would have resented me resenting him. Contrast that with the unconditional adoration he'd presumably found in Laurel, and – well. I'd got what was coming to me.

'Good men don't go running off after other women just because they're a bit bored with their wives,' I finished lamely.

'I'm not trying to justify what he's done. But I wonder whether, in time, you might come to understand it. And in the meantime...'

I nodded slowly. Of course, she was right.

I was going to have to accept Laurel's presence. That, and make sure that whatever total sum of happiness was left in my husband's life would at least come partly from me and the kids, and not all from her.

FIFTEEN
LAUREL

'I feel like the fat, speccy short-arse at a speed-dating event,' complained Harry, my colleague and closest work friend. 'There's no way any of these kids will come and talk to us.'

'Come on, chin up,' I said. 'There must be two hundred kids here. Surely at least a couple of them are interested in a career in nursing.'

'I wouldn't bet on it.' Harry ran his hands through his glossy blond quiff and adjusted the NHS lanyard that hung round his neck. 'Have you scoped out the competition?'

I had. 'True. There's an investment bank over there, an AI software development outfit over the other side…'

'A luxury hotel chain two stalls away.'

'And just in case any of these little darlings do fancy working in a caring profession…'

'We've got the Royal Veterinary College right next to us.'

We laughed.

'See?' Harry rolled his eyes theatrically. 'No chance. We're like Cinderella if she went to the ball pre the fairy godmother's intervention.'

For the hundredth time, I rearranged the stack of blue-and-white 'Choose Nursing' leaflets on the shelf behind me and fixed the bright, encouraging expression back on my face.

'Still,' I said, 'at least it's got us off the wards for the day.'

Harry brightened. 'And at least we get to knock off early. I've a hot date tonight. A man I met in the actual flesh, can you believe it? And not even off Grindr. He's a barista. Our eyes met over my long black and the rest is history – or I hope so, at any rate.'

'You can serve caramel lattes at your wedding,' I suggested.

'And bacon baps,' Harry said. 'He gave me one on the house. That's when I got the bottle to ask him out. His name's Moussa and he's from the Ivory Coast. He's ever so fanciable.'

As Harry continued to describe Moussa's hotness, I felt my thoughts drifting into melancholy. The world he was in – one of hope and excitement, of blind faith that the One was out there somewhere, just waiting for you to find them – felt impossibly remote to me, like it had been in a different lifetime when I was last there.

Harry lowered his voice. 'How's your fellow doing, anyway, Laurel?'

I sighed. 'He has good days and bad days. You know how it goes. But I try and tell myself that every day's a gift. All the guff we tell our patients' families. But it's kind of different when it's you.'

'You're not buying your own hype,' Harry chided, but his voice was kind. 'Tell me again about your first date. I love that story.'

'It wasn't a date,' I objected. 'Come on, give me some credit. I knew he had a wife and I'm—'

'Not that kind of girl.' Harry raised his eyebrows cynically.

'Exactly. Well, I wasn't. But we'd been messaging, because I put his blanket in my bag by mistake when we went to the pub, and I needed to give it back.'

'Because it was Missoni. Although you didn't know that until you sent me a picture of the thing and I was like, Laurel, that would have cost the thick end of five hundred smackers.'

'Exactly. But it took ages for my splint to come off and then he was busy at work. But by then he'd told me he was into cycling too, and I said I was really missing it but the fall had knocked my confidence.'

'And he said, "Let me help you get back on the horse."'

I sighed, remembering. Of course I should have said no, and returned Gray's blanket to him some other way. But when he told me he was planning a fifty-kilometre cycle in Epping Forest on a Sunday, and it was my day off and near my home, and the weather forecast promised glorious sunshine, I found I couldn't resist his invitation to join him.

Besides, he had my bike and it just made sense. Didn't it?

So I met him at the appointed spot, handed over the blanket and watched as he unloaded our bikes from his car. We set off, the trees and tracks and sparkling sky unfurling around us; I was conscious of only the pleasure of being out there on this gorgeous spring day, the cool air stinging my lungs, my body working again like it was supposed to, my confidence returning with every thrust of my legs.

He hadn't lied – the route was tough, with one challenging ascent after another. I'd kept up my fitness as best I could while I was signed off with my broken wrist, but I could feel myself labouring to keep up with him.

'You okay there, Laurel?' he'd asked.

Damn it. I wasn't going to be patronised by some man on a ten grand trophy bike. I put my head down and forced my legs into overdrive, slowly gaining on him, then drawing level, and then, just as we crested the hill, shooting past him.

Gasping for breath, we stopped, the breeze suddenly cool against my sweating face.

'And then he kissed you,' Harry said.

'That's right.'

'And you realised you were that kind of girl after all.' He sighed. 'Naughty Laurel. Not that I blame you. So romantic.'

'Yeah, that's what I thought too.'

Romantic. That's exactly what it was. In that moment, all thoughts of Gray's wife, his children, even my own morals, had fled my mind as if they'd been blown away by the wind. Nothing existed except Gray and me, his body and mine, our lips and tongues and his hands moving over my sweating back, sliding under my windproof jacket and over my skin so I gasped with desire.

'We can't,' I said. 'Not here.'

'There's no one to see except birds and rabbits,' he pointed out.

'I know. But still.'

He smiled. 'I'll ring you.'

And he had – the next day. We'd met up the following Sunday for drinks in a pub he'd suggested and I'd agreed to, neither of us acknowledging that he'd chosen it because it was on the opposite side of London from his home. At first, the meeting had been awkward as hell. We were both driving, so neither of us could drink. We ordered Diet Cokes and then – as much to give us something to talk about as anything – some food.

When it came, the steak was overcooked and leathery, the chips soggy and each plate adorned with a wrinkled grilled tomato.

'I'm sorry, Laurel,' he said. 'This is awful.'

I laughed. 'I've had far worse in the hospital canteen. Besides, it reminds me of going out to the Berni Inn when I was little. Massive treat.'

'Oh God, me too.' He grinned. 'Only ever on my birthday, because it was too dear.'

'The desserts! Lemon cheesecake with sultanas.'

'Are you mad? Ice cream sundae all the way.'

Suddenly we were laughing, united in our shared memories. It surprised me – from what I'd seen of Gray's house, his car and his bicycle, I'd expected him to have come from a background of wealth and privilege. But soon we were comparing notes about Findus crispy pancakes, chocolate concrete after school dinners and bags of scraps from the chippie.

'I was sixteen before I tasted garlic,' I told him.

His smile faded. 'Oh, things were a bit different for me by then. I went to a posh school.'

But before I could ask him more about that, he said, 'Shall we get the bill?'

So we did. As we were leaving the pub, he took my hand and led me to his car, opening the passenger door for me. I got in without a word; he drove away, and we found a lay-by and had sex in the back seat.

Maybe not so romantic after all.

I managed a half-laugh and Harry looked at me sympathetically. I could imagine the thought going through his mind: *Shit. She's not going to cry, is she?*

Then he said, 'Hold up. Looks like we've got a customer.'

A girl was approaching our stall. She was in her school uniform, like all the others, and, like almost all the girls, her tie was hanging loose round her neck, her skirt was rolled up to just below her bum cheeks and her hair fell in loose waves down her back. She was wearing the expression I'd always seen in teenage girls when they approached me in uniform: half deferential, half embarrassed, with a sprinkling of bravado as she tried to pretend the other two feelings weren't there.

'Good morning,' Harry said chirpily. 'How are you today?'

'Are you interested in finding out more about a career in nursing?' I asked.

The girl nodded. 'I mean, kind of. My mum says I'd be signing up for a life of drudgery, low pay and cleaning up other people's sick.'

There was something familiar about her – her dark eyes, her hesitant smile. I could have sworn I'd seen her before somewhere, but I couldn't think where.

I laughed. 'Well, there's a bit of that. But the nurses' union – the Royal College – has fought hard recently for better pay and conditions. You might have seen that on the news. And once your career starts to progress it becomes a bit different from what you might think. There are so many different specialisms.'

'This QR code right here will take you to a link that tells you more about them,' Harry said, handing her a leaflet.

'What's led you to think of going down this route?' I asked.

'I...' she began hesitantly, 'I've always liked helping people. And recently... I dunno. I suppose I've seen what it's like when people really need to be helped.'

I smiled and she smiled back. The smile transformed her face – lighting it up in a way that made me smile even more.

'That's just the best start,' I said. 'The health service is crying out for people with your kind of mindset.'

'We're holding an open day at Princess Margaret's Hospital over the summer,' Harry said. 'You should come along to that. Laurel and I will be there with loads of our colleagues, and you'll be able to see more of what clinical work is like from the inside.'

'I'd like that,' she said.

'And we have opportunities for work experience too,' I added. 'I know it's not always easy, depending on your family background. But you need to remember that nursing is actually highly competitive, and like any degree course you'd need to put in the strongest application you can.'

The girl nodded. I could see something change in her face – almost an awakening.

'I'm doing science, maths and biology at GCSE,' she said. 'And English too, obviously. I like studying. I'll talk to my mum and' – there was the slightest hesitation – 'my dad, and come to the open day if I can.'

'It would be lovely to see you there,' I said. 'My name's Laurel Norton, by the way. Laurel with two Ls.'

I pointed to the badge on my chest and smiled again.

'Nice to meet you, Laurel and' – she peered at Harry's name badge – 'Harry. I'm Lulu Graham.'

Lulu Graham.

Oh my God. Of course. It was with Gray that I'd seen her face, on the wallpaper of his phone in a smiling photo with her brother and mother. There'd probably been photos of her up in the house as well, framed portraits on the wall or snapshots attached to the fridge, but I hadn't noticed those – I was too wary of Anna to risk being caught noticing anything.

Gray had told me his children's names and ages, and occasionally shared his pride in them and his worries about them – feisty Lulu, growing up too quickly for comfort; awkward Barney, who still hadn't quite found his tribe. It had never crossed my mind that I would meet either of them – certainly not now, not here.

Harry pressed an assortment of leaflets on her, and she thanked us before turning to walk away, already studying them closely and scanning the QR code on her phone.

I heard Anna's voice – her mother's voice – as clearly as if she was speaking over my shoulder.

Stay the hell away from my children.

SIXTEEN

ORLA

13 May 2024

Lately, whenever I leave my house or arrive home, I find myself glancing at the door to number eight. It's as if I am expecting to see the blinds drawn in mourning or something else – something more symbolic: the wings of the angel of death casting a shadow on the smooth paint, a black cross daubed upon it, or even wilting, cellophane-wrapped flowers tied to the railings on the square, as happens when a fatal accident or murder has taken place.

But every day there has been nothing; only sometimes Gray's carer's car parked outside, or the slim, dark-haired woman – the other woman, Gray's lover – approaching the door for her regular visits. I feel relief that he is still alive, that the loss that awaits that family has been averted for the time being, but also a kind of horror that their ordeal is continuing.

I have been doing what I can to help, but it feels like so little. Dropping in to sit with Gray for a while, saving articles from *Frieze* magazine that I think might interest him to read aloud. Inviting Anna for lunch or a glass of wine. I have wondered about approaching Laurel and offering some words of comfort to her too, but that seems too intrusive, too presumptuous – and also perhaps disloyal to Anna.

I am in unfamiliar territory. I don't know what to do for the best, what is expected from a good neighbour, from a friend, from a person who tries to live life honestly and decently.

Yesterday, though, I was presented with what felt like an opportunity to make a difference to the Grahams, even if in a small, insignificant way.

It was late afternoon and I had been for a walk, the heavy rain that had fallen earlier having eased off, leaving sparkling clarity and a rainbow arching over the glass towers of the City. On my return home, I saw Barney Graham sitting alone on one of the benches in the square.

He is a tall lad, fair-haired like his mother, awkward and gangly like so many boys just entering their teens. His football was on the ground between his feet, but there was no one there for him to have a kick-about with. Instead, he had headphones in his ears and was staring at nothing.

Taking the headphones as a sign that he didn't wish to be interrupted, I raised a hand in greeting and carried on by. But when he saw me he removed them, stood up and came over to the gate.

Hello, Barney, I said. How are you?

He rubbed his nose with the back of his hand, and I saw he'd been crying. He said, Okay, thanks Orla. I mean, you know. Dad and stuff.

I nodded, as awkward and at a loss for words as he was.

Then he said, I was listening to music. Debussy. I've started learning the piano at school, and our teacher played us one of his pieces today. It's... I'd love to play like that someday.

I smiled. There's no reason why you shouldn't, if you work hard.

That wasn't true, of course. I myself am completely tone deaf and could never play – or indeed even identify – Debussy if I spent a lifetime trying.

I can't practise at home, he said. Dad hates it. When I was in primary school I learned the recorder and the noise drove him crackers.

I said, I'm not surprised – the recorder's not the easiest instrument to listen to at the best of times.

Barney said, Right? and laughed. Besides, we don't have a piano. Mum would get me one of those keyboard things if I asked, but it doesn't feel... with Dad and stuff...

Then an idea struck me. You could come and practise on my piano, I said. Well, it's Beatrice's – my daughter's – but she wouldn't mind. I bought it for her but she's not living at home any longer, so it's just gathering dust really.

To my surprise, he agreed enthusiastically. He came in with me, accepted a cup of tea and a scone heaped with blackberry jam, and then I showed him the piano in the front room and he sat down, suddenly looking like a boy who'd arrived in a place where he was meant to be. For the next half hour I listened as the notes began to flow more surely and confidently, with fewer pauses, repetitions and muttered oaths from Barney.

Then he came and found me in the kitchen, thanked me and said he should get back home.

It was nothing – or at best it was the smallest thing. But I hope he will come again. I told him he is welcome any time. I hope my home, the keys of that piano and the music can become a kind of refuge for him.

SEVENTEEN
ANNA

'Are you sure you're up to having it here?' I'd asked Gray three days before. 'We can easily change the plans. Orla would host, or Sarah or Cathy.'

'I'm not missing my daughter's sixteenth birthday party, Anna.' He pushed himself up on the pillows, his face mutinous.

'I'm not saying you should miss it. Of course not. I just thought it might be easier...'

'To cart me next door? Or to Richmond? Don't be ridiculous.'

'I... Okay. You're right, of course. But if it gets too much you must just say, and we'll get you upstairs. Promise?'

So Gray had promised, and Lulu's party was going ahead as planned.

She and Barney had been up the previous evening until late, cutting out bunting from green and white paper – balloons being deemed environmentally unacceptable, and pink babyish – and strung it up from the exposed beams in the dining room. I'd baked a three-tier cake with a not-very-successful attempt at ombre icing. Bottles of champagne, wine, beer and soda water for Aperol spritz were chilling in a zinc tub on the terrace. Cathy's husband, Richard, had volunteered to man the barbecue.

And Lulu had modelled her dress for me – a vintage find from eBay, which she'd altered thanks to Orla's sewing machine.

'It's awfully short,' I'd told Gray, perching on the edge of his bed. 'You can practically see her knickers.'

'She's sixteen, Anna. She can wear what she likes.'

'It's precisely because she's sixteen that I don't want her wearing what she likes.'

'It's a family party. Stop pearl-clutching.'

So I'd stopped, and told Lulu she looked beautiful in the strappy satin '90s number, which showed off the smooth curves of her legs and arms, and which thankfully she'd elected to wear with her usual trainers instead of high heels.

Barney moved an armchair from the family room through to the kitchen, where the folding doors were open to the garden. Richard and I helped Gray downstairs and made him comfortable there, a rug over his knees even though the day was warm.

'Christ, I feel like an old man,' he grumbled.

'Better than feeling like a cold man,' I said as cheerily as I could. 'Do you want a drink?'

He hesitated. 'I'll wait a bit. Don't want to be shitfaced when I make my speech.'

An hour later, the house had filled up with people. Lulu was handing round snacks, her little cousins trailing admiringly behind her. Three of my recently divorced friends were getting stuck into the rosé and exchanging online-dating horror stories. A group of our neighbours were getting stuck into the Pimm's and exchanging house renovation horror stories. Barney was drifting between the television, which was showing the cricket, and the food. Orla had pulled a chair over to Gray and was talking and laughing with him.

I approached them, a bottle of champagne in my hand. 'I think it's about time for you to do the honours.'

'Before I get too pissed?' he said.

'Before everyone else does,' I corrected, although what I had wanted to say was, *Before you get too tired.*

'Right you are. Make sure everyone's got a drink, send our first-born over and I'll get cracking.'

With Orla's help, Gray got to his feet. I poured him a glass of fizz and handed him a teaspoon and he pinged the glass. Lulu put down the platter of blinis she'd been carrying and moved over to her father, standing shyly beside him. The room fell silent.

'Family and friends,' he began, clearing his throat. 'Thank you all for being here with us today. As you all know, this has been a hell of a year for us as a family, particularly for Anna, my wife and my rock. But we're not here to talk about all that – tempted as I am to make every occasion all about me, I'm not going to be doing that today.

'Because today is all about our daughter, Lulu, who turned sixteen a week ago. When she was born, she took my breath away – and that was after I'd fainted on the delivery room floor.'

There was a murmur of laughter, and Gray carried on. 'I couldn't believe that Anna and I had created something – *someone* – so absolutely perfect. Sixteen years later, I don't think she's perfect any more – maybe if you could put your dirty clothes in the basket like your mother asks, darling.'

'Daaaad,' Lulu protested, although she was beaming.

'But she still takes my breath away. Lulu is beautiful. She's clever. She's hilarious. She makes the world's best cheese toastie. Everyone who meets her loves her – except maybe that religious studies teacher she had in Year Eight. And most of all, she's the kindest, most loving daughter we could have dreamed of.'

The room had fallen silent; all I could hear was the crackling of the coals on the barbecue and the sound of Augustus slurping up a bit of smoked salmon that had fallen on the floor. Then Orla sniffed and Lulu let out a half-sob that might have been a hiccup.

'I know...' Gray began, and then seemed to choke up himself, before carrying on. 'Just to briefly address the elephant in the room. I know I won't see Lulu's eighteenth birthday or her twenty-first. I won't get to make a speech on her wedding day. But I don't want anyone to be sad about that – not today, anyway. Because today is about celebrating the life of this gorgeous girl, who makes me and Anna so proud every single day.

'We love you, little Lulu. Happy birthday.'

Someone started singing 'Happy Birthday to You', and everyone else joined in seconds later. I sang myself – sang my heart out, not wanting my daughter to know in that moment that it was breaking.

By midnight, all the guests had left. Orla had stayed to help me clear up, before departing for number five an hour before. The leftover food was packed away in the fridge ready to be raided by the children in the morning. The cake had been reduced to a few crumbs on its stand. The impressive haul of presents was stacked in the family room ready for Lulu to open the next day. The bunting was curling on its strings, but I'd decided to leave it up for the kids to enjoy for another few days. Gray's carer had been and helped him into the shower and back to bed.

I poured myself a final glass of red wine, checked that the back doors were locked and went upstairs. The first floor was in darkness; I could see a faint glow from upstairs where Lulu was awake in her room, up late texting her friends, and could hear the faint splash of water from the bathroom as Augustus drank from his bowl, thirsty after all the smoked salmon.

I didn't knock on the bedroom door in case Gray was asleep, but opened it as silently as I could and crept in. He was lying down, his face as white as the pillows, but his eyes were open.

'Hey.' I sat down next to him, putting my glass on the bedside table. 'How are you feeling?'

'Knackered.' He eased himself higher on the pillow and I could see lines of pain flicker across his face. 'But not too sore. The meds are kicking in.'

'You smashed it today. I was really proud. Hopefully you'll sleep well.'

I passed him the water, but he didn't take the glass; instead, he guided my hand to his lips and kissed it. It was just the slightest brush of his dry lips, but it brought a lump to my throat.

'Hopefully,' he said. 'Morphine dreams are wild – better even than coke.'

I tutted, hiding my emotion as I knew he was hiding his. 'I'm not sure you're meant to enjoy it.'

'I reckon I can enjoy whatever I want at this point.'

'True.' I rested a hand on his shoulder. 'Gray? Today made me think – what do you want to happen for your funeral?'

His eyes were drifting closed, but he opened them again and said indistinctly, 'I told you. Chuck me in a plain pine box and take me to the tip, and then everyone get pissed down the Crooked Billet.'

'Right. I know that's what you said. I just wanted to make sure you hadn't changed your mind.'

'A deathbed conversion?' He turned over, pulling a pillow from the other side of the bed and hugging it to his chest. 'Not likely.'

That should be me, I thought with a stab of anguish. *Me he's holding while he sleeps. I should be with him, for however many nights we have left.* But I couldn't ask him if he wanted that – I was too afraid of what the answer might be.

'There's nothing special you want, though?' I persisted. 'No particular music or anything?'

'Fuck, no,' he said. 'None of that maudlin shite.'

I half-laughed, then asked, 'What maudlin shite did you have at your mum's funeral? Can you remember?'

He turned over again, still clinging to the pillow. The sleepiness was gone from his eyes now; they were wide open, dark and trippy-looking from the morphine.

'Jesus, Anna. I don't know. Probably "Ar Hyd y Nos".'

'A what now?'

'It's a Welsh lullaby. Everyone has it – it's a massive cliché. Like English people having "Jerusalem" at their weddings.'

He closed his eyes and sang faintly, 'Holl amrantau'r sêr ddywedant, Ar hyd y nos, "Dyma'r ffordd i fro gogoniant", Ar hyd y nos.'

I felt as if a heavy weight was being pressed on to my chest. 'I remember that. You used to sing it to Lulu and Barney when they were babies.'

'No I didn't. You're imagining it. I never sing.' A flicker of sadness flashed across his face. He turned on to his side away from me. 'I need to sleep, Anna.'

'Okay.' I stood up. 'Call me if you need anything. And – like you said, pine box, no music. But maybe not the council tip.'

'Thanks, Anna,' he murmured. Then, half-muffled by the pillow, I heard him say, 'I love you.'

That weight pressed on me again, feeling as if it might crush the life out of me. 'I love you too.'

I got up and left him for the spare room, which I couldn't quite bring myself to think of as my room. I washed my make-up off, cleaned my teeth in the en-suite bathroom and got into bed.

But I couldn't sleep. I lay there, staring into the darkness, thinking of that song, which had sounded so familiar. The song Gray said he thought had probably been played at his mother's funeral, which he'd sung to Lulu and Barney at night.

He had. In spite of his denial, I could remember it clearly – the darkened house, still a building site, the smell of paint and plaster dust everywhere. Me lying in the bath exhausted, fretting that somehow we were poisoning our baby daughter with airborne chemicals. And Gray's voice drifting from the bedroom, low and sweet, accompanying his steady footfalls as he paced up and down with her.

He was right – he never sang. But he'd sung then, when he was soothing our babies to sleep, and I'd loved him for it.

And even if my memory was playing tricks on me – even if it was something else he'd sung to them, even if he couldn't recall what music had played at his mother's funeral – how come he remembered the lyrics so clearly, years later after Lulu and Barney were born, and still now, every word, in a language he no longer ever spoke?

EIGHTEEN
ORLA

7 June 2024

Through my open window, I can hear the rattling of bins as Anna takes out next door's recycling. The sound makes me sad, because it always used to be Gray's job to do that and I would often hear him calling out a good morning to a passing neighbour or whistling, surprisingly tunefully, over the clattering of bottles.

Now I know I will never hear him whistle again, and I cannot recall when it was that the task passed from him to Anna. I am thinking of him now, imagining him lying there in his bed by the window, hearing the same sound I am hearing from my front room.

I feel so helpless, being a witness to what is happening to that family. But I am doing what I can: having Barney round here most afternoons to play the piano; taking round home-baked scones and asparagus from my garden, although Anna is a better cook than I am, and she tells me Gray's appetite has dwindled almost to nothing; listening when they seem to want to talk.

Yesterday, though, I was given a task of my own to perform, by Gray himself. Anna had asked me to go and sit with him for an hour in the afternoon while she took the children to whatever activities they were doing after school. He would probably be asleep, she said, she just didn't feel right leaving him alone for long any more.

But Gray wasn't asleep. He was propped up on the pillows, his laptop on his thighs. His hands were resting on the keyboard in a way that reminded me vividly of the way Barney's look when he has been wrestling with a particularly challenging piece on my piano.

I wondered whether I should tell him about his son's visits. I wondered whether he can hear the music drifting across from my home to his as clearly as I can hear the crescendo of tumbling glass bottles into the Grahams' recycling bin.

He looked exhausted. But he greeted me with a smile and said he was glad I had come.

It's good to see you, I said. Is there anything I can do for you?

He said yes. He said he had been waiting for me to come. But it wasn't a cup of tea he wanted, or his pillows fluffing.

He asked me to go to the room next door, the room he uses – or used, because I fear he will never go in there again – as his home office, and switch on the printer on his desk. I obeyed, and seconds later I heard it click and hum as it pulled a sheet of paper into whatever feeder mechanism it has.

Is it working? I heard him call anxiously. Temperamental bloody thing.

I assured him it was. There were envelopes in a drawer, he said, and asked me to bring him one, along with a pen.

I did. Then I watched as he folded the sheet of paper into thirds, slipped it into the envelope, sealed it and hand-wrote an address on it.

Will you post this for me, please, Orla? he asked. After... you know.

I said I would.

And Orla – don't tell Anna. Please.

Before I could agree, he reached out and shook my hand – a peculiar thing to do, given we have been friends and neighbours for almost twenty years.

It felt like a pact, that handshake. It felt as if I have signed up to some sort of agreement, or even a conspiracy – like the phrase forcing my hand. He had entrusted me with something secret: something he does not want his wife to be aware of. I feel deeply uneasy about that: I have held on to my own secrets for far too long to welcome other people's.

But I will do as he asked. I have no choice – do I?

NINETEEN

LAUREL

It looked like a meal prepared for a poorly child. On the tray was a boiled egg with a crocheted egg cosy covering it, a plate of toast buttered and sliced into strips, an orange cut into pyramids, a glass of milk and three chocolate Hobnobs. There was also a tiny glass vase – actually, I saw when I looked more closely at it, it was an empty tonic-water bottle – holding a single, perfect red rose.

When I'd arrived at the house a few minutes earlier, I'd seen a profusion of identical roses blooming in the beds in the garden square. Anna must have been out and picked it, perhaps after she put the egg on to boil and pressed the lever on the toaster.

'You may as well take this up for him,' she said dismissively, as if I was the hired help. 'He won't eat much.'

She looked shattered. Her hair was unwashed, scraped back from her face with a scrunchie in the same dark red as Lulu's school uniform. There were dark hollows under her eyes and her jeans hung loosely on her hips.

'Of course.' I picked up the tray, doing my best to smile encouragingly. 'Boiled egg and soldiers – if that doesn't tempt him, nothing will. You should make one for yourself – sit down for a bit.'

Anna looked at the open box of eggs on the kitchen counter as if she'd only just realised it was there. 'I'm not hungry. And I really don't need self-care tips from you, thank you.'

Her words stung, and I had to bite back a sarcastic retort. There was no point in rising to her anger – not only would it get me nowhere (except possibly slung out into the street without having seen Gray), but her feelings were totally understandable. She was furious – with me, with the world, no doubt with Gray himself – and I couldn't blame her for it.

'Did he have a bad night?' I asked gently.

She sat down on one of the stools by the counter, as suddenly as if she was a puppet whose strings had been cut. 'They're mostly bad now. The carers come and get him ready for bed, then again in the morning, but it's the time in between.'

'I know,' I said. 'It's not easy.'

'It's like when the kids were babies.' She pulled a square of paper towel off the roll and looked at it the same way she'd looked at the eggs, then folded it in half and blew her nose. 'Except I'm twelve years older, I don't have a husband to help me, and...'

I waited. It was almost as if she had forgotten it was me she was talking to.

'And with babies everyone tells you it'll get better, but this won't. At least, not until...' She trailed off, not wanting to say the words that were on her mind as they were on mine.

I felt emotion welling up inside me, sweeping away my careful veneer of composure. I was angry too. I was hurting too. And I was full of self-loathing because, in spite of all Anna was going through, I envied her. I was jealous as all hell of the time she was getting to spend with Gray when I wasn't – jealous in a way I'd never been before I knew the hours and days he had left were finite in number.

I put down the tray, pulled a tissue out of my pocket and dabbed my eyes. Anna watched me coldly, as if by my display of weakness I was trying to detract from her own pain.

'You should take that up before it gets cold,' she said.

'Anna – let me know if there's anything else I can do to help. Please.'

Her lips tightened and she shook her head. She wasn't letting me in – wasn't granting any more privileges than she already had. 'You can let yourself out and leave the tray in the hallway.'

I said, 'Okay,' again, turned away and set off up the stairs.

Gray was awake, sitting in an armchair by the window, next to the bed. The curtains were open and the morning light fell across his face. It had only been a week since I last saw him, but the change in him was noticeable – shocking, even. His cheeks were hollow, and the veins on his hands stood out like twisted strings. I could see his abdomen swollen with ascites, pushing against the fabric of his pyjamas. The skin on his feet above his slippers was bone white.

But when he saw me, he managed a smile.

'Room service,' I announced, stepping through the door. 'Would you like this on your lap?'

'Stick it on the bed for now,' he said, 'and come here.'

I did as he asked, squatting down next to him so he could fold me in his arms. There was still strength in him, as if all the power from his wasted muscles had been absorbed, concentrated into bone and sinew. When he kissed me I could smell his familiar aftershave and toothpaste alongside the other smell – the smell of acetone or pear drops on his breath, which was familiar too, in a different way.

We held each other for a long time, until my Achilles tendons were screaming from squatting.

'You should eat your breakfast,' I said at last.

He looked at the tray. 'I can smell those roses through the window. I wonder if Anna will ever be able to enjoy them again.'

I didn't know the answer to that, but I didn't need to respond because his train of thought had already moved on.

As I settled the tray on his legs, removing the speckled brown egg from its woolly hat and carefully slicing off the top, he went on, 'I thought we'd be able to sleep together again. Well – not sleep, but...'

'I know what you mean.'

'Just a couple of weeks ago, I was lying here with a massive hard-on, imagining you walking in and taking your clothes off. But you didn't come that day.'

'I must've been working. Damn – I missed out on the fun.'

He dipped a piece of toast in his egg and ate it, then took another. 'I suppose that ship has sailed. And we wouldn't have done it anyway.'

'We couldn't have. Not with Anna here. Not even if she wasn't. It wouldn't be right.'

'I know. I wouldn't have expected you to. Funny – that night at Eldercombe Manor was the last time, and we had no idea.'

My heart twisted with sadness. 'And the time before that – in my room at Mel's flat.'

'The penultimate time. And before that…'

'The Premier Inn. Scene of our most passionate moments.'

He smiled and ate half another toast finger. 'Shame I left it so late to level up the romance.'

'You didn't.' I leaned forward from my perch on the bed so our knees were touching. 'It all felt pretty damn romantic to me. Even the Premier Inn.'

'Even the time in my car by the McDonald's Drive-Through in Barking?'

'Especially that,' I teased. 'I'll never feel the same way about a Philly Cheese Stack again.'

He laughed, pushing the tray away. 'I'm done here. Eat some orange, if you can, so Anna won't feel hurt.'

I put the tray back on the bed and took a piece, holding my hand under my chin to catch the juice as I bit into it.

Gray said, 'Laurel.'

I reached for his hand and held it, feeling the stickiness transfer from my fingers to his, waiting for him to say what he needed to say.

'That's not going to happen now. You and me having a final shag. Is it?'

'I don't think so.'

He nodded. 'I think it's time for me to move to a hospice, don't you?'

I took a breath, trying to steady myself and find the right words. 'It's time whenever you want it to be. Or not at all, if you'd rather stay here.'

'The kids are struggling.' He spoke as if it was an effort to admit it. 'I see Lulu's face when she walks in here to see me, and it kills me. I hear Barney stop outside the door and not come in, because he can't face seeing me. And it's too much for Anna. She thinks she's coping but she's breaking. I can tell. She's only holding it together for them.'

I could tell too. 'There's more help available if you need it. She can speak to the district nurse. There's Hospice at Home, or even just a respite stay.'

'Except it wouldn't be a respite, would it?' he asked.

'I don't know, Gray. Prognostics is tricky, your oncologist will have told you that. No one knows.'

'Could be weeks, could be days,' he said.

'I'd be surprised if it was days,' I said gently. 'But...'

'Not months, either.'

'No,' I said. 'Not months.'

'Then it's time,' he said. 'Best to get it done when... Before there's some kind of crisis. I don't want the kids...'

He stopped, pressing a hand over his eyes.

'I get it,' I said. 'This'll be their home for a while yet.'

'That's right. I want Lulu to bring a boyfriend home from uni for Christmas and not have to be like, "And this here's the room where Dad carked it." I don't want Barney having nightmares. I want this house to be somewhere they'll always remember feeling safe.'

'You must do whatever feels right. It's totally, one hundred per cent your decision.'

'I don't want...' He paused, taking a breath that I could hear was unsteady. 'I don't want it to hurt, Laurel. I'm fucking terrified of that. It's bad already, sometimes, but what happens later, if I can't tell people it's hurting?'

God. I'd given this reassurance to many people before – the families of patients, mostly, occasionally friends whose loved ones were dying and thought that I was somehow the fount of all knowledge on the subject. But giving it to Gray was harder than almost anything I'd ever done before.

'Palliative care is really good.' I hated the way those words sounded – bland and professional, with nothing of the sick, churning sadness I was feeling inside. 'You'll have all the pain relief you need.'

'Does that mean I'll be off my tits on morphine?'

I laughed. 'Yeah, basically.'

'Laurel...' He hesitated, turning over my hand and tracing a pattern on it, a simple right angle, like the letter L, down and to the right then to the left and up again. 'Do people... in your experience, when they're dying and on morphine, do they say things without meaning to?'

'I guess...' I spoke slowly, weighing each word, wanting to be as truthful as I could but also not knowing the full truth; wanting to reassure him but also not wanting to lie to him. 'I guess sometimes they do. But the thing is, by that stage, most people aren't very lucid. It's like when you talk in your sleep, or you've just woken from a dream and you're not sure what's real. It doesn't always make a lot of sense.'

He sighed. 'I think I've decided. And I'll have a nap now. Can you...'

'Give you a hand getting back to bed? Sure. Let me put this out of the way.'

I picked up the tray, put it down on the floor by the door and turned back the covers. I helped Gray to his feet and on to the bed, although he was so light I could have lifted him easily. I plumped his pillows and made sure the pyjama top was smooth under his back.

Then I sat down next to him again, cleaned the orange juice off both our fingers with a wet wipe, and took his hand in mine.

'Laurel.' He looked at me, his eyes fathomless with fear. 'Will you be with me when I die? Will you hold my hand like this?'

I wondered if he knew how badly I wanted to promise him anything, even if I wouldn't be able to keep my promise.

'But Anna...'

'She's doing so much for me,' he said. 'I can't tell her it's not enough. I can't tell her how scared I am. I can't tell her I know she's not coping.'

'I understand,' I said. 'Don't worry. I'm here. I've got you. I love you.'

'I love you,' he murmured, his eyes closing.

I waited until he was asleep, then got up, took the tray and left the room, full of dread for the conversation I was about to have with Anna.

As I descended the stairs, I thought, *What is it you don't want anyone to hear you saying, Gray?*

TWENTY

ANNA

When Laurel came into my kitchen, carrying the tray I'd specifically asked her to leave upstairs, I was standing in the open doorway to the garden, my vape in my hand. The smell of it mingled with the scent of the honeysuckle that was blooming around the doorway. The robin I'd been watching hop along the fence, watched also by Augustus, took flight when it heard the rattle of the tray on the counter, and my brief moment of peace was over.

'Anna.' I heard her tip the half-eaten breakfast into the food-waste caddy and start running hot water over the plates. 'I wondered if you've got a moment? Gray ate a bit; he's asleep now.'

I tucked the vape into my jeans pocket and pulled the back door shut as I turned around.

'Yes?' *Offer her a coffee? Don't offer her a coffee.* But I couldn't help myself. 'Would you like a drink? A coffee, I mean. It's a bit early for an actual drink.'

'Just a glass of water would be lovely, thank you,' she said guardedly, folding her arms across her chest. 'I'm on shift at one.'

As if she'd thought I was serious about having an actual drink. Or known I was serious. Or was so virtuous that even the mildly stimulating effects of caffeine were too daring for her to contemplate before work.

I poured two glasses of water from the fridge and handed one to her. There was no homemade shortbread to offer this time, only a single scone left from the batch Orla had brought round the previous day.

'Thank you,' she said again, smiling and perching on a stool by the island.

I watched her. Her hands were folded in front of her, the nails short and unpainted, the skin dry. She sipped her water, then wiped away the ring of condensation it had left with her sleeve. *Make yourself at home*, I thought bitterly. *Any friend of Gray's is a friend of mine. Not.*

We looked at each other, both of us silent for a moment. Not for the first time, I allowed myself to wonder, *What did he – does he – see in her?* If she'd been twenty years younger than me it would have all made more sense. If she'd been some glamour-puss with nail extensions and hair extensions and no doubt a full Hollywood wax, I'd have kind of got it.

But she wasn't. She was just an average-looking woman, with her layered shoulder-length brown hair and the scattering of freckles across her cheeks. Only her figure was exceptional: the tiny waist, long, muscular legs and round, tight buttocks that girls a few years older than Lulu put in serious gym time to achieve.

Gray had never particularly liked slim women, though. I remembered when I'd been heavily pregnant with Barney, hot and clumsy as a beached whale, him grabbing me from behind, his hands reaching for my breasts, murmuring, 'Look at you. You're a goddess,' before sweeping me off to bed.

'Anna,' she began. 'I... I hope you don't think I'm speaking out of turn here. I know how difficult it is for you having me come here, and I'm sorry. I know how tough all this is for you.'

I watched her, almost enjoying her discomfort. Then she seemed to gather herself, calling on some resource of inner poise or training or sheer bloody-mindedness.

'I'm not a palliative care specialist,' she went on. 'I work in A&E. Before that I was in the ICU. I've seen a lot of families go through incredibly difficult times with their loved ones. And as... well, speaking as a professional, there's something I thought I should mention to you.'

'Go on,' I said, facing her across the kitchen island, my forearms resting on the cool marble. I met her eyes, like I was daring her to come out with what she was clearly afraid of saying.

'I wonder' – she took a long breath and let it out again – 'whether it might be time for Gray to move to a residential care setting.'

'You mean a place where he'd live. As opposed to this, which is what?'

'I mean a hospice,' she said. 'Gray is... His care needs are increasing. You know that, Anna. It can't be easy having him at home. He knows how much of a burden this is placing on you and the children.'

Part of me knew that what she was saying was true. Over the past week, I'd become increasingly conscious of just that burden, and I knew it would only grow heavier.

But who was she to tell me this? What right had she to even notice what was going on in my home, with my husband? Who had appointed her Gray's spokeswoman?

Barely able to keep my anger in check, I said, 'What are you talking about?'

'I'm sorry, Anna. I don't want to impose. Perhaps it's something you and Gray could discuss, though.'

'What – you think my husband and I haven't maybe – just maybe – already touched on the subject of him dying?'

'Of course I know you've—'

'Let me tell you something, Laurel. Because you've been here to see Gray – what, five times? I've been here day in, day out. I've seen how what he wants changes. First he wanted jelly so I got him jelly. Then he didn't want that any more so I got him custard. Then it was rice pudding until he didn't want that either. Then it was chicken soup and I stood here boiling bones for fucking hours and now I've got a freezer full of the stuff that he can't eat.'

'I know,' she said. 'It must be—'

'You don't know.' I took a gulp of my water and banged the glass down on the counter. 'You've got no fucking idea because all you do is swan in and play games with him for an hour. He needs me. I'm looking after him.'

'You're managing wonderfully. It's just that—'

'One thing he's been absolutely clear about, Laurel. All the time, ever since he got diagnosed with this evil bastard of a disease – even when he's off his face on morphine and can't remember my name – is that he wants to die here, at home, with his family around him and his cat on his bed. Like Terry Pratchett. That's what he said.'

'People change their minds.' She was still speaking calmly, but I could see her hands trembling as she lifted her glass to her lips. 'When they realise what it's like for the family. It's not uncommon—'

'I don't think *he's* changed his mind,' I spat. 'I think *you've* changed it. I think you've persuaded him that what you want is what he wants. Because you want to be with him – now, when it's getting close to the end. You want to get your claws into him and take him away from his wife and his children just when he's going to be taken away from us anyway, because you couldn't manage to take him away from us before.'

Abruptly, she started to cry. 'That's not what I want. Honestly, I never wanted that. I never wanted any of this to happen.'

'Oh yes, you did. Don't play the victim here, Laurel. People don't fuck married men by accident. You didn't slip on a banana skin and – whoops – there you were in his bed. Don't give me that shit. I'm not stupid.'

Laurel took a tissue out of her pocket and pressed it to her eyes. She wasn't wearing any make-up; if she had, it would have been running all down her face.

'Okay,' she said, straightening her shoulders. 'I understand. I won't mention it again.'

But I wasn't finished. 'You think you know him, don't you? You think, after – what? A year? – you know him well enough to make decisions about what's best for him and our family. Well, you don't. You don't have a clue about Gray. I've known that man for twenty years, warts and all. You think he loves you, don't you?'

'I...' she stammered. 'Anna, he's never said he doesn't love you. Not even once.'

'That's because he doesn't know what love is,' I spat. 'Doesn't have a clue. Love him all you want, you'll only get your heart broken same as I have.'

Two bright spots of colour appeared in her cheeks, and I could see she was angry now, as well as blindsided by my sudden attack. But somehow she still managed to keep her voice calm.

'We're both going to get our hearts broken,' she said. 'You and me. There's no getting away from that.'

Her words silenced me because there was no hiding from the truth in them. She was right – there was no point in squabbling over a dying man like a pair of hyenas at a kill. It was ugly – it was shameful. It was futile.

'I think you should go now.' I was trembling, but the worst of my rage had passed. I felt like I too might start to cry. I wanted my vape. I wanted that drink.

'I was going to come again the day after tomorrow,' she said. 'Is that still...'

'Come,' I spat. 'I can't stop you, can I? I can't refuse to give my dying husband what he wants.'

'Thank you, Anna,' she said, almost humbly.

Then she turned and left.

I can't refuse to give my dying husband what he wants. I couldn't, and therefore I knew I would speak to Gray and find out whether he had changed his mind. And I was fairly certain that the move to a hospice would take place.

Already, I was regretting what I had said to Laurel – feeling that I had failed Gray, been disloyal to him, slagged him off when he couldn't defend himself. And in spite of what I'd said to her, I knew that if she was able to feel, after his death, that her love for him had been true and pure when mine hadn't, she would have won.

TWENTY-ONE
ORLA

14 June 2024

I am sitting here in the dark writing these pages with a sense of foreboding. What happened yesterday feels like my fault, although I know it is not. I did all I could – there were circumstances beyond my control. It may all still work out.

But deep down, I feel as if it will not. I feel as if I have failed – that I acted too late and Gray himself made his request of me too late.

It was yesterday afternoon, one of the few rainy days we have had this glorious summer. I had called round at number eight as I have done every afternoon this week, with a jar of jam for Anna and some beeswax lip salve for Gray. When I went upstairs to see him, he was awake and lucid. He has been sleeping more and more recently, whether because of the drugs or the disease I do not know. Often I can do nothing except sit in the chair by the bed and chat nonsense to him – anecdotes about the goings-on of the neighbours, the infighting in the local historic buildings Preservation Trust, yet another trendy new cocktail bar opening on the main road.

They say hearing is the last sense to go, and I hope my words bring some comfort.

Certainly, I don't believe he will be writing letters on his laptop again. But he clearly remembered that visit – just a few days ago, although it feels like longer.

The approach of death does strange things to the passing of time, I am learning. It moves slowly, then terrifyingly swiftly. And then, I suppose, it stops altogether.

As soon as I sat down, Gray said that he had been hoping I would come. They're moving me to the hospice today, he said.

I said I knew, and that it was good to see him awake.

But he didn't seem to be in the mood for pleasantries. He needed my help, he told me. He needed me to do another favour for him. I agreed willingly.

I need you to call my solicitor, he said. Have you got your phone?

I had. A moment later it pinged and vibrated in my hand, and I saw that he had sent me a contact.

He had already left a message for her – Claudia James, her name is, according to the contact which is now saved on my phone – but she was unavailable, out of the office at a conference all day.

He didn't want Anna to know, he told me, but there was an amendment he wanted to make to his will. A bequest. Something he had only recently decided to do.

I said, Of course. I agreed to try and call Claudia myself. I did last night and I will again this morning, as soon as the day has properly begun and it is reasonable to call anyone.

But then Gray's speech became disjointed, as if he was falling asleep or the drugs they are giving him through patches on his skin were kicking in. He tried to explain what it was he wanted his solicitor to do, but I struggled to make sense of it.

At one point he broke into song, then his eyes closed and he fell silent.

I can see why he was worried – why he asked me to make that

call for him. Wills can only be changed by those of sound mind, and I know – and Gray knows – that whenever his solicitor contacts him, he might not be able to explain to her what it is he wants to do.

For all I know, it may already be too late.

TWENTY-TWO

ANNA

Across the road from the hospice was a restaurant that sold burgers and fried chicken, as well as – crucially – white, rosé and red wine by the carafe. A mere glass wouldn't have been enough; two glasses would have meant having to summon the waitress to order a second, and a bottle would have been shamefully excessive. But a carafe was perfect – 375ml, just enough to take the edge off.

I'd taken the edge off at lunchtime over a chicken Caesar salad I hadn't been able to eat, and now (having checked that the waiting staff had changed shifts) I was taking it off again over an early dinner with Lulu and Barney.

We'd spent the past hour sitting by Gray's bedside. I'd told him about the mouse Augustus had brought in through the cat flap that morning, which had taken refuge under the kitchen island before I could catch it or the cat could murder it. Lulu had told him about her friend Aisha's break-up with her boyfriend. Barney had told him about a stag beetle he and Orla had found in her garden, which he'd taken a photo of on his phone and would show Gray when he woke up.

'Mum.' Barney took a noisy slurp of his Oreo milkshake, then poked at it with the straw, looking down into the glass rather than at me. 'Do you think Dad might get better? I mean, I know the doctors and everyone say he won't. But Joachim at school was saying there was a man at his church who was given days to live, and the pastor prayed over him, and he got up and he was fine.'

Oh Joachim, you little fool. Why did you do that? Spread lies and fantasies and give my boy false hope?

I reached across the table and he took my hand, his fingers chilly from the glass. 'Dad's not going to get better, darling. I don't know what illness the man at Joachim's church had, but it wouldn't have been pancreatic cancer. That's something people don't just get better from.'

'Miracles don't exist really, do they?' Lulu muttered, poking at the lemon slice in her fizzy water. 'Dad said once they're just lies people tell themselves to feel better.'

'Miracles aren't like science,' I attempted to explain, trying to keep my voice even. 'Sometimes people want to believe in them, but they can't be proved. Or if they can, it's because there's a rational, scientific explanation behind them. I only really believe things when there's evidence to back them up, and your dad's the same. But there are people who like to believe in things that can't be explained that way, like Barney's friend's family.'

'Joachim says faith can move mountains,' Barney mumbled, letting go of my hand and picking up some chips.

'The most important thing faith does is make people feel better,' I said, wishing with sudden despair that I had it myself, so I could feel better. 'And there's one thing we can all have faith in right now, and that's that your dad is getting the very best possible care in the world where he is.'

They were both watching me intently. I knew they were listening to every word I said, their own faith in me as their mother still strong. *Don't fuck this up, Anna*, I willed myself.

'He's not in pain. He knows he's safe and he knows we love him. I've got faith in that, and that's how I'm managing to endure this. That and you two.'

I reached across the table and held my children's hands. Barney's fingers were greasy from his chips, and Lulu had a smear of ketchup on her knuckle. In that moment, I loved them so much it was like a knife in my heart. If I could have eaten them to protect them, like a stressed-out mother hamster, I would have done in that moment.

'What'll happen to us after Dad dies?' Barney asked, his eyes fixed on his plate.

'What do you mean, what'll happen?' I asked gently. 'What are you worried about happening?'

'I mean, I know we won't be orphans.' He managed an awkward half-grin. 'Because we'll still have you, Mum. But you don't have a job, and Dad does – Dad did. Will we be poor?'

'Don't be absurd, Barney,' Lulu said. 'Why would we be poor?'

But I could see a flash of alarm in her face, and I knew that although this prospect hadn't occurred to her before, now that it had, it scared her.

'Of course we won't be poor,' I said. 'Don't worry about that for one single second. Your dad has insurance policies – one that pays off what's left on the mortgage, and another one that... well, life insurance, that he took out in case something like this ever happened. Not that we thought it ever would, but that's what things like that are for. And Carl's buying out Dad's share of the business, although he's going to pay that off over a few years.'

'Will we be rich, then?' Barney asked.

'We're comfortable already,' I answered firmly. 'We're incredibly fortunate – you both know that. Your dad's worked hard all these years and we're in a far, far better position than many families. And that isn't going to change. We'll get to stay at Damask Square for as long as we want. You'll both get to go to university if you want to, just like we planned. And eventually there'll be some money for both of you to put down deposits on homes of your own or go travelling or whatever it is you want to do.'

And thank God for that, I thought. Thank God for all the boring, meticulous financial planning Gray did and I went along with; for the fairly sizeable inheritance from my grandfather, which had allowed us to put down the deposit on the Damask

Square house, even though the renovations had since eaten up all my remaining capital and I hadn't worked in years.

But it didn't matter – everything was shared, ours and the children's.

But what if Gray had changed the will? Changed it to include Laurel somehow, at our children's expense? The idea made me feel sick.

As if my thoughts had summoned her, there she was outside. Laurel was waiting to cross the road to the hospice, her hands on the handlebars of her bicycle, the afternoon sunshine illuminating her face; she was half-smiling, as if something good was about to happen to her.

'Mum?' Lulu said. 'See that lady over there? She came to our careers fair at school. She's a nurse. Do you think she works at the hospice?'

'No,' I said. 'She doesn't. She's a friend of your father's.'

'Really?' Lulu stood up, crumpling her paper napkin and dropping it on her plate. 'That's wild. I'm going to go and say hi.'

Before I could stop her, she'd hurried out of the restaurant, and I saw her run across the road and over to Laurel.

TWENTY-THREE
LAUREL

I was with Gray when he died – but also, I wasn't.

The whole day – that bright, peaceful summer day, with the leaves on the plane trees barely stirring in the breeze, a cloudless blue sky like an upturned bowl overhead and the rooms in the hospice almost insufferably hot – I'd played a weird kind of tag with Anna and her kids.

I had taken some time off work – three days, which was the maximum compassionate leave HR would allow me for someone who was not quite a partner – and spent as much of them as I could by his bedside. Mostly, that meant night times, when Anna and the children went back to Damask Square to sleep if they could. But during the day, when the children were at school, Anna and I moved in and out of his room as if we were doing some kind of dance, only neither of us knew what the steps were meant to look like.

There had been one encounter, one time when our paths crossed, when I was arriving after work to see Gray, and his daughter came running over to me, having recognised me through the window of the restaurant where she was having dinner with her mother and brother.

'Laurel.' She stopped by my side, out of breath, looking like she'd been crying. 'It's Lulu. I thought I recognised you.'

I felt blood flood to my face, as if I'd been caught doing something inappropriate. I couldn't look towards the restaurant across the street where I knew Anna would be, sitting and watching.

'This is so random, seeing you here. Mum said you're a friend of Dad's.'

If Anna had said that, I could only go along with the half-truth. 'That's right. How are you doing, Lulu? You and your brother?'

She sniffed, her tears not far from the surface. 'We're okay. It's just... you know. It's a lot.'

'I know.' I wanted to touch her, offer some sort of physical comfort, but the knowledge of Anna's eyes on me prevented me. 'I'm so sorry you're all going through this.'

'Thanks.' She flashed a brief, painful smile. 'Have you come to see Dad? We can all go in together.'

'I...' I was torn between my longing to see Gray and my knowledge that I couldn't – not now, not when his wife and children were there. It was out of the question. 'I think maybe he shouldn't have too many people with him at once. He needs to be kept quiet. I'll come back a bit later.'

After that, I gave my number to Precious, the nurse who mostly looked after Gray, and asked her to text me when the coast was clear. She agreed with the sad smile of a woman who'd seen this sort of thing before.

There were rooms in the hospice where families could stay overnight, but because I wasn't family and Anna had her own to look after, neither of us used them. I cycled there from Mel's flat after sleeping in my own bed, feeling a fleeting sense of freedom and joy as I breathed in the still-fresh air, parakeets and gulls wheeling overhead.

When I arrived at the hospice it was seven in the morning. The smell of tea and toast permeating the corridors. The people who were on days arriving smiling and rested and taking over from their weary colleagues, the rattle of plates coming from the kitchen and the first trill of the phone as people began to call to ask, *How is she? Did he have a good night?*

I knew hospitals – their rhythms and their moods. I could tell as soon as I walked in that the night had been good – there had been no deaths. Not Gray's and not anyone else's. Relief flooded me.

I said good morning to Precious. 'How is he? Did he have a good night?'

'Very peaceful.' She smiled warmly. 'Would you like to go in? I'll bring you some toast.'

'Thank you – that would be amazing.'

She brought me toast that had gone a bit leathery but tasted fine once I'd smeared a load of Marmite on it, and a cup of overstewed tea, which is how I like it anyway. While I ate I held Gray's hand, and in between bites I talked to him.

'It's absolutely gorgeous out,' I said. 'It reminds me of that day when we cycled out to Kent, remember? We stopped on the edge of that apple orchard to eat our lunch, and there was no one about, so we thought we might get jiggy, and then we realised there were bees absolutely everywhere. I said you'd have a hell of a time explaining at home how you'd got stung on the bollocks, so we left it. I wish we hadn't, now.'

I saw Gray's face flicker and felt his hand squeeze mine – just the faintest pressure, but I knew he was listening.

I'd told myself I was used to death, but I was quickly realising I wasn't.

'We used to talk about where we'd go on holiday,' I went on. 'I've never been to Disneyland Paris, and I was dead keen on it – I still am, if I'm honest. But you said you'd been through it three times with your kids, and you'd rather chew your own arm off than go again. If I ever do go, I'm going to take a photo of you with me, just to spite you.'

That ghost of a smile crossed his face again and he opened his eyes.

'Well, that got your attention,' I said. 'Do you need anything? Water?'

He nodded.

'Let's get you sat up.' I adjusted his position on the pillows and held a glass to his lips. 'There are some mints here too, and Precious will be along to do your mouth care soon, I expect.'

I snapped open the can of Smints and held out one to him. He managed to take it between thumb and forefinger and guide it to his lips. When I saw him swallow, which was getting difficult, I leaned over and kissed him. I'd never kissed him good morning before, I realised. Perhaps I never would again.

'Marmite,' he said.

'Oh God, I taste of it, don't I? Sorry about that.'

'Like Marmite.' He smiled. 'Hate bananas.'

'They're gross, aren't they? Slimy devil penises.'

He managed a croaky laugh.

'I'll be in and out all day,' I carried on. 'Anna will too. You don't have to worry – there'll always be someone here. It's like a relay race.'

Except in this race, there was only one possible end and no winners. Silence fell between us, and I sought to fill it with something other than the gloomy thoughts that rushed into my mind if I allowed them to.

'I got a text from Lulu yesterday,' I told him. 'It's so random – she came to our stand at the careers fair I did for work, and then she saw me arriving here the other day. She asked for my number, to find out more about becoming a nurse. She's a great kid.'

He smiled. 'The best.'

Before I could say anything more, there was a tap on the door and Precious glided in. She didn't have to say anything; I knew what she meant by her careful smile. Anna had arrived. Anna had been asked to wait in the lobby on the pretext of Gray getting some personal care, so I could slip out the back without seeing her.

'Thanks,' I mouthed, then I said to Gray, 'I'm going to head off for a bit. I'll be back soon, okay? I love you.'

'Love you,' he murmured.

I knew there would be a last time he said that to me, but I didn't know it was then.

I bought a coffee and found a park nearby and sat on a bench, my face turned up to the sun. My eyes were closed but I could see the brightness through my eyelids and feel the warmth soaking through my T-shirt.

Gray had been taken outside the day before, Precious had told me, when Anna was there. I hoped he'd enjoyed the sunshine. Had he been uncomfortable? Would Anna have remembered he liked to suck on chips of ice sometimes?

Stop it, Laurel, I said to myself. Anna knew him. She'd loved him for twenty years, and I had for just eighteen months. So I made myself stop thinking, and I waited on the bench until Precious texted to tell me the coast was clear.

Gray slept deeply for most of the afternoon. I chatted to him a bit, but when he didn't respond I stopped – there was no point disturbing his rest. So I sat quietly by his side, holding his hand until my arm went numb and my shoulder started to ache, then I moved the chair to the opposite side of the bed and held his other hand.

At four, Anna came back with the children. Precious had gone off shift and Desmond had taken over, and I guess she hadn't briefed him about me, so I was still sitting there when the door opened.

I jumped to my feet. 'Sorry. I was just leaving.'

Gray's son looked at me curiously. I hoped he hadn't seen me holding his father's hand.

Anna said, 'Yes. How is he?'

But before I could answer, Lulu said, 'Hi, Laurel. Is it okay if I text you about the hospital open day?'

'Of course.' I was conscious of Anna's gaze on me. 'I'll look forward to seeing you there.'

'It'll be busy, though,' Lulu went on. 'Maybe we could meet before? Have a coffee or something?'

'That would be nice.' I reached out and touched her shoulder. 'Take care of yourself in the meantime. And your dad.'

Then I legged it across the road, had a fried chicken burger and a Coke, and waited until I saw their car turn out of the gates and drive away before going back.

The radio was on when I entered the room – LBC, playing on Gray's phone. I switched it off and sat down, telling him I was back and taking his hand. I could feel no answering pressure, so I spoke to him only occasionally, telling him that we were almost ready to exchange contracts on my new flat and that I'd hopefully be moving in in a few weeks.

'It's a shame you never got to see it,' I said softly. 'Maybe if I'd had my own place, we could have spent more nights together. That would've been fun, right?'

Gray's hand gripped mine with sudden intensity and his eyes opened, wide with alarm. 'Joel?'

I was bewildered. What was he talking about?

'What about Joel?' I asked.

'The operation. Is he okay?'

Then I realised. He must be remembering coming round from the anaesthetic after the surgery to remove his kidney – confused, as patients at the end of their lives sometimes were, slipping back into the past because the present was fading away and there was no future.

'Joel's fine,' I reassured him, stroking the paper-dry skin of his hand. 'He's recovering well. You did a wonderful thing, Gray. You're a brave man.'

'It was nothing.' His voice was quite clear. 'Not compared to...'

Then his words faded away, and soon the pressure of his hand relaxed and he fell asleep.

I must have done too, upright in the uncomfortable chair, Gray's hand still in mine.

I was still holding it when I woke, roused by the first music of birds in the trees outside. It was still dark; my watch told me it was just after four in the morning.

Apart from the sound of birdsong, everything was quiet. Everything felt peaceful and serene. Only one thing had changed: Gray had stopped breathing. I hadn't been aware of it; I'd heard nothing. His hand in mine was lifeless, but still warm from my own skin.

Stiffly, I got to my feet. Gray's face was still, peaceful. I went to the window and opened it. Some of the older nurses in hospitals still did this, to allow the soul of the departed to go free, and it was the last thing I would ever do for Gray.

I felt cool air on my face and heard the dawn chorus more clearly.

He was gone.

TWENTY-FOUR

ANNA

I wasn't with Gray when he died, because Laurel was.

I had more or less made peace with the idea that I might not be there, and explained as best I could to the children that when they said goodbye to their father in the evenings, it might be for the last time.

Each night, when Gray was in the hospice, I'd sit by their beds and talk to them, sharing memories of their father I'd never told them about before. They listened to the stories and smiled, perhaps realising that I needed to tell them as much as they needed to hear them. Sometimes they added stories of their own: *Remember when Dad made brownies for the school bake sale and they were still raw inside and I had to pretend they were a special gourmet recipe? Remember when Augustus was a kitten and got stuck up the tree in Orla's garden and Dad climbed up to get him and then he was too scared to get back down, and we thought we'd have to call a fire engine to rescue them both?*

When I woke up on Wednesday, I didn't know that it would be the last day. I got the children off to school and drove to the hospice. Gray was in his room, awake; Laurel was nowhere to be seen. Our agreement might be an unspoken one, but we were both abiding by it. She had the nights and snatches of the days when I was with the children; the rest of the time was mine.

But I was almost sure I could detect her presence in the room. I caught a hint of the scent of her shampoo, there was a plate by the bed with toast crumbs on it, the top was off the canister of mints I had bought and the vinyl seat of the chair felt warm when I sat on it.

I put my hand on the sheet where it covered Gray's knee.

'Hello, you. You look like you slept well. The kids are at school, but they'll be along later to see you. They're starting to wind down for the summer holidays now. We've still got those two weeks in Portugal booked – do you remember? We decided not to cancel until we were sure what would happen. I don't know whether we'll end up going. The children might need a break, but they might prefer to stay home. I'll play it by ear, don't you think?'

I chatted on for a while, but he didn't respond. I could hear him breathing steadily and evenly. Occasionally his closed eyes flickered, and I wondered if he was dreaming – those wild morphine dreams again. I picked up his phone, found one of his favourite podcasts and began to play it with the volume turned down low.

Watching his sleeping face, I tried to memorise every detail of the man I'd loved for twenty years. There would be a time soon when I would see it and it would no longer be the face of a living, breathing man. Everything that made him Gray – his desires, his memories, his secrets – would be gone.

I was suddenly overwhelmed with the craving for a proper cigarette – not my vape but the real thing. How many times had Gray and I smoked together, guiltily enjoying the pungent, deadly hit of nicotine, the plumes of our exhales mingling together?

Too many times to count – the first of which was the day we met.

It was in the summer of 2003, at my cousin Lucy's wedding. I was twenty-three, too young for many of my friends to be getting married just yet, so Lucy's wedding felt like a distraction from my normal social life. She was eight years older than me; I'd be attending with my younger sisters and my mum and dad.

Cathy and Sarah had been jealous, I remembered, because I was a bridesmaid and they weren't. They watched enviously as I walked up the aisle clutching a corner of Lucy's train through a sea of flowers and hats. My uncle handed Lucy over to her groom, and I took my seat in the front row. Almost immediately, I felt a tap on my shoulder and heard Cathy whisper, 'Look at him. Hot.'

I followed her discreetly pointing finger and saw the guy who was filming the wedding video: a stocky blond man, wearing a leather jacket in spite of the heat, moving around the room as swiftly and lithely as a tomcat, so intently focused on his work that he might have been filming on Oscar-contender movie rather than a provincial wedding.

'I saw him first,' I whispered back.

Then the ceremony got under way and we couldn't say anything more until it was over, and after that we were whisked away for photographs and canapés.

But I kept an eye on the video guy, and when there was a break in the proceedings I saw him slip away, so I slipped too.

I found him in the rose garden, smoking a cigarette.

'Hi,' I said. 'Got a light?'

I had one in my bag, but he didn't need to know that. He offered me his packet of fags, and I took one, leaning in for him to light it for me.

'Not sure you should be fraternising with the help,' he said, 'being a bridesmaid and all.'

'But I'm the help too,' I assured him. 'I'm the bride's cousin, by the way. My name's Anna.'

'Gray,' he said.

'Great name.' I smiled.

'It's more of a nickname, actually. So are these all your family?'

I laughed. 'Not all of them. Come on – there are lots of us, but not two hundred. My mum and dad are here, though, and my two sisters, and my granny and grandpa. And there are other cousins about – there are fourteen of us altogether.'

'Wow.' His deep brown eyes widened with something like longing. 'What's that like?'

I laughed. 'Carnage, mostly. You should see our family Christmases.'

'I'd like to. Let me know if you ever have room for waifs and strays.'

'There's so many of us we probably wouldn't notice a gate-crasher,' I joked.

By the end of the night, he'd taken my number. The following Monday he called me, and on the Friday night we went out. He took me to a fancy cocktail bar in Soho, where a client of his was apparently a member and had swung him a guest pass.

And that December, he *did* join my family for Christmas – not as a gate-crasher but as my boyfriend. I remembered his face on that day too, when he'd walked into the crowded room and seen all the assembled faces, not the same but similar, heard the laughter and chatter, smelled the roasting turkey and the woodsmoke from the fireplace.

'You're lucky, Anna,' he said. 'So lucky to be part of this.'

'You are too, now,' I told him.

It was six months after that that he asked me to marry him, and less than a year later we found the house on Damask Square and started our own family.

Later that day, I returned to Gray's bedside with the children. They talked to him, telling him about their day at school.

Lulu glanced at her phone. Barney's stomach rumbled – he hadn't wanted the sandwich I'd offered him after school. Normally he would have been at his cricket practice, and Lulu would have been at her dance class, but instead we were all here, in this limbo that we longed to end but dreaded ending.

At last I said, 'I suppose we should get home.'

But then Gray opened his eyes.

'Hello, darling,' I said. 'Lulu and Barney are here with me.'

'Hi, Dad,' Lulu said, forcing a smile even though I could tell she wanted to cry.

'How are you feeling?' Barney asked, as if part of him was still expecting that miracle.

'I love you,' Gray said. He sounded as if his mouth was dry.

'We love you too, Dad,' Lulu croaked, gripping his hand, tears suddenly streaming down her face.

'Dad – we're here,' Barney said, and I knew what he meant was, *Please stay with us*.

I stood up and went to the window, looking out over the grass and up to the sky rather than at my husband and children. I could hear the faint rustle of the pillowcase as Gray turned his head to look first at one of them and then at the other. I could hear Lulu's sobs and Barney sniffing. Then I turned back and leaned over the bed, my arms around their shoulders, the three of us huddled close over Gray as if the four of us were squeezing in for a family selfie.

There'd be no more of those. I didn't want there to be. I didn't want my children to remember their father like this.

'Take care of them, Anna,' Gray murmured.

'I will,' I said. 'I promise you I always will.'

'Take care,' he said again, his voice almost a croak now, 'of your mum. Like I did.'

'We will, Dad,' Lulu whispered.

'Promise,' Barney said.

Gray said one more word. 'Mum.'

As his eyes closed, I saw tears beginning to trickle down his cheeks. I didn't want the children to see that – I wanted them to remember this as a calm time, a peaceful time. I didn't want them tormented by the memory of him in pain or distress. I stroked his face, brushing away the tears with my fingers until they stopped flowing.

When his breathing had settled and he was quiet again, I said, 'I think we should go home.'

I said goodbye to Gray and told him again that I loved him, and waited while Barney and Lulu did the same. None of us knew for sure, but I think we all felt in our hearts that it would be the last time.

TWENTY-FIVE

ORLA

18 June 2024

I am writing these pages not in my own home as usual, but three doors down, in the kitchen at number eight. I was woken at five by a knock on my door and realised almost immediately what must have happened, so I called out of the window that I was on my way, dressed hastily and ran downstairs, picking up my bag with this notebook in it before I opened the door.

Anna was standing on the doorstep as if the last movement she'd made was to raise her hand to the knocker. She looked frozen, although the morning was already warm. I reached out to her, and she took a step forward, almost falling into my arms.

Is it over? I asked.

I felt her head move against my shoulder as she nodded. She told me that he had died early this morning, and that Laurel was with him. She asked me to wait at her house until the children woke up.

You don't have to tell them, she said.

They'll know, I thought.

She said, I'll come back as soon as I can and get them. I just want to see, first...

I understood. She needed to see Gray's body before she decided whether the children should – to say her own goodbyes in order to know what form theirs should take.

She has probably never seen a dead person before. I am twenty years older than she is and I have only once, when old Mr Isaacs passed away ten years ago.

We are both lucky, I suppose. Many women our ages and younger will have seen death over and over, laid out bodies, drawn down blinds, comforted the bereaved and been comforted themselves. She may want to spare her own daughter that experience – that rite of passage, I suppose it is – until later.

I followed her to her house, and she let me in. Help yourself to coffee, she said.

So I did, and now I am sitting in her warm, silent kitchen with Augustus on my lap, waiting for the first sounds from upstairs. I will answer the children's questions as best I can, prepare them for the news their mother must break to them. I will wait here, I suppose, for the district nurses to come and remove the hospital bed that was installed upstairs and restore the room to a normal place to sleep. I will offer to help with the funeral arrangements. I will cook meals and portion them into Tupperware for Anna's freezer.

I will do what I can.

And at some point I will have to ask Anna whether Gray's solicitor received my message and whether she got there in time. Whether or not the change he wished to make to his will was made in time, and what that means for the family.

They have made this house into a beautiful home – a showpiece. I remember Gray showing me around when it was completed and ready to be photographed for *Architectural Digest*. He was so proud of what he and Anna had created, and rightly so. They were happy here, I know, before life and death got in the way.

I hope they will be happy again. I hope that, in time, the children will recover from the loss of their father and Anna will recover from her husband's betrayal of her. I hope she will realise that it was right for him to tell her – that it was the only thing he could have done, that the secret could no longer be kept.

I can hear footsteps upstairs now. It is time for this day to begin again – for the Graham family to face this next chapter in their lives and whatever it will bring.

TWENTY-SIX
ANNA

There's no pretty way of saying it: I was drunk at my husband's funeral.

In the two weeks since Gray's death, I'd woken up each morning with a sense of leaden dread, realising simultaneously that, one, I had a fucking shite hangover and, two, Gray was dead. Again. It was as if, each time, the knowledge that he had died and that I had a pounding headache and a mouth that tasted like the inside of the kitchen food-waste caddy descended on me as freshly, as horribly, as if I hadn't known it before.

It had started the morning after he died. Well, strictly speaking the morning after that, because the first morning I had been stone-cold sober, thanks to some premonition that I might have had to get up in the middle of the night and drive to the hospice to see him for the last time. But the day after that, the nineteenth of June, was what I think of as the first of the death hangovers.

I was woken by Lulu coming into my room – the spare bedroom, still; I didn't know when, if ever, I'd be able to face moving back into the room I'd shared with him.

'Mum,' she whispered. 'Mum? Are you awake?'

I was now. 'What time is it, darling?'

'Half past six. I couldn't sleep.'

There was no point admitting that, thanks to a couple of hefty belts of twenty-year-old Armagnac after the children had gone to bed, I'd slept like the dead. So to speak.

'Come here, sweetie.' I pushed the duvet aside and Lulu got in next to me, snuggling up like she hadn't done in years. She was wearing the knickers and crop top she'd slept in; she smelled of yesterday's deodorant, and her skin was like warm satin under my fingers.

'Mum? Remember how Dad used to blow his nose after he showered every morning?'

Did he? Maybe he did. The sounds of Gray's morning ablutions had become so familiar, such an invisible part of the fabric of my days, I hadn't noticed them in a decade or more – only this year, when he'd sometimes been sick in the mornings and I'd say, *Jesus, are you okay?* And he'd say, *Think so. Fucking acid reflux again.*

Should you see a doctor?

Nah, I'm all right.

So long as you're not pregnant.

Ha – chance would be a fine thing.

'Every morning, like a foghorn,' Lulu was saying. 'When I was little, it was just a noise Dad made. Then I started thinking, Gross! If I had a friend for a sleepover I'd be like, God, how embarrassing. And I woke up this morning and I realised I'll never hear it ever again.'

She started to cry, and I pulled her close and held her, perversely glad that my banging head and churning stomach were distracting me for the time being from the other, deeper pain I knew would descend eventually.

Somehow, we got through that day. The kids were off school. Sarah came over and made mushroom omelettes for lunch because she said we needed to eat. There were calls to the undertakers. A huge flower arrangement came from Gray's work, with a card signed by all the staff that made me cry. Orla brought round a vegetable lasagne, and I found myself thinking that if I had to cook dinner, I'd have an excuse to have a glass of wine.

But putting Orla's stoneware dish in the oven and making a salad counted as cooking, I told myself two hours later, cracking open a bottle of rosé.

The following Monday, the children went back to school. Cathy and Sarah were on top of the funeral arrangements. My mum, who'd stayed for the weekend, had gone back to Herefordshire because she said she couldn't leave the dogs with Dad any longer.

The flood of sympathy cards had slowed to a trickle by then, but when I heard the familiar rattle of the letter box and the thump of paper landing on the doormat, I still assumed that the postman had brought today's instalment – like having taken out a subscription to a particularly grim periodical, I thought, and not being able to cancel it until the introductory offer period was over.

I walked upstairs from the kitchen, where I'd been sitting staring vacantly out at the garden wondering whether eleven o'clock was too early for a drink, and picked up the stack of mail from inside the front door. There were a couple of leaflets from curry restaurants on nearby Brick Lane, an official-looking letter from Gray's bank – which I'd wait to deal with until Cathy or Sarah was with me for moral support – and four plain white envelopes, their contents slim and rigid.

Cards, of course. I ripped open the first one, glanced at the tasteful image of a pond at sunset and read the stilted, careful words of sympathy inside, from the mother of a child Lulu had been best friends with in primary school. The second was similar, from the family of Jack Isaacs, who used to live in the flats near Damask Square. The third was hand-painted, a watercolour of the front of our house before we'd begun the renovations. Although the edges of the paper were worn and curling and the paint faded, I could see the skill that had gone into its creation.

I opened the card.

Dearest Anna

I painted this years ago and I suppose I intended to give it to you and Gray, but it slipped my mind. I was so sorry to hear of his death. He was the sweetest, funniest man and you and the children must miss him desperately. I am thinking of you and hope we can see each other when I'm back in London. Perhaps this will remind you of happier times.

Much love,
Beatrice

Orla's daughter. A typical Beatrice gesture – a mixture of care and thoughtlessness, emotion felt sincerely but expressed clumsily. It made me sad that Gray would never see the painting – he would have loved it.

I walked back downstairs and propped the painting up on the mantelpiece to show the children, then turned to the final envelope, feeling an immediate jolt of shock. On it was handwritten not my name, but 'Nigel Graham'.

No one had called Gray 'Nigel' since the officiant on our wedding day.

I remembered asking him on our first date if Gray was a nickname, and if so what his actual name was.

'Humphrey,' he'd said.

'Oh, come on. Really?'

'Okay. Aloysius.'

'Stop it!'

'Sorry. It's Percival.'

Then our drinks arrived and we'd changed the subject, and it hadn't been until our first holiday together, when I saw it in his passport, that I found out. When I asked him about it then, he'd laughed, half-embarrassed, and said, 'Come on, Anna. If you were called *Nigel*, wouldn't you change it as soon as you could?' And I'd had to admit that I would.

But whoever had sent this card still knew Gray as Nigel.

I slit open the envelope with a kitchen knife, not tearing it with my thumb as I had the others, and took out the card inside. No tasteful pond here, no muted watercolours on cartridge paper or tree clad in autumn foliage.

It was a white card embossed in silver. The number 25 was in the centre, surrounded by hearts and champagne flutes, their bubbles merging with the sparkly hearts and drifting towards the top of the page.

A silver wedding anniversary card. Except Gray and I had been married for only eighteen years and known each other for just twenty-one.

My hands were shaking as I opened it. The writing inside was elegant, written in royal-blue ink from a fountain pen.

Nigel

You might prefer to forget, but I haven't. I think of you every day and hope you're embracing them all in health and with happiness.

Love you still
J

The words shocked me like a kick to the stomach. Someone who loved Gray – who had loved him when he was Nigel. Whose love had begun or been consummated or formalised twenty-five years before. A woman whose name began with J, who Gray had never mentioned to me, not even once.

Someone – I found myself rummaging through Gray's work bag, finding a spiral-bound notebook and laying it open on the kitchen table next to the card to make sure – whose handwriting bore a striking resemblance to Gray's.

I checked the back of the envelope, but there was no return address. I studied the postmark and saw that the card had been posted in Edinburgh, a city I couldn't recall Gray ever having visited.

I needed a drink.

I was alone with Augustus, and cats don't judge, so I made a gin and tonic and went and sat in the garden. Never again, I thought, would I hear Gray say, *We should give that shed a sand and a coat of paint*. When he said, *We should...* like that, it meant one thing: it was a job that was officially his, which he was delegating to me but which I would passive-aggressively not do, and so it wouldn't get done. He'd first said it about the shed three years ago; it was still unpainted and now was likely to remain so.

I'd never be able to ask him who J was and why he meant so much to her that she had thought of him every day for twenty-five years.

What must that be like? I wondered. Would I look back twenty-five years from now and realise I had thought of Gray every single day? Would I still feel this edge-of-a-cliff, terrifying grief, which switched without warning to anger? Did J, whoever she was, think of Gray with that same impossible, conflicting mess of emotions?

The only thing that got me through those days was the prospect of dulling the ache each evening with several glasses of wine, so that at least I would be able to sink into oblivion for six hours, even if on waking my head throbbed, I felt sick and the fresh reality of Gray being gone hit me just as hard as it had the previous day.

On the day of Gray's funeral, when Sarah arrived at half past nine in the morning, she found me in the kitchen pouring a gin and tonic.

'Anna!' She looked at me with horrified pity. 'What are you...?'

'Just got to take the edge off,' I muttered. 'It's Gray's funeral, after all. It's what he would have wanted.'

I took a sip, the alcohol hitting me like a brick concealed inside a pillow.

'Are you okay, love?' My sister moved round the kitchen island so she could see my face. 'I mean, of course you're not okay, but... Is this...?'

'I've been hitting the booze too hard,' I admitted. 'It's not forever. Just until today. It's not a thing. Don't worry.'

She looked at me, concern written on her face as blatantly as a graffiti tag. Then she reached out and squeezed my shoulder before hurrying upstairs to check that the kids were up.

I finished my drink and went upstairs to get ready. On the floor above, I could hear Sarah speaking gently to Barney and the shower running. I showered myself, put on some slapdash make-up and dressed in the floral silk wrap frock Gray had always liked. I'd lost weight since I wore it last, and I had to secure the neckline with a safety pin.

'Mustn't get your tits out at your husband's funeral,' I muttered to myself. Not that it mattered. Not that anything really mattered, except putting one foot in front of the other for the next few hours, until it was tomorrow and I could start afresh, scrape my life together and carry on.

'Standing room only,' I said, stepping through the chapel doors half an hour later. The interior was dark after the brilliant sunshine outside, but I could see rows and rows of people, squeezed shoulder to shoulder on to the padded seats. More were standing outside, where a PA system would broadcast the service, and still more would be joining via a Zoom link.

It had all been arranged. Probably some of it by me – I couldn't remember. It must have been me who'd issued the instruction not to wear black, because Gray had always liked bright colours – so it was my fault that entering the chapel felt like stepping into a kaleidoscope.

Richard held my arm and steered me to the front row of seats, and I took my place between Lulu and Barney. I could smell flowers, but not see any – we'd asked for donations to the hospice instead. It must be my perfume, the Anaïs Anaïs I'd worn on our wedding day and never used any more.

I closed my eyes and kept them closed while the celebrant

went into her welcoming patter. I opened them when Carl came up to the front to read 'Dirge Without Music'. He must have responded to my email asking him to do a reading and suggested that, but I couldn't remember agreeing or ever having read the words until I saw them printed on the service sheet I was holding.

'More precious was the light in your eyes than all the roses in the world,' he read.

I wondered if Gray had felt that way about Laurel. I wondered if he'd ever bought her roses. I hadn't seen her in the chapel when we came in – but then it was so dark I hadn't seen anyone distinctly.

I found myself hoping she was there. Gray would have wanted her to be there.

At last it was over. Lulu had started to cry about halfway through and was gripping my hand, a soggy tissue pressed against my palm. Barney's face was blank, as if he'd never be able to feel anything ever again.

I needed a wee and another drink, equally badly.

I stood up, relieved to find that I could walk quite steadily back through the rows of faces, some contorted with weeping, some grave and still, some wearing careful, supportive smiles. I was okay until I got outside, and then the sunshine hit me, my eyes went funny and I felt my legs disappear from underneath me.

TWENTY-SEVEN
LAUREL

There was no room inside the chapel, so I listened to Gray's funeral from outside, gathered around a screen with the other people who couldn't fit inside. Not that it made much difference – from the moment the celebrant kicked off the proceedings by saying, 'Friends and family, we are gathered here today not just to mourn a death, but to celebrate a life,' I started to cry and didn't stop.

Even when she said, 'The life of Nigel Graham, husband, father, friend, colleague and neighbour,' my tears only intensified: I hadn't known his first name, although I'd always half-assumed it must be something other than Gray. I had been so peripheral to his life, even that most fundamental fact about him was news to me. I was shut out, and not just literally.

I had known, during that last hour I had spent sitting with his body before Anna arrived, that this would be the end – the last time I could be alone with him. Precious had known it too, embracing me and saying softly, 'I'll let you know when it's time.'

We both knew what she meant: time for Anna to arrive, time for my wishes and Gray's to take a back seat, because he was dead and I would have to relinquish him, permanently now, to the people he truly belonged to, to the life that I had only been an illicit, secret part of, to the death that I couldn't change.

Anna must have spent the past two weeks planning all of this. The rainbow colours the invited mourners were wearing; the poem I could hear being read by a man introduced as Carl, Gray's business partner; the venue for the drinks afterwards. Planning it all must have been awful for her – but was it worse than not being able to be part of it? I couldn't and never would know.

Still, I was envious. She had the status of being his wife. She could elicit sympathy without being ashamed. She'd be sent cards and flowers, and people would share their memories of Gray with her to make her feel less alone, to show her they had loved him too.

All I had were the memories of the time I'd had with him. How many hours, I wondered, had we actually spent together in those months? Not that many. In total, they probably added up to less than ten days. But every moment had been filled with joy – it was when I wasn't with him that the bad stuff had happened: the guilt, the loneliness, the pain of missing him.

Now the good part had ended and only the bad remained.

I heard Carl's voice reading or reciting the last line of the poem he or Anna had chosen: 'I do not approve. And I am not resigned.'

I didn't and I wasn't. But there was nothing I could do about it. Gray was dead. I would never see him again. That was that.

At last the ceremony ended. Someone announced that there'd be food and drink at the Crooked Billet and everyone was most welcome, but I sensed that probably didn't apply to me. I decided to leave – slip quietly away, perhaps go for a long bike ride and lose myself in the pain of pushing my body to its limits.

I'd get out of the black suit I'd bought for the occasion, not realising that everyone else would be in bright summer clothes more suited to a wedding than a funeral.

As I turned to go, the door of the chapel opened and Anna stepped out, flanked by her children. I turned away, not wanting her to see me, but seconds later I heard a cry of alarm and the unmistakeable sound of a body falling to the ground.

'She's fainted,' someone said.

My training and my instinct kicked in. I took a step forward, then hesitated, but it was too late.

'Laurel's here.' Lulu Graham had spotted me. 'She's a nurse. She'll know what to do.'

She reached out and gripped my arm as if it was the only thing stopping her falling herself. I could see terror in her eyes, and I knew what she must be thinking: *Not Mum as well as Dad.*

'Hey.' I put a hand on her shoulder. 'Don't worry. She'll be fine. We've got this.'

'Are you sure?' Her voice trembled. I could see she'd been crying and was about to do so again.

Instinctively, I put my arms around her and held her close for a moment.

'It's okay, Lulu love,' I said. 'I'll make sure your mum's looked after.'

She gulped. 'Thanks, Laurel.'

Then we let each other go and I squatted down next to Anna's prone body, awkward in my high heels, abandoning any hope of making a discreet getaway.

Lulu's was just one of the faces peering down at Anna and me, variously shocked, anxious and plain old curious. I could see two blonde women, almost indistinguishable from each other and so like Anna they could only be her sisters. There was an older woman with stylishly cut grey hair, slender in a rose-coloured silk dress. And Gray's son too, his face frozen with shock.

I only looked up for a second before turning my attention to Anna.

'Anna, can you hear me?' I asked. Her chest was rising and falling. Her pulse was even.

Maybe she had fainted; maybe she had lost her footing descending the steps in her platform sandals and banged her head or winded herself. Mostly, though, the smell of gin on her breath, barely concealed by toothpaste, told its own story.

'Is she all right?' The woman in the pink dress had squatted down next to me. 'Is she hurt?'

'I don't think so.' I met her eyes and she nodded, understanding without me needing to say anything. I raised my voice. 'If you wouldn't mind all moving back a little, please. Me and...?'

'Orla.'

'Laurel.' I smiled at her briefly. 'Me and Orla will try and get Anna sitting up.'

'It might be an idea to get people moving off to the pub,' Orla said, turning to the small group that had gathered round. 'Laurel and I will take Anna home and get her medical attention if she needs it.'

'Come on, darlings.' One of Anna's sisters put her arms round Lulu and Barney, steering them away. 'Mum'll be fine. It's the stress of the past few days, poor love. I'm sure she'll join us when she's feeling better.'

Orla and I leaned over Anna's prone form, gently helping her to sit up. There was a bump on the back of her head, swelling already, but no blood. Her eyes were open but glazed and unseeing. I gave her a sip of water from the bottle in my handbag, and Orla called a taxi on her phone.

It was only then that I was able to look up and see into the chapel through the still-open doors. The rows of seats were vacant now. A ray of sunlight illuminated the front of the space where the celebrant and the readers would have stood. Where Gray's coffin would have been, there was now only emptiness.

Half an hour later, we'd got Anna home. She was conscious, talking and able to climb the stairs on her own – just very, very drunk. I left Orla to settle her in bed, found paracetamol in the bathroom and a bag of frozen peas in the kitchen, and poured a glass of water before going back upstairs to the spare bedroom, where I guessed Anna must have been sleeping alone during Gray's illness – or perhaps even before that; I had no way of knowing.

Orla met me in the doorway.

'Poor woman,' she murmured. 'I'm sure she wouldn't want...'

'Anyone to know?' Orla nodded, and I went on, 'Strictly speaking, given she's been drinking, she ought to have medical attention. But...'

'She's got it,' Orla said. 'From you. I've taken her dress and shoes off. She wouldn't mind – we've known each other long enough. I've been their neighbour ever since they moved in. And you...?'

There was no point in lying, but at the same time I found it almost impossible to tell the truth.

'I was...' I began. 'Gray and I were...'

Orla nodded. 'I knew there was someone. They both told me – Gray and Anna. When you said your name I knew who you were.'

I said, 'I'm sorry. I really am. Sorry for what we did and now...'

'Sorry that he's gone. We all are. But for you it must be different. Harder.'

Her words brought a lump to my throat, but now wasn't the time to cry. I thanked her and stepped past her into the bedroom, where Anna was lying still, breathing heavily, covered by the duvet.

'Anna,' I said. 'It's Laurel. How are you doing?'

Her eyes flickered and opened. They were unfocused and bloodshot, but her pupils looked normal.

'Laurel,' she muttered. 'What the hell are you...?'

'You fell and bumped your head. Do you know what day it is?'

'Friday. Gray's funeral.'

'That's right.'

'My head fucking hurts.'

'I know. Can you sit up and take some tablets?'

I put my arm around her shoulders and helped her into a sitting position, then handed her the water and paracetamol and waited while she sipped and swallowed.

'What an idiot,' she said, her words slurred. 'I've made a right fool of myself.'

I shook my head. 'It's okay. No one will mind. You should rest and not worry about anything.'

'The kids…?'

'They're with their aunt.'

'Cathy or Sarah?'

'I don't know,' I admitted, reassured by her relative lucidity. 'One of your sisters, anyway. They're just like you.'

She managed a smile. 'Gray loved my family. He said becoming part of it was the best thing about marrying me. Maybe that was a red flag.'

I shook my head. 'He loved you very much. You and the children. I've always known that.'

She looked at me with a hint of the spiky aggression I was used to seeing. But she didn't have the strength to sustain it.

'Why did you do it, then?' Her tone was weary – almost resigned. 'If you knew he loved us so much?'

'I suppose in the beginning I didn't,' I admitted. 'I knew he had a wife and children. I can't hide from that. But I didn't know… I didn't know you.'

'I suppose he told you his wife didn't understand him.' Her lips twisted into the sarcastic half-smile I was beginning to recognise.

I shook my head. 'He never said that. He never said anything bad about you. Just recently – a few weeks ago – he told me you were an amazing mother.'

Her face sharpened. 'He did? Why did he tell you that?'

Because I told him I wanted to be a mother. But I couldn't reveal that to Anna.

'I can't remember,' I lied. 'Something about his own mother, maybe.'

'What did he tell you about her?' she demanded.

Now I wasn't lying – or hardly at all. 'Nothing. He never mentioned her apart from that one time.'

I know about mothers, he'd said. *I had a shit one.* That was all. I hadn't asked him about it at the time – it hadn't seemed important. But perhaps it was.

'He owed me everything, you know.' Anna's anger didn't seem to be directed at me any longer, but elsewhere. 'This house, our family, everything he wanted. And he could have thrown it all away, because of you.'

'I'm sorry,' I said. 'Sorry for what I did. What me and Gray did.'

Abruptly, the fire went out of her, and she lay back down on the pillow.

'I'll tell you one thing, Laurel,' she whispered. 'I don't think I ever really understood him at all.'

TWENTY-EIGHT
ANNA

I didn't speak to Orla for a week after Gray's funeral. I didn't speak to anyone, really, apart from the children and my sisters, who rang every day to make sure I was okay. The melting-away of well-wishers that I'd been warned might take place once the funeral was over had indeed happened, and I welcomed it. I didn't want to see anyone.

The truth is, I was embarrassed. I had done that unforgivable thing and Made a Scene. Possibly even worse than that – Made an Exhibition of Myself. I was embarrassed by what had happened. I still couldn't quite piece it together – I'd fainted, or collapsed, or passed out, I wasn't sure which. If it hadn't been for that, I'd have been able to hold it together, I was sure. I'd had a few drinks, but I'd been fine.

But collapse I had, and – the details were hazy, but not hazy enough – Orla and Laurel, of all people, had come to my rescue, got me in a taxi and put me to bed. When eventually I'd come round, finding myself with a filthy headache and my underwear still on but my dress and shoes removed, I'd been too mortified to get myself up and show my face at the pub for Gray's wake.

I'd found Orla downstairs, drinking tea in the kitchen, and thanked her for her help but assured her that I was fine, that one of my sisters would drop the kids round and probably stay the night so there was no need for her to wait. Laurel, to my relief, had already left.

Two days later, I slipped a card through Orla's letterbox thanking her for her help and apologising for my behaviour, but I didn't knock on the door: I was still deep in the Fear, dreading to know what she thought of me.

But when someone lives three doors away, you can't avoid them forever. The kids' school had broken up for the summer holidays. Lulu had taken herself off to a cheerleading taster camp with her friend Aisha, but Barney had a day-long cricket coaching session and needed to be dropped off.

I was parking the car against the railings of Damask Square on my return when Orla's door opened and she stepped out of her house.

'Good morning.' Smiling warily, I climbed out of the car.

'Anna.' Orla reached out her arms to me and I found myself stepping into her warm, fragrant embrace. 'Thank you for the card. You didn't have to. I've been thinking about you, but I thought you might need some space.'

It was typical of her to have guessed that space was exactly what I had needed.

'Would you like to come in?' she asked gently.

'I...' Suddenly, the prospect of the morning on my own, with nothing to do but wait for Cathy or Sarah's call, felt unthinkably bleak. 'Yes, please.'

'I bought some pastries from the new Turkish place that opened next to Imran's shop,' Orla continued, leading the way into her kitchen. 'They're really rather good. Have you had breakfast?'

I hadn't, so I found myself seated at Orla's kitchen table – which was littered as usual with recipe books, sketch pads, packets of seeds for the garden and two drowsy cats – accepting a coffee and a börek.

'How have you been?' she asked. 'The days after the funeral's over... it must be hard. Lonely.'

A lump coming to my throat, I nodded. 'I'm all right. My sisters are looking out for me, and the kids keep me busy, and Mum's coming down again this weekend. And there's all the stuff – you know, the admin stuff. Insurance and making sure all the direct debits are going through and things like that. I'm keeping busy.'

Too busy to be hitting the gin at eight in the morning. But I didn't say that, and Orla didn't ask.

'There was something, Anna...' she began uncertainly. 'I wanted to ask – but there didn't seem a right time, with Gray's death being so sudden in the end.'

'It was sudden.' I sighed. 'Only five days after he went into the hospice. I still wonder if that was the right decision, but I couldn't...'

'I doubt it would have made much difference,' Orla said. 'Surely not? And better quick than the alternative. But still – a shock.'

I nodded. Already, those days were a blur – a blur of pain and panic and avoiding Laurel and feeling utterly helpless in the face of what was happening.

'What was it you wanted to ask?' I sipped the last of my coffee, turning the cup round on its saucer as if I was trying to read my fortune in the few grounds that drifted across its base.

'Oh, Anna. This is difficult. Before he left here, Gray asked me to do something for him. A favour. And I... I'm afraid that was just before the ambulance arrived to take him and there wasn't time that day. I fear I let him down. I wanted to talk to you about it.'

'What did he want?' I asked. 'Whatever it was, I'm sure we can fix it.'

'It's...' She hesitated, and then her words came out in a rush. 'He wanted me to ring his solicitor. He wanted a last-minute change to his will. I did get hold of her, the next day, and she said she would contact him. But I don't know if it ever happened.'

His will. I remembered sitting in the café with the children and the prospect crossing my mind that Gray might change it – alter it in favour of Laurel. I hadn't let that worry take hold at the time, but now it did, as if it had been waiting to pounce, biding its time.

Frantically, I tried to sort through the jumbled memories of those days. If Claudia James had visited the hospice, I'd have known, surely? Someone would have told me, if I hadn't been there at the time. And besides...

'I don't think he could have done,' I said slowly. 'He was – by that stage, he was sleeping so much. He was on a high dose of morphine. I doubt any lawyer would have judged him to have capacity to change something like that.'

'That's what I was afraid of,' Orla said sadly. 'I'm so sorry, Anna.'

'You don't have to be sorry.' My hands were gripping my coffee cup so hard I worried it would shatter. 'Orla – tell me. Was it to do with Laurel? Was it to leave her something in his will?'

'No!' If I'd doubted her honesty, the expression of absolute horror on her face would have erased my misgivings. 'God, no, Anna. Nothing like that. He wanted to make a bequest to a charity.'

'To a...' I released my hold on the cup, hearing it rattle on the saucer. 'Well then there's nothing to worry about. It's easily done. I can just make the donation myself. I expect our accountant will have something to say about the most tax-efficient way to do it, but it'll be quite straightforward. Assuming he told you what charity it was, that is.'

I thought of the donations Gray had made while he was alive. He'd been a sucker for signing up for direct debits when chuggers accosted him on the street or knocked at the door, and each month a steady but substantial trickle of money had left our account. Plus at the end of the tax year he'd made more substantial donations: to Shelter, to Centrepoint, to Cats Protection. When he'd done an Ironman triathlon a couple of years back, he'd raised money for Kidney Research UK.

Any of those were welcome to an additional chunk of cash, so long as it wouldn't leave me unable to fund the children's university fees.

'I...' Orla began. 'I'm not sure. I remember what he said. I wrote it down, just in case.'

She reached into the worn leather satchel that hung over the back of her chair and took out her purse, unzipped it and extracted a scrap of paper, glanced at it and handed it to me.

'YMCA?' I read. 'Really?'

Orla shrugged helplessly, raising her palms to the ceiling. 'That's what he said. At least, that's what he ended up saying. He started with the Y and then YC and then YA and then he started singing the song – you know.'

I did. Almost involuntarily, I found myself doing the hand gestures.

Orla smiled. 'Gray did that too. I wasn't sure – it seemed unlikely that that was what he meant. But it must have been, mustn't it?'

'I suppose so,' I agreed. 'And – thanks, Orla. I'm glad you told me. I'm glad everything's all right, between – you know. After the other day.'

'Take care of yourself, Anna. Remember I'm here.'

She hugged me again and I thanked her for the coffee, then went back next door and straight into Gray's office.

I sat down in the leather chair at his desk and switched on the computer.

TWENTY-NINE
LAUREL

For the first time, I inserted my shiny new key into the shiny new lock and turned it. The door swung obligingly open, and I stepped inside.

I was greeted by the smell of paint and the sight of a billion dust motes dancing in the afternoon sunlight that flooded through the windows. In a few minutes, the man with a van I'd hired to bring my boxes of stuff over from Mel's place would arrive; later this afternoon, after a trip to Ikea, he'd bring yet more boxes, this time of flat-pack furniture for me to assemble.

For now, though, the flat was empty – a bland shell waiting to be turned into a home. It felt airy and spacious, although I knew that once the furniture was in place it would feel a lot smaller. There was a living room and kitchen in one, a bedroom overlooking what would eventually become a communal garden, and a bathroom, the walls tiled in the jade green I'd chosen on a whim.

I'd buy plants, I decided. I'd put up a rack on the wall for my bike to live on. I'd choose new bedding – pink, maybe, in a floral design with leaves to match the green of the plants.

I'd have a housewarming party, inviting friends over to admire my new home.

It would be home. It would have to be.

But Gray would never see it. He'd never kick his shoes off, sit down on the bed and hold out his arms for me to join him. I'd never cook him a meal and serve it on my new white plates. He'd never emerge, dripping and fragrant, from the shower. I'd never greet him at the door or kiss him goodbye there.

There would never be traces of him there: clean clothes he would bring so he had something to change into after we'd been for a bike ride together or had sweaty sex; a spare charger for his phone; a toothbrush to stand alongside mine on the shelf above the basin.

I'd said, *It'll be easier when I have my own place.* Apologetic, because he was a proper adult with a home of his own, and I was sharing with Mel and it didn't feel right to bring my married lover over to spend the night. *Yeah, it'll be easier*, he'd agreed, remorseful because even when Anna and the children were away, he didn't feel right having me round to the house on Damask Square.

One of the main reasons I'd decided to take the plunge and buy a flat of my own was that it would make it easier to see Gray.

But it would never happen now. It would never be easier.

The loss of him was like a hole inside me that refused to heal – a chronic wound. I wished I had something of him here, some token that would serve as a concrete reminder of him. Not the earrings he'd given me, or any of the other little gifts: the L'Occitane hand cream he'd bought me when my skin was chapped and dry from washing in disinfectant at work; the book of cycle rides he'd promised we would do together; the cashmere socks that had kept my ankles warm all last winter.

Those things were mine now. They were reminders of him, but they weren't his; they'd never been part of him. I wished I'd thought to ask him for something – anything – a piece of clothing, a handwritten note, a lock of hair.

I had nothing. I thought of all his possessions that Anna would have to sort through, deciding what to donate to charity shops, what to keep and what to throw away. I imagined myself rummaging through their bins and coming away with some trash or treasure for myself, but I knew I would never do that. I imagined writing to Anna and asking if there was anything she could spare, but I knew I'd never do that either.

Gray's things weren't mine, and Gray himself had never been mine.

I was shaken out of my gloom by a knock on the door and the arrival of Piotr, with his permanent smile and his impressive biceps, who'd lugged my boxes up five flights of stairs because the lift was temporarily out of order.

I thanked him profusely and tipped him lavishly, and he set off down the stairs again, still smiling, promising to return in two hours, depending how bad the traffic was in the Dartford Crossing. I set about arranging my clothes in the built-in wardrobe, conscious of how shabby and grubby everything seemed to look on the bright new shelves, even though it had all seemed perfectly okay when I'd taken it out of Mel's spare bedroom the day before.

I tore off the bubble wrap from the framed photographs and placed them on the mantelpiece in the living room: me with my mum and dad, me and Justin on his wedding day, me holding my tiny newborn nephew, me and Mel in pink sparkles on a hen night.

There were none of me and Gray – those were only on my phone, and looking at them was too painful still.

There was nothing of Gray here – nothing of me and him together. There never would be.

But there was something of him that hadn't died. The thought came to me quite suddenly, along with the name I'd only heard once and not even expected to remember.

Joel.

Out there was a part of Gray that was still alive, performing its biological function inside the body of another man. The thought was almost fantastical. Somewhere, there was a scar that was the twin of the one I'd seen on Gray's abdomen the first time we'd had sex. I'd only asked about it afterwards – *What happened there?* – even though I knew the answer.

I donated a kidney, he'd said, quite casually, as if it was the most normal thing in the world to do. *A good friend of mine was ill, and I had the chance to make him better. So I took it.*

And this Joel – whoever he was – had taken a part of Gray.

Joel. There could be hundreds or even thousands of them in the country – if he still was in the country. If he was even still alive – I knew very little about the prognosis for kidney recipients, but I guessed that it wouldn't be universally positive, especially not after so long.

He'd been ill. Probably he was still ill, requiring ongoing monitoring and medication to stop his body rejecting the organ that had been Gray's. Ill with what?

It had been a long time since I'd qualified as a nurse. I hadn't properly studied in years – not since I finished my master's degree. But now, I felt a rush of what I'd felt back then: curiosity. An urge – almost a craving – to know more, understand more.

I wanted to find out why Gray might have donated an organ to Joel – why Joel had needed it; whether it was still doing its job.

It was just a kidney – but to me it was fascinating because I wanted to know what had led to it being transplanted from Gray's healthy body to his friend's ailing one. More than that – it was important, significant, precious even, because it had been Gray's and I'd loved him.

I had nothing of his. The earrings he had given me had never really belonged to him, never been a part of him. But someone, some man named Joel, had something that had fundamentally, viscerally, been Gray's. I wanted to find it – find the man in whose body it had been for twenty-five years.

I didn't know how I could do that – I didn't even know whether it would be possible. I didn't know whether Joel was still alive. But I was determined to find out.

THIRTY
ANNA

When I sat down at Gray's computer after saying goodbye to Orla that afternoon, I felt a horrible sense of guilt. It was as if I was expecting to hear his footsteps on the landing outside and then his voice saying, *What the hell are you doing on there, Anna?* as I spun guiltily around in the chair, too late to shut down the computer.

I knew that wouldn't happen, but I noticed that my palms were sweating as I logged into his operating system. That presented no difficulty: his password, B@rn£y followed by the six digits of Lulu's birthday, was secure enough but easy for me to remember. He'd shared it with me a few years back.

YMCA, Orla had said. Why had he chosen to donate to them? He'd never been a churchgoer, never shown a particular interest in the upliftment of young people. Perhaps I would find some evidence that he had donated to them before – one of his many direct debits, or an email newsletter he had signed up to.

His personal and work email accounts had been open on the screen, both with several thousand unread messages. Before his last day at Flick London, Gray had set his out-of-office message to an innocuous few lines saying that he was no longer with the agency, and that Carl could be contacted in his absence. I wondered if it had been updated again following his death, but there was no way to find out short of emailing him myself, which I couldn't bear to do.

I did a simple search for YMCA on both accounts, but found nothing whatsoever. Then I found myself looking through his calendar to see whether his assignations with Laurel were noted there, made private so I couldn't see them, but doing that had made me feel so grubby and sad that I pushed back the chair and left the office, closing the door behind me and leaving the computer to put itself to sleep.

It was two weeks before I returned to Gray's desk. The days had fallen into a sort of weary rhythm: the children, apparently not disappointed by my decision to cancel the booked holiday to Portugal, were out most of the time – Barney playing cricket with his pals or playing Orla's piano, Lulu meeting Aisha at the gym to practise the moves she'd learned at her cheerleading camp.

I didn't choose that – I wanted them here, close to me, safe. I wanted to be there if they needed to talk or cry. But what they needed seemed to be the company of their friends, the resumption of normal teenage life after the long weeks of their father's illness, and there was nothing I could do but respect that.

I slept late most mornings – that is, after waking at three o'clock in a puddle of sweat and lying there, fighting the horrors of a low-level (or, quite often, high-level) hangover for a couple of hours until sleep mercifully reclaimed me. It was often half past nine or ten o'clock before I made it downstairs, where I'd make myself a piece of toast and Nutella and a coffee, only to discover that both had gone cold while I sat staring blankly out at the garden.

What Orla had said had niggled at my brain relentlessly, unassuaged by the five-hundred-pound donation I'd made to the YMCA from my own phone, just in case that was what Gray had meant after all.

YMCA. Why?

Had they supported Gray somehow after his mother's death?

Was whoever had sent the silver anniversary card connected to the organisation? Did they commemorate membership that way, like Alcoholics Anonymous, I wondered, absent-mindedly going to the fridge and pouring a glass of wine.

The answer had to lie somewhere in Gray's past. I'd barely scratched the surface of his email account – it was time to delve deeper. I took my wine upstairs, sat down at Gray's Mac and logged on.

His past – his mother. Almost automatically, I found myself typing her name into the search bar at the top of one of the open windows on his screen. The search returned one result: a PDF file entitled 'Louisa Graham'.

It was Lulu's birth certificate. A scan of the pale-yellow, red-printed official form, completed in an almost childishly neat hand-writing by the registrar, documenting that Louisa Celeste Graham had been born to Nigel Graham and Anna Christine Graham on the twenty-fourth of May 2008 at Homerton Hospital.

I remembered the conversation we'd had, walking home after the scan appointment that had confirmed we were having a daughter.

'We can call her Celeste, right?' I'd asked, giddy with excitement. 'It's the best girl's name ever. Pretty and feminine but also serious. Unusual, but easy to spell. It's the perfect name. I've always thought so.'

Gray reached out and took my hand. 'Anna. I realise it's you who's going to push this baby out of your fanny and everything. Seriously, it's your choice. But...'

'But you think naming our daughter after a fictional elephant is a terrible idea?' I turned to him, ready to die on that hill.

He smiled. 'Not at all. It's a nice name. It's just...'

'Just what?'

'I'd really, really, like to name her after my mum. I'm sorry. It just feels like the right thing to do.'

I felt all the excitement drain out of me. How could I argue with that – with the right of a dead grandmother to be memorialised in her son's firstborn child's name? With the right of Gray, bereaved when he was barely an adult, to honour his late mother in that way?

'What was her name?' I asked.

He told me. My first thought was, *It could be worse.* At least it wasn't Sharon or Tracey. My second was, *We can always end up using her middle name.* But when our daughter was born, Gray had cradled her in his arms, gazing down at her with adoring pride, and said, 'Hello, little Lulu,' and I'd been so flooded with hormones I thought it was the cutest name ever.

Louisa. I moved the mouse, clicked back on to Gray's personal email and typed the name into the search bar there. A full page of results came up: evidently Gray had corresponded with a Louisa Martin at our mortgage brokerage; a Louisa van der Walt at the optician where he bought his contact lenses; and a Louisa Clift who'd organised a surprise birthday party for her partner, a friend of Gray's. He'd also received a promotional email from a wine merchant inviting him to a tasting of German wines, one maker being named Louisa; enquired about booking a Villa Louisa for a stag weekend; and bought me a lingerie set called Louisa in black, size 32F.

It was on the second page of the search results that I found what I was looking for. It was an email in his drafts folder with no subject line, with the recipient's email address louisagraham2903@hotmail.com.

The mouse felt slippery with my sweat as I clicked it. The email was blank. It contained no text at all, just that email address in the 'To' field and Gray's in the 'From'. It had never been sent, but the date the draft had been saved was the twenty-fifth of May 2008.

The day after Lulu's birth. Gray had wanted to email his mother, to tell her she had a grandchild named after her. But he hadn't. He hadn't for the same reason I hadn't emailed his work address – because he knew she was not alive to see it.

I searched again, this time copying and pasting the email

address, but there were no other emails to or from Gray's mother, and no more drafts. There had been no point – Gray must have realised that.

I cancelled the search and returned to the main inbox. In the preceding two weeks, since the last time I'd come up here, more emails had arrived. The first five pages of them were now all unread, and I wasn't going to read them. Instead, I tapped the mouse on the bar that told me I was viewing messages 1 to 50 of 54,671 and selected 'Oldest'. The first email he had received was in 2003, around the time that he and I met.

But before that, he must have had another email address – a Yahoo one or a Hotmail one perhaps. I had no way of accessing that – no way of knowing who Gray might have contacted in the years before we met.

No way of knowing who J might have been. No way of reading emails he'd exchanged with his mother before her death. No way of searching for messages to or from the YMCA.

We'd never visited Swansea, where Gray grew up, because he'd said there was no point, nothing left for him there. He must have loved his mother – he'd insisted on naming our daughter after her. But as far as I knew he had never laid flowers on her grave or been to the place where her ashes were scattered.

I shut the laptop and left the study, closing the door behind me. The answers weren't here. They were in the places that had shaped Gray as a child. That's where I needed to look.

THIRTY-ONE
ORLA

7 August 2024

I am writing this at the table in the garden. It is already warm and has been light for well over an hour – it was before five when I was woken by Aengus and Iseult playing tag on my bed, frantic to be allowed outside to lay waste to the bird population. Now, of course, having had their breakfast and a lengthy wash, they are stretched out on the flagstones in the sun, only rousing occasionally to scold furiously at a magpie.

And for me, the day stretches ahead, almost featureless. The house is empty except for me and the cats – there are no lodgers, no meals to cook, no responsibilities. Only Barney will come this afternoon to spend an hour or two at the piano.

Unlike my daughter, I have no ear for music, but I can tell that he is improving. Not only that – there is a visible change in him when he sits down at that piano. It's as if two things are happening to him at once: first, the weight of sadness that bows his shoulders when he arrives seems to lift; as soon as his hands touch the keys a smile appears on his face and by the time he leaves he is lighter, freer. And second, the gawkiness and awkwardness of his early adolescence leaves him, replaced by assurance – almost cockiness –

that reminds me of his father. His entire body seems to be saying, *Look at me! I'm good at this!*

I wonder why Gray didn't discover this gift and nurture it – why there is no piano in the front room of number eight like the one I bought for Beatrice to play. Even if, like me, he didn't care a jot for music and actively disliked classical music, he cared about his children very deeply. To deprive Barney of something that will bring such pride and happiness for the child's whole lifetime seems bizarre to me – almost cruel.

But perhaps this talent and passion of Barney's has only revealed itself now. Maybe some boys are late bloomers. I grew up in a household of women; I went to boarding school with girls and only met my own daughter when she was a young woman of twenty-two – boys are a mystery to me.

And so is his late father, in his own way. I knew Gray as Anna's husband, Lulu and Barney's father, my neighbour. A successful man who had turned his creative passion into a thriving business. But the funeral brought home to me that his life before he and Anna moved to Damask Square is a total blank: Gray never spoke to me about his past. And at the funeral, although there were dozens of people there to pay their respects – friends, neighbours, colleagues, Anna's sisters and their husbands, Anna's mother and father – there was no one who might have known him as Nigel.

Anna must know his history, or at least some of it. But she has never spoken to me about any in-laws, either, nor any old friends of Gray's. I wonder why.

THIRTY-TWO
LAUREL

'Well, I'd call that a success.' Harry stacked up the last few leaflets and put them in the box. 'We'll have more nurses than we can shake a stick at in a few years, if that lot were anything to go by.'

'Careful what you wish for.' I tried to echo his upbeat tone, but the truth was I was exhausted: fatigued from my sleep being interrupted by dreams of Gray, then spending the rest of the night scrolling futilely on my phone looking for clues to how I might track down Joel. Weary of putting a brave face on things at work, given that few of my colleagues knew of Gray's existence, never mind his death. Worn out from providing care and sympathy to other people when I didn't feel entitled to claim any myself. 'It's not like we can afford to pay the ones we've got.'

'True.' He winced. 'Anyway, I think I can just about stretch to a half of lager down the Crown and Castle – fancy it?'

'God, yes. I could murder a drink. And I don't know about you, but if I never see another teenager in my life, it'll be too soon.'

'I couldn't help noticing,' he remarked as we made our way to the locker rooms, 'that your girl didn't turn up. Your fellow's daughter, who we saw at the school earlier in the year?'

'Lulu.' I frowned. All day, I'd been looking out for her, trying to spot her among all the other teenage girls who'd turned up to the hospital careers open day. But I had been disappointed – not just because speaking to her would have given me a longed-for connection, however tenuous, to Gray, but because... Well, because of *her*. Because she was his child and she would be suffering even more than I was. I could picture Gray's face lighting up in a smile and him saying, *Ah, so you saw my girl? How is she?*

Now, I wouldn't have the luxury of imagining that conversation with him.

'No, she didn't show,' I said to Harry. 'Shame, really. But the schools only went back last week – I guess she's busy. But she texted me a couple of days ago and said she'd see me here. I hope she's okay.'

'A sixteen-year-old with better things to do on a Saturday than hang out with the likes of us.' Harry turned one way into the men's locker room while I turned the other into the women's. 'Hard to imagine, really, but here we are.'

I laughed. 'See you in ten minutes.'

It was more like fifteen by the time I'd showered, changed and applied some lip gloss, but soon we were sitting at a table in the pub garden, a jug of sangria and a bowl of chips between us.

'Starving.' Harry dipped a few in the paper tub of ketchup and shoved three of them into his mouth at once. 'God, talking all day takes it out of you.'

'I'm more thirsty.' I gulped some sangria. 'My throat feels drier than when I did a hundred-k cycle last weekend.'

It had been an unsuccessful attempt to escape my thoughts and subdue my body into sleep, but I didn't tell Harry that.

'Get you, Miss Fitness Influencer. Wasting your weekends doing that, when you could be doing things that are actually important.'

'Like what?' I asked.

'Like holding a housewarming for your nearest and dearest. You've been in that flat – what, six weeks now? And have we been invited round for so much as a cup of tea? Have we fuck.'

'I know, I know.' I took a long sip of my drink and dunked a chip into ketchup. 'I'll get around to it, I promise. It's just all a bit new. I'm not ready to have people spilling red wine on my sofa, treading crisps into the carpet and being sick in my shiny toilet.'

'All wrong.' He shook his head in mock reproof. 'Anyway. How are you, darling girl? Bearing up all right?'

If I was honest, I was struggling. Some mornings it took all my energy to get out of bed, and a few times when I'd managed that, I'd had to call in sick so I could spend the day crying on the sofa. Once, after an elderly patient had passed away peacefully surrounded by her family, I'd had a full-blown panic attack.

Cycling felt like the one thing that kept me sane, because it was the one time I could imagine I was close to Gray again. And Lulu's absence that day was hitting me harder than I wanted to admit to anyone, even Harry.

Feeling the sting of impending tears, I pushed my sunglasses down off my forehead.

'I'm okay,' I said. 'Just about. You know – one day at a time. But I'm not going to lie – it's hard.'

Harry nodded sympathetically, waiting for me to carry on.

'I keep thinking,' I said, 'about the guy who Gray donated his kidney to. You know, if it hadn't been for that, he might have been able to have treatment. The cancer would probably still have killed him – pancreatic, you know, it's a fucker. But if he could've had a few rounds of chemo he might still be here. I could have had another couple of months with him. And his wife and kids, obviously. And instead, there's someone out there walking around with a bit of Gray inside him, still alive. Or at least, I hope he is. If he is, then – you know. It wouldn't have been for nothing. Not that it would bring Gray back.'

Harry reached across the table and took my hand. 'You poor love. It's tough, isn't it? But you know a donated organ's not like a book that you're meant to return to the library, right? Once it's gone it's gone.'

I took my sunglasses off and wiped my eyes with a paper

napkin. 'I know. The surgeons would be kept pretty busy if they had to check them in and out every two weeks.'

Harry laughed. 'You're not wrong. It's quite a thing though, an altruistic donation like that. Was the guy related to him?'

'Just a friend, apparently. Someone he knew in secondary school. Gray never talked about it much – I think they lost touch soon after. But I got the impression... This is going to sound weird.'

'Go on.'

'I got the impression it was – not like paying a debt, like in those urban myths that go round online sometimes. But because he felt like he owed the guy something, in more of a moral sense.'

I could remember what he had said, quite clearly. It was one of the nights we'd spent at the Premier Inn – or not a night, because Gray would need to be home by about two-thirty. We'd been lying in bed, the remains of a Chinese takeaway surrounding us. Gray was wearing his boxer shorts, and I was still naked, because he said there was nothing sexier than me eating chicken fried rice with no clothes on.

The top of the scar was visible above the waistband of his underwear, and I ran the blunt end of a chopstick lightly over it.

'So what happened?' I asked.

He knew me well enough for me not to need to elaborate on the question, and I knew him well enough to expect the kind of answer I'd got.

'I was at a party and I met this hot Russian girl. She kept buying me drinks and then she invited me back to her hotel room. I thought it was my lucky night – and then I woke up in a bath full of ice.'

'Come on!' I urged. 'Tell me what really happened.'

He reached over and pulled me close against him. 'You going to have that last spring roll? There's nothing to tell. I had a mate who needed a kidney, and I had a spare one, and it felt like the least I could do.'

'What was wrong with him?'

'His kidneys were fucked, obviously. Now come here,' he

breathed as he pulled me down on top of him. 'We've still got twenty minutes until pumpkin o'clock.'

'What do you mean, a moral sense?' Harry said now. 'Are you saying he was pressurised into it somehow?'

'No! Not that at all – at least that's not the impression I got. More like he was so grateful to the guy, he'd do that willingly. "It felt like the least I could do", was what he said.'

Harry poured the last of the sangria into our glasses. 'He sounds like one hell of a man, your Gray.'

'He was. But what I want to know – what I can't help thinking – is, if the recipient is still alive, how can I find him?'

Harry shook his head. 'There are definitely ethical safeguards around that kind of thing.'

'I know, but – there can't be that many people who received donor kidneys in around 2000, right?'

'About three-and-a-half-thousand transplants are performed in the UK a year,' Harry said. 'I read a thing about it as part of my CPD.'

'Okay. That's a lot.'

'You'd only need to rule out three thousand four hundred and ninety-nine of them,' he said. 'But maybe – if you knew what the condition was – there'd be support groups, that kind of thing. You could track him down that way. If they were mates, he'd want to know how Gray was – that Gray had died.'

'Yes,' I said slowly. 'But there are loads of conditions it could be, right?'

'Diabetes, glomerulonephritis, autosomal dominant polycystic kidney disease, lupus, Fabry disease…' Harry rattled off.

'Glad someone was paying attention in their CPD.'

'But you're not going to be able to find him. You know that, right?'

I did know – but somehow I needed Harry to say it.

'Why not?' I asked.

'Patient confidentiality. Come on, Laurel. You don't need to have done your CPD to know that – it's been drummed into us since day dot.'

'I could try, though. If I don't get anywhere lurking on online support groups, I could ask people.'

Harry raised his eyebrows. 'Like who?'

'I don't know. People who know about kidneys. Specialists.'

'They're bound by patient confidentiality too,' he pointed out.

I sighed. 'I guess. So then I'll just go back to spending my evenings counting the walls of my flat.'

'Walls unsullied by the presence of any guests,' Harry said pointedly.

'Shut up. I'll buy you another drink here instead.'

'Deal,' he said.

I got up to go to the bar. Harry had certainly poured cold water on my hopes of ever tracking Joel down through online research, and I knew he was right – it was an impossible quest.

There was only one person who I felt sure would be able to help me, and that was the one person I could never ask.

Anna.

THIRTY-THREE
ORLA

6 September 2024

It was not so long ago that I wrote that my house was empty apart from me and the cats, but this morning I have an unexpected guest.

The events of last night were so strange and unexpected that when I woke up this morning I believed for a moment that I had dreamed them; then I opened my bedroom door and saw the door to the room that used to be Beatrice's – and still is, the bed kept permanently made up in case of one of her unannounced visits – was closed. So I have returned to bed with my notebook to record what happened before the details elude me, and to decide what I should do.

First, I heard the sound of a car engine being revved with unnecessary and unsociable vigour so late at night. I heard its door open, a blast of loud music and a man's voice raised in laughter. There was something about the series of sounds that was aggressive – threatening almost, like a dog fox barking to assert his territorial claim.

The door slammed closed. The car engine revved again, and I heard a screech of tyres as it pulled away, then total silence descended once more. I lay still for a moment, half-wondering if I had imagined the noise, or if it had in fact not been so loud at all but merely seemed that way in the otherwise still night, and then I drifted back into sleep.

But I was woken again by a knock on my front door, and I jerked upright, fully awake now, startled and almost afraid. I am a woman in my sixties, alone in this big house and, I suppose, vulnerable. Normally I do not feel that way at all, but last night I did. I switched on my bedside light and peered out of the window, but thanks to the portico over my front door I could see nothing – the street below seemed deserted.

The knock came again, less timid this time.

Hastily, I pulled on yesterday's clothes and hurried downstairs, the cats trailing behind me, blinking in surprise but amenable to the prospect of an early breakfast. I had my phone in my hand, my finger on the emergency call button just in case.

But when I opened the door, it was Lulu Graham standing there.

She was wearing her usual jeans, extravagantly ripped and slung low on her hips, and a top cropped so high it almost exposed her breasts, the fashion now that is becoming on only the very young. Her make-up was heavy – or it had been; now it was blurred and smudged – and her long hair dishevelled. Her eyes were wide with alarm and something else I cannot now identify.

I'm sorry, Orla, she whispered. Sorry to disturb you. But I didn't know what else to do.

Feeling almost lightheaded with relief, then prickled with concern, I told her it was all right, and invited her to come in.

She told me that she'd lost her keys, that Barney was out with a friend and her mother... She hesitated. Her mother must be asleep, she said.

Asleep, I wondered, or something else?

But I didn't get a chance to respond. Lulu kept talking, jabbering almost, her words coming in a rush.

I tried calling and texting her but she didn't wake up, she said. I was going to go and find a café or something and wait until morning but I feel – I didn't feel safe out there. So I knocked on your door. I hope it's all right.

I assured her that she had done the right thing, and offered her a hot drink; I could see that she was shivering, although even at what my phone told me was three a.m., the night was warm.

Just a glass of water, please, Orla, she said. And to use your bathroom, if that's okay?

Poor girl – the need for the loo would have made her wait out in the street feel even more urgent.

She hurried upstairs, and I fetched a glass from the kitchen and waited on the landing for her to emerge. She seemed calmer when she did, although her eyes still had that wide, hyper-alert look.

Gently, I suggested that she might feel better if she got some sleep, and we could get her home in the morning, and she reluctantly agreed to stay.

So I put her to bed in Beatrice's room, and I expect she will be there for a good few hours, sleeping as only an exhausted teenager can. Now I will need to figure out what to say to Anna – whether to dissemble about the time Lulu arrived home, whether to tell her about that car and the man's voice.

THIRTY-FOUR
ANNA

'Where were you?' My voice came out angry and shrill.

'I was at Aisha's. I told you, Mum. We were talking. We were messing about on TikTok. I lost track of the time – her mum and dad were in bed and it was too late to ask for a lift home. I knew you'd go off on one if I stayed over and you wouldn't want me getting a bus home so I got an Uber.'

I looked at my daughter. Her skin was peachy and glowing, but there were violet shadows under her eyes – partly tiredness and partly last night's make-up. She was still wearing yesterday's clothes and, when I'd pressed her body against mine in a hug that was almost frantically tight, I'd noticed that she smelled different from usual – a hint of sourness, a fragrance that wasn't hers.

I'd woken up at nine that morning with a pounding head. The house was silent. I'd overslept. As soon as I moved, Augustus jumped up off my pillow and began yowling for his breakfast.

'Has no one fed you?' I muttered in confusion. 'Hold on.'

I pressed my throbbing head into my hands, trying to recall the night before. Barney had been staying over at a friend's place. Lulu had been out. Loneliness descending on me like a weight, I'd made myself a vast, ice-cold dry martini and then another, then opened a bottle of wine – and then another. I'd longed to cry, but tears wouldn't come, so I'd found an old DVD Gray had filmed of the children when they were small and put it on to watch, hoping it would jerk me out of my numb inertia. But it hadn't – all it had done was remind me how happy we had been, how innocently oblivious of what was going to happen to us.

It was too much to bear. The way I'd felt then – so full of joy and hope and confidence – was too different from how I felt now, lonely and resigned and bitter. And it told me nothing about what Gray's life had been before those days, when he stood with his camera filming Lulu chasing a bumble bee in the garden, me pushing Barney on a swing in the park, tiny Augustus furiously attacking his own tail.

There were no answers there, on those silver discs of memories. There had been nothing on the computer in Gray's study. But there might be some elsewhere in the house. There was some stuff of Gray's, up in the loft in storage boxes. His emails might have post-dated him meeting me, but those boxes didn't. I could go up there and investigate.

I'd gone upstairs with my bottle and glass, determined to make a start. But I must have got sidetracked, and sat down on the bed and gone to sleep. Or blacked out.

'Just a second,' I told the still protesting Augustus. 'Let me check on Lulu, then I'll give you breakfast.'

But when I eased my daughter's bedroom door open, expecting to see her sprawled on the bed deeply asleep, the room was empty.

She wouldn't have got up without seeing to the cat – he wouldn't have let her.

I snatched my phone from my bedside table, finding that the battery had given out at some point during the night. I connected it to the charger, feeling sweat breaking out on my palms as I tried again and again to bring it to life. Then I saw five missed calls from Lulu at just after three in the morning.

It was only when I saw the text message from Orla telling me that she was safe in a spare bed over at number five that my panic turned to rage.

Lulu hadn't been with Aisha last night. She was lying – I knew it and she must know I knew. But I wasn't blameless. My phone had died, and I hadn't seen her calls. She was home now, and safe – but what if she'd been in trouble and needed me?

'TikTok or no TikTok,' I said firmly, 'you can't be getting cabs home at three in the morning. It's not safe. You shouldn't have left Aisha's place at that hour – you know that. You can't have an eleven-thirty curfew on weekends if you're not going to be responsible about sticking to it.'

Lulu bit her lip. 'I know, Mum. I'm sorry. I just didn't think.'

I pressed my hand to my throbbing head. I was handling this all wrong, but I didn't know what else to do. 'Next time, you need to think. Set an alarm on your phone for when it's time to come home, phone me and I'll collect you.'

She nodded meekly, and I could see her hoping that that might be the end of it.

'I'm going to have to ground you,' I went on. 'No going out during the week for two weeks, or on weekends for the rest of the month. And after that, you'll be in by ten again. Once I've seen you sticking to it, we'll have a rethink. Okay?'

'Okay.' Something flickered over her face – relief, I realised. Relief that I hadn't challenged her on her lie, hadn't threatened to ring Aisha's parents and ask whether she'd actually been there at all? Or something else – relief that she'd be prevented from doing whatever it was she'd been doing?

'And you'll buy Orla a decent bunch of flowers out of your allowance,' I told her.

'I'd have done that anyway,' she replied sharply.

That at least was true. Lulu had always been thoughtful. Her impulsive generosity reminded me of her father – her father, who she'd lost. Her grief must be terrible, but she wasn't talking to me about it, perhaps because she wanted to protect me from the intensity of her feelings.

'Sweetie.' I reached across the sofa and put my arm round her. 'This has been a horrible time for all of us. You know you can talk to me about stuff – if you're worried about something, if there are things going on in your life you need help with.'

'I know, Mum.' She snuggled her head briefly into my shoulder.

'Just because Dad died, it doesn't mean there can't be other things to deal with that are difficult as well.'

'I know. Thanks, Mum.' She wiped her nose on the sleeve of her jumper. Then she whispered, 'I miss him.'

'I miss him too.' But it was also more complicated than that now. I missed the Gray I thought I'd known.

'There aren't even that many photos of him.' Lulu glanced up at the television, where the DVD I'd played the night before was still paused on a frame of three-year-old Barney at the top of a slide, his sister waiting at the bottom to catch him. 'Because he was always behind the camera, not in front of it.'

'You know,' I said, 'there's a box of Dad's old stuff up in the loft. When we moved in here, I brought loads of crap with me – clothes and photos and books and letters. All sorts. But he just had the one box. When we were doing up the house I went through my old things and got rid of a lot of them, but Dad never wanted to do that. And it didn't take up much room so I just left it. We could have a look through it, if you like. There might be photos of him from when he was a little boy. School reports, stuff like that.'

Please say you'll do this with me.

Lulu's face turned to me, hopeful and eager. 'Yes. Let's do it. But, Mum...'

'What, darling?'

'Before we go up there, I'd really, really like a shower and eggy crumpets. You know, like you used to make sometimes when we were poorly?'

'Eggy crumpets.' My alcohol-soured stomach let out a massive rumble. 'You know, that's exactly what I feel like too.'

. . .

'I haven't been up here since I was, like, six,' Lulu murmured, looking round at the boarded-out loft. 'It's like Narnia.'

I knew what she meant, even though magical lands don't usually feature cans of paint stacked along the walls, Christmas decorations packed away in their boxes and crates of children's old clothes and toys.

'Oh my God,' Lulu breathed. 'Is that Cobbles?'

'It certainly is.' I pulled back the sheet, revealing the battered dapple-grey painted coat of her old rocking horse. One of the cheek straps on his bridle was broken and his mane and tail were yellowing and tangled, but his eyes were still bright, the worn leather of his saddle still glossy.

Lulu knelt down in front of him. 'Hello, you. Ah, Mum! I can't believe he's still here. I can't believe I'd forgotten all about him.'

'When we redid your bedroom, we talked about passing him down to your cousins for them to play with, but you weren't having it,' I said. 'You thought he was too babyish to have in your new room, and Barney never really played with him, but you wouldn't let us donate him to the charity shop. So we put him up here.'

Lulu's eyes were bright with tears. 'Poor Cobbles. Do you think he's lonely up here? Do you think he thinks I don't love him any more?'

Shit. What do I tell her about the emotional life of an old toy horse?

'I think he's enjoying a well-deserved retirement,' I hazarded. 'Maybe one day, if you ever have a daughter, we can take him off to some specialist toy restorer and get him spruced up again, and it'll be like a total new lease of life for him.'

'Like on *The Repair Shop*. Remember, Mum, Dad was obsessed with that show during lockdown.'

'Him and half the country,' I said. 'But yes, just like that. He'll be quite safe here until you need him again.'

Or until I decided I could no longer stay in the house on my own. But there was no point in raising that prospect now, not when

Lulu needed so badly to feel that her home and her memories would be here forever.

But she seemed satisfied with my fudged promise. 'Now where's that box of Dad's stuff you were talking about?'

'I hope it's here somewhere. It's possible he chucked it out at some point, but I don't think so.'

I squatted down in front of the low cupboards that had been fitted beneath the eaves and eased open a door. Inside were four cardboard boxes, their sides still unfaded and the tape that sealed them fresh. On two of their lids, in Gray's sloping capitals, 'DVDs' had been written with a Sharpie; the others were labelled 'Videos'.

I burst out laughing. 'Your bloody father.'

'What?' Lulu asked.

'We had a massive row about these a few years ago. I don't know if you remember, the bookshelves in the front room were absolutely stuffed with the things. Old movies, DVDs, box sets – he never watched them. He said they'd be worth a fortune if he put them on eBay, but I knew that was nonsense, and anyway he'd never get around to doing that either.'

'So he put them up here?'

'He told me he'd taken them to the charity shop. In fact he swore blind he had. But he stashed them up here instead, the bugger.'

'Poor Dad. I think you were mean, making him get rid of things he wanted to keep.'

I sighed. 'Maybe I was. But he got his way, didn't he? And now it'll be my job to get rid of them at some point.'

'But not now?' Lulu asked anxiously.

'Not now. Don't worry.' I closed the door and opened the next one along. 'Here we go.'

The box I'd pulled out looked quite different from the others. Its greige cardboard was faded and caked with dust – a reminder of the time, which felt as if it had lasted years, when the house was a building site and everything in our lives had been dusty. The tape that had once sealed it was dried out and peeling away. The long-dead corpse of a spider slipped out from beneath one of its flaps, making me and Lulu recoil.

'I hope there aren't more of those in there,' she said with a shiver.

'There won't be,' I promised, although I was far from sure. 'Do you want to take this downstairs or look through it now?'

Lulu hesitated. 'Let's open it here.'

The desiccated tape pulled away quite easily from the top and sides of the box, and I eased open the flaps. Inside, I could see the back cover of a book, dark blue but faded around the edges, as if it had spent hours in bright sunlight. The borders of the pages were yellowed and curling.

Lulu lifted it out and read the title on the front cover. '*Sixty Famous Solos. Classical Piano Sheet Music.* That can't have been Dad's. Dad hated classical music.'

But beneath it were more books of sheet music – more than a dozen of them. *Chopin's Complete Preludes, Nocturnes and Waltzes. Beethoven's Moonlight Sonata. Ultimate Piano Solos. Classical Piano Masterpieces for Intermediate Players.*

I pulled the books out of the box, mystified. Beneath them was a brown A4 envelope with 'Nigel Graham' written on it in faded handwriting I didn't recognise. I opened the flap and peered inside, then extracted a sheaf of stiff paper. There were eight sheets of it, in slightly different colours and printed in slightly different typefaces, but all bore the same logo in the top right: that of the Associated Board of the Royal Schools of Music, and each certified that Nigel Graham had passed his practical examination, from grades one through to eight.

I sifted through the pile, once and then again, studying each certificate as if there'd be some anomaly there – some other boy's name, some obvious alteration that had been made. The text seemed to swim in front of my eyes, but when I blinked it was still there, still the same.

Gray. The man who'd ask me to turn the radio off if he walked into the kitchen when I was listening to Classic FM. The man who'd feigned an attack of the flu when a client had invited him to the opera. The man who'd come reluctantly to church when we spent Christmas with my parents, but would only mouth the words to the hymns.

And yet, between the ages of ten and eighteen, he'd been not just musically capable, but apparently gifted.

'Mum,' Lulu asked slowly. 'Why did Dad never call himself Nigel?'

'I'm not sure. When I first met him, he told me his name was Gray. That's what everyone called him. I guess he thought it was a naff name and he'd rather be called something a bit cooler.'

'And why did he – I mean, he always said he hated classical music. When I tried to learn the violin in primary school he'd leave the house if I was practising.'

It was true. I remembered Gray's expression – almost agonised – when Lulu had brought a borrowed violin home from school. *Can she not?* he'd demanded.

'It did sound a bit like a cat being tortured, to be fair,' I teased.

Lulu giggled. 'I know, right? But Dad – he passed all those exams. He must've been seriously good at the piano.'

'Maybe he lost interest,' I said. 'People do, like you not being into ballet any more.'

But my daughter's face told me she was unconvinced – and she wasn't the only one.

This wasn't about some certificates packed away in a box and forgotten. It wasn't about a name changed in early adulthood. It was about the erasure of a whole childhood – a whole past. Whoever Nigel Graham had been, he didn't seem like he was anything to do with Gray – the man I'd fallen in love with and married. The father of my children. The husband I'd lost so recently.

What else was there about him that I didn't know?

THIRTY-FIVE
LAUREL

We all called him Dr Swinging-Dick. Of course, being a surgeon, he was Mr Swinging-Dick, but that didn't have quite the same ring to it.

Harry and I had had a conversation in the pub a couple of years back about what he would have been christened, if he'd had the choice or had known the lofty destiny that was in store for him.

'Rupert Ponsonby-Goldfinger,' I suggested.

'Billy Big-Bollocks,' said Harry.

'That's too similar to Swinging-Dick,' I objected. 'Blaize Lifesaver.'

'Swift Scalpel-Nurse.' Harry giggled.

'Or Jesus Nexttogod. But he'd have had to be Spanish for that.'

'Not John Smith, anyway.'

Laughing and rolling our eyes, we'd moved the conversation on to the next snippet of hospital gossip.

Lots of surgeons have big egos – it's a thing. Not all of them, of course – Mel and I sometimes played bingo over the *Nursing Times* when we read interviews with surgeons, seeing how many times clichés like 'modest demeanour' and 'humble beginnings' would get trotted out. Mel had even dated a surgeon a few years back, and he was a totally normal guy, apart from (she told me after they broke up) liking being tied up in bed and being told he'd been a very naughty boy.

No one who valued their career would ever call John Smith a very naughty boy. Or even John, come to that – he was Mr Smith even to people who'd been working with him for decades. Now in his early sixties, he was tall, silver-haired and distinguished. He played experimental jazz during surgery, treated the patient like they were his guest at a posh dinner party, and had once called a junior doctor a 'hapless fucking wankbadger' in front of the entire team.

Because he worked in the transplant department, our paths rarely crossed, for which I was thankful. But I needed insight into organ transplants, and perhaps even a clue as to how I might go about tracing Joel.

After finishing my shift, I changed out of my work clothes and into my cycling-home ones, and headed up to the third floor, where the directory had told me Dr Swinging-Dick's office was located.

There was a chance he would be there, but it was also possible that he'd be in theatre, or in a meeting, or even off on annual leave at his second home in Provence. The ward was relatively quiet that evening. The inpatients had been given their evening meal and settled for the night; the late shift had taken over from the day one. A ward sister was standing by the desk scrolling through notes on her computer screen.

'Hi,' I said, trying to sound more confident than I felt.

She looked at me enquiringly, immediately identifying me as staff rather than a lost visitor, or a day patient who'd found herself on the wrong floor.

'Evening. What can I do for you?'

'I'm Laurel Norton. I work downstairs in A&E. I was hoping to have a chat with John Smith.'

'Dr Sw— Mr Smith? You're in luck. He's in his office.'

'Great! Where do I find that?'

'Down the corridor on the right. But you'll need to be quick –

he's not operating until tomorrow, so he'll be off home in a few minutes.'

I thanked her and headed off, hurrying along the corridor past a series of grey-painted doors, some with names stencilled on them, others identifiable only by printed-out names stuck on with Sellotape, or in some cases with the names crossed out and others hastily hand-lettered in biro.

But I found his easily enough. It was one of the stencilled ones, 'Mr John Smith' in black capitals against the chipped paint.

I knocked.

Instead of an invitation to come in, the door opened instantly and the man himself stood there. He was tall, over six foot, and lean in the way men of a certain age are who watch their diet like hawks and go on lots of walking holidays. A tweed jacket was slung over his shoulders. His hair was silver and carefully brushed, and he carried an expensive-looking leather laptop bag in his right hand and what I assumed were the keys to his sports car in his left, on which he wore a plain gold wedding ring.

Startled, I took a step back. 'Good afternoon, Mr Smith. I'm sorry to bother you.'

'Whatever it is, you'd better make it quick,' he said. 'I've got seats at the theatre in forty minutes.'

'I will.' Intimidated more by his abrupt manner than his presence, I frantically tried to get my thoughts in order. 'I was wondering if you would help me – if you could let me know if there's any way of finding out who received an organ transplant from someone.'

He frowned. 'Both donors' families and recipients are able to make written contact via the transplant centre. Cards and messages of thanks and good wishes are duly passed on.'

'Yes, but... this was some time ago. As far as I know, no one made contact afterwards, and anyway the donor and the recipient knew each other.'

He'd begun to brush past me, but now he stopped, as if I'd

caught his interest. 'Are you saying this was a living donor, not a deceased one?'

'Yes. An altruistic donation.'

'In that case, and if the two parties were already known to each other, I'm afraid I don't see the issue here, Ms...?'

'Norton. Laurel Norton. The donor recently passed away, you see, and I'm trying to trace the recipient.'

'Was this a family member of yours?' he asked, leaning a shoulder against his office door and looking down at me.

'No. A... friend.'

'Then, Laurel, surely the thing to do is ask the donor's family who the recipient was. It doesn't seem particularly fraught with challenge to me.'

'I don't know whether the family know either. And anyway... it's complicated. It's difficult for me to ask them.'

'You appear to have a high level of interest in a matter that – purely as an impartial bystander – looks to me like none of your business,' he said.

I felt my face flame with embarrassment and indignation. I was getting nowhere with this man. His reputation as an arrogant prick was clearly richly deserved.

Walk away, Laurel, part of me urged. *You're wasting your time here – and he clearly thinks you're wasting his.*

'The thing is, Mr Smith.' I took a deep breath and tried to sound calm and reasoned. 'The donor and I... we were close. We were in a relationship for a year before he died. I feel as if making contact with the friend he donated his kidney to would help me to process my loss.'

His face softened slightly. 'And he was estranged from his family, hence your inability to pursue this through them?'

I thought about lying – that would have been the easiest thing to do. But honesty seemed to be having the desired effect, so I told the truth.

'No. He was... He was married, you see.'

'I see.' He drew the word out as if it had more than two Es on the end. He was looking at me differently now – almost speculatively. 'And the transplant took place a while back, you said?'

'More than twenty years ago.'

'And was this in England or Wales? Or, for that matter, north of the border or in Northern Ireland?'

I realised I didn't know the answer to this. 'I think it might have been Wales.'

'Well, Laurel.' A smile flickered over his face, but it was without warmth. 'This sounds as if it could be an intriguing investigation to pursue. We must consider patient confidentiality, of course. But I could perhaps do a little detective work on your behalf, if you were able to furnish me with some more details.'

'That would be amazing,' I said. 'Thank you so much, Mr Smith. I really appreciate it. Could I email you, maybe? I don't want to make you late for your show.'

He shot his cuff, glancing at his heavy gold watch. 'Indeed. I must be off. But do give me your number, Laurel. We can discuss this more – perhaps over a drink and dinner.'

Then he winked at me.

The wink told me everything I needed to know. Whether or not he was actually willing to help, there would be strings attached – strings in which I wasn't willing to become entangled.

'I... Perhaps I could email you?' I gabbled. 'I'd rather keep this professional. If you know what I mean.'

His face turned cold as stone and I realised I had messed up. I'd acknowledged his desire to overstep boundaries but also – far worse – I'd bruised his ego.

'Young lady,' he said, 'I think you'll find that your initial request to me was far from professional. You know where to find me should you change your mind.'

I gazed at him, unable to find any words. But I didn't need to – he was already shouldering me aside, heading off with long strides down the corridor.

THIRTY-SIX
LAUREL

To say my encounter with Dr Swinging-Dick left me bruised would be like saying a patient was bruised after a collision on the motorway at eighty miles per hour. It wasn't like I'd really been expecting him to be able or willing to give me a definitive answer. It wasn't like I'd hoped he would say, 'Nigel Graham? I remember carrying out that surgery like it was yesterday!' or anything like that. But I'd hoped for something – any sort of clue that would give me another avenue to explore.

And I'd left with nothing. Worse than nothing.

His suggestion that we talk over dinner hadn't been threatening or even particularly offensive – I'd dealt with far worse before. But my reaction to it had startled me – the idea that he, a senior colleague, could exercise some sort of *droit du seigneur* over me was bad enough, but what had really disgusted me was the sight of that gold wedding ring gleaming on his finger.

Gray had worn a wedding ring too. I'd seen it the very first moment we met, when he extended his hand to help me up from the pavement outside his house. The fact of him having a wife and a family had always been just that – a fact. Something about him I'd found out at the beginning and simply accepted. It had meant that we couldn't see each other as much as we'd have liked to. It had meant that the future of our relationship had been uncertain at best. It had meant a weight of guilt that I'd internalised and become accustomed to so quickly I ceased to notice it.

It was my guilt, my shame, my problem to deal with. But what about Gray's? I'd heard Mel's warning – *He's not a good man* – but I hadn't really listened. I'd been too invested to care what my friend thought of him – and besides, she'd never met him; she didn't know him like I did.

But if Dr Swinging-Dick was sleazy and a cheater, had Gray really been any better? For all I knew, I wasn't the first woman he'd had an affair with. There could have been other women, younger women, colleagues, women he was in a position of power over, who he'd slept with and betrayed his wife with.

I didn't want to see him that way. I'd always managed not to see him that way, because he was Gray – he was different and special and he loved me. But was it – was *he* – really so very different after all?

If I looked at the bald facts, it was extremely hard to see how.

Stopping at a traffic light, a crowd of my fellow hi-vis-clad commuters surrounding me, and a wall of buses, cars and lorries behind me, I made an abrupt decision. Instead of carrying on straight as I'd intended, I edged through the forest of bikes to the left-hand side of the junction, wobbling and apologising. I turned off the main road, rode round three sides of a square and rejoined it at the junction I'd previously passed, this time heading south and then east, instead of north.

Navigating easily from memory, I rode back past the hospital, on through Islington and the City, until I reached Damask Square.

It was a warm September evening, and still light even though it was gone eight o'clock. As I chained my bike to the railings surrounding the garden square, I noticed roses still blooming in the beds inside. The surrounding houses and flats had their lights on, but many of the curtains and blinds were not yet drawn – although those in number eight were, I saw with relief.

I noticed a glow coming from inside number five, as if a light had been switched on at the back of the house while the front room remained in darkness.

You're welcome to come and knock on my door, Orla had told me, when I'd said goodbye to her after settling Anna in bed. That had been the day of Gray's funeral – almost three months ago. I hadn't taken her up on her offer, but now here I was – drawn back to the square.

My legs feeling wobbly with fatigue, I approached the door and knocked. A few seconds later, I heard the quick tap of approaching footsteps. A brighter light illuminated the fanlight above the door, which opened after a moment.

Orla stood there, a look of polite enquiry on her face, wearing yoga trousers and a crop top, a cashmere jumper slung over her shoulders. I caught myself wondering how old she was – surely in her sixties, yet she dressed and moved like a much younger woman.

A smile broke out on her face when she saw me, the lines it revealed confirming my guess at her age.

'Laurel. I hoped you'd come, and here you are. Come in.'

Suddenly conscious of my dishevelled appearance and the sweat I could feel trickling down my back under my luminous pink cycling jacket, I said, 'If you're sure it's not a bad time?'

'Of course not. The cats and I were making dinner, and I was going to open a bottle of wine. Would you like to join me?'

I realised then how hungry I was. 'That sounds lovely. If you're sure?'

She didn't answer, but stepped aside with a welcoming gesture, and I followed her through the house to the kitchen at the back. The glass doors to the garden were open. In the fading light I could see a profusion of flowers, both wild and tended, and the smell of wet foliage drifted in. Two cats, one tortoiseshell and one tabby, came hurrying to meet us with eager mews.

On the kitchen table were a white jug of roses, a frosted bottle of wine and a loaf of bread, still fragrant and steaming on the metal sheet it had been baked on.

'Stop complaining, you two,' she scolded the cats, scooping

food into two bowls. 'What will Laurel think of your manners? There you are then.'

Orla put the bowls on the floor and the cats buried their faces in them, crunching noisily. She pulled the cork out of the wine and poured two glasses, and I sat down on one of the wooden chairs.

'Now,' she said. 'You must tell me how you've been.'

I took a breath and a sip of wine. 'Okay. But also not okay.'

She nodded, turning to the kitchen sink and beginning to wash some lettuce. 'Grief is like that.'

There was something about the tranquillity of that kitchen, something about Orla herself, that made it easy for me to talk. I found myself telling her how I'd become consumed with the need to know about the recipient of Gray's kidney transplant, how it had led me to my encounter with John Smith earlier that evening and the doubts that had arisen in my mind about Gray himself as a result.

While I talked, Orla made salad, sliced bread and arranged butter and cheese on plates. We finished our wine, and she refilled our glasses. Then she joined me at the table.

'I knew Gray for a long time,' she said. 'But it also felt like I barely knew him at all. There were so many parts of him that were closed off – that I don't think he ever opened up about, even to Anna.'

'Did he ever speak to you about his friend – Joel, the transplant recipient?'

'Only very briefly. Enough for me to form the impression that they'd been close, but weren't any longer. Not that there'd been a rift, more that Gray had moved on. Or moved away – not just literally but emotionally, as if he needed to put distance between himself and whatever Joel represented.'

'But you don't know what that was – or why?'

She shook her head. I spread butter on a piece of warm bread, the nutty fragrance rising from it as the butter melted and soaked into the crumb.

'There may have been something,' she said, her head tilted to one side as if she was trying to dislodge a buried memory. 'Something he said to me once – or didn't say. It was connected to music, I think.'

'Gray hated classical music.'

She smiled. 'That and bananas. It'll come to me, Laurel, and when it does I'll let you know.'

After that, we talked about other things. Mostly, I just sat, basking in the comfort of that house as if I was a cat myself, until I started yawning hugely and realised that it was time for me to go home.

I was unchaining my bike from the railings when I heard voices approaching, one soothing, almost wheedling, the other raised in shrill anger. The voices themselves were familiar but the tones were so foreign it took me a moment to realise who they were – Anna and Lulu.

'I'm not being unreasonable,' Anna was saying. 'Come on, darling. You know what you did was—'

'Literally the crime of the century, according to you,' Lulu snapped back. 'Because you never stayed too long at a friend's place and you never lost track of time and you never ran out of charge on your... Oh wait, you didn't even have mobile phones then. Which is why you just don't get it.'

'Lulu, come on. I was sixteen once. Okay, I didn't have a mobile. But I had friends and parents and rules I did my best to break. And boyfriends. And if I—'

'God, why do you have to make everything about sex? For fuck's sake, Mum. That's just gross.'

'I'm not making everything about sex. And don't swear at me.'

'What else am I supposed to do when you're trying to ruin my life?' Lulu's voice was trembling now, at the pitch of emotion where anger was about to give way to tears. 'I hate you. I wish Dad was here.'

I heard the sound of running feet and she appeared round the corner, her hair flying and her face already streaked with tears.

When she saw me she looked startled, then embarrassed, then

muttered, 'Hi, Laurel,' before slotting her key into the door, bursting in and slamming it behind her.

There was no way to escape before Anna saw me. My stomach dropped – I'd been caught on her home turf, and I'd overheard her fighting with her daughter.

Anna approached number eight more slowly, almost wearily. She was looking down at the ground, and for a second I considered ignoring her and hoping she wouldn't spot me after all. But that was cowardly and pathetic.

I stepped away from the railing, wheeling my bike like a barrier between us. 'Good evening.'

'Laurel.' She didn't look pleased to see me, but she didn't look furious, either. 'Sorry. We've been out.'

'I...' I wasn't sure what would be worse: her believing I'd come to see her or her knowing I'd been to visit Orla. 'That's okay. I was just about to head home. I had a drink with Orla.'

Anna grimaced. 'Always such a tonic. I might drop in on her myself. I take it you overheard that pleasant little chat with my daughter.'

I thought about denying it, but there was no point. 'Some of it.'

'Well.' She looked at me coldly. 'I'm glad I could give that bit of insight into our family life.'

I blushed. I knew what she must be thinking – that I would be feeling smug and vindicated at this evidence that Gray's family wasn't perfect. That I'd witnessed Anna scolding her daughter and might imagine her scolding Gray too.

Desperate to convince her that I didn't see things that way at all, I said, 'My niece is that age. They'd try the patience of a saint.'

Reluctantly, Anna cracked a tired smile. 'Tell me about it. Sweetness and light one minute, spitting hellcats the next. I keep telling myself she's growing out of it, and then something like this happens.'

'I can imagine.' She must have been shaken by the row, I thought, to be unbending like this to me, of all people. I kept my voice neutral. 'It must be a difficult time for all of you.'

Abruptly, Anna seemed to remember who she was talking to, and her familiar prickliness returned. 'Yes. We'll be all right. We'll get through it... as a family.'

It was a clear *keep-off* message. I swung my leg over my saddle and was about to pedal away when I heard myself saying, 'I could drop her a message, if you like. Take her out for a coffee. She's got my number, from before the hospital open day.'

Something stopped me adding that Lulu hadn't turned up to it – from the gist of their conversation, I suspected that Anna might not know that, and I didn't want to inflame things between them even more.

'What? You want to have some sort of cosy chat with my daughter? Exchange reminiscences about her father? Is that it?'

'Anna!' I understood her wariness, but the idea that I might reveal the nature of my relationship with Gray to his daughter shocked me. 'No! Of course not. Not that.'

'All right,' Anna agreed reluctantly. Then she stiffened further and added, 'It's not like I can stop you. Or her.'

'Okay.' I ignored her coldness. 'I'll do that. Take care, Anna. Have a good evening.'

I pushed down on the pedal and rode away towards home, leaving Damask Square and its inhabitants behind me – for the time being at least.

THIRTY-SEVEN

ORLA

20 September 2024

Memory is a perverse faculty! For the past week, I have been racking – or is it wracking? – my brains on Laurel's behalf, trying to recall the incident with Gray that I mentioned to her, which might or might not have been the clue she is searching for. Now, as I lie here hastily filling these three pages as the sky outside my bedroom window lightens, it is there in my mind, as clear as if it had always been there.

It was Iseult who reminded me. She has taken to waking me in the mornings by standing on my chest, reaching out a paw and tapping my face, then – when that is ineffective – extending a claw to prick my skin. It is just what my Maud used to do. Lying here, resistant to being woken, I let my thoughts drift to my old cat, with all her quirks and foibles, and a picture – or rather a film, for it was fully there with movement and sound – came back to me.

It was after a meeting of the historic buildings Preservation Trust two years or so back. Somewhat guiltily, I'd roped Gray into joining the society, hoping he would be an ally against the faction that supports allowing a supermarket chain to take over Imran's shabby newsagent shop. We had sat through the meeting together, and afterwards I invited Gray back here for a drink by way of thanks.

I sat him down in the chaise longue in the living room. On the table there was a pile of glossy magazines: Beatrice, my musical daughter – so unlike me in that regard – subscribes to *The Strad*, and while she was abroad she asked to have them delivered here. While we were chatting, Maud strolled into the room, slightly stiff and arthritic as she was by then, before taking a leap up on to the table.

Poor soul – she must have misjudged her distance or forgotten that the glossy pages were there, because she landed on top of the pile and it – and she – went skidding to the floor. She was fortunately unharmed and, as cats do, immediately set to washing herself, as if to convince us that that was exactly what she had intended to happen.

We laughed, and Gray got down on all fours to gather up the scattered magazines while I went to the kitchen to fetch some ice. While I was there, I could hear him remarking dismissively about their contents.

Rachmaninoff's Second – God, who'd want to sit through that?

Philip Glass must be the most overrated composer of all time.

I remember Blodwyn Griffiths playing when she was sixteen and she's still at it, poor woman.

When I returned with glasses, ice and a bottle of single malt whisky on a tray, I found Gray sitting by the fireplace, a page open in front of him, staring at it as if he had seen a ghost.

Are you all right? I asked. Would you like a splash of water with this?

For a moment it was as if he hadn't heard me. Then he shook his head as if to banish a bothersome fly, closed the magazine and replaced it on the pile.

I will be when I've had a drink, he said. Just a blast from the past.

But his face was quite white, and he drank his whisky like it was medicine.

We continued our conversation, and the incident – which had only been fleeting – passed from my mind completely. A month or so later Beatrice returned, and I handed over the magazines along with her other post.

What did he see in the pages that day? I will send Beatrice a message and find out whether she still has that collection of journals – likely she will, because she is quite the hoarder.

I feel as if I am close to finding a missing piece in the puzzle Laurel is trying to solve.

THIRTY-EIGHT
ANNA

It was four days after Lulu and I opened Gray's box in the attic, and I was sitting in his study, a glass of wine by my side and a pile of papers next to me.

Apart from Gray's music certificates, the box hadn't yielded much in the way of secrets. Below the envelope containing them, Lulu and I had found another holding six old school year-group photographs.

'Oh my God,' Lulu had shrieked when I handed them over to her. 'Which one's Dad?'

Then we'd heard Barney's voice calling from below, 'What about Dad?'

'Come up here, Barn,' Lulu said. 'Come see what me and Mum've found.'

My son scrambled up the ladder and joined us in the loft, flopping down on the floor next to his sister. He was wearing board shorts and a Queens Park Rangers shirt, and he smelled like he'd been playing football.

'Sheesh, Barney, you stink,' she said. 'Look at these.'

Heads together, the two of them peered down at the first of the photographs. Looking at it upside down, I could see that the year printed at the bottom was 1990. There were three rows of boys in the picture, the middle ones standing, the front ones seated and the back row presumably standing on a bench. There were perhaps thirty of them in total, all identically dressed in grey trousers, maroon blazers and maroon-and-gold striped ties.

They must all have been about the same age as Barney.

'Is that Dad there, in the middle row behind the teacher?' Barney asked.

'No way!' Lulu argued. 'He's wearing glasses, and Dad never did, did he, Mum?'

I remembered Gray complaining, just a few months back, that it was getting hard to read PDFs on his phone. *I'll need spectacles like an old man, Anna*, he'd said. He'd never need them now. He'd never be an old man.

'He wore contact lenses,' I said. 'But he would've worn glasses back then, probably. Could that be him, there on the end of the front row?'

'Fuck off!' Barney said. 'Sorry, Mum. I mean, that's never Dad.'

But I wasn't so sure. I leaned in closer: the boy whose face had caught my eye was one of the smaller ones – one of the late developers. He was sitting a little distance away from the child to his left, as if the photographer had told him to budge up but he'd ignored the instruction. The blazer he was wearing was unbuttoned, unlike the others, and I could see inches of white cuff showing below its sleeves. There was a similar gap between his trouser hems and his shoes, revealing an expanse of grey socks.

There was something – something about the angle of his head, the way his chin was tucked down almost into his chest, his eyes peering upwards to look into the camera, that was Gray. It was the same tilt I saw whenever I looked at the framed photograph on the mantelpiece from our wedding.

It was a look that betrayed whatever lay beneath Gray's confidence. A look that said, *I'm not sure I should be here.*

'You know what, Mum, you might be right.' Lulu turned the photograph around and handed it to me. 'Let's see the next one.'

'There he is again, second row,' Barney said, pointing his finger at the photo. 'He's taller now. He looks more like Dad this time.'

There was a boy standing behind him, resting his hand on his shoulder – the only one in the second row doing so.

Lulu and Barney had reached the last of the pictures now, charting the progress of the boy who might have been Gray into a young man, beginning to be handsome, who we all agreed was by far the most likely candidate.

'So what else is there in that box?' Barney asked.

I pulled out another envelope. 'School reports.'

'Gimme.' Lulu grabbed them, pulling one out and reading at random. '"If Nigel wishes to pursue his geography studies to A-level, he will need to pay some attention to his coursework." Poor Dad.'

For a moment, her face was alight with laughter. I knew she was imagining that when Gray came home from work, she'd tease him about it, ripping the piss, telling him he didn't have a leg to stand on next time he reminded her to do her homework, maybe even saying, *'Pot, black, kettle. Nigel.'*

Then I saw her realise that she would never be able to do that. The smile vanished from her face as if it had never been there – as if she'd forgotten how to smile and would never remember again. *You will, my darling*, I promised her silently, as our eyes met in shared anguish. *It might not feel that way now, but you will.*

She stood up, wiping her eyes with the cuff of her jumper and dusting off the seat of her jeans. 'Mind if I take one of those photos, Mum?'

'Of course not. Do you want one too, Barney?'

'Uh... yeah. Guess so. Is there anything for lunch, Mum?'

Now, I was reading through the school reports again. St Gwbert's, it appeared, had been a selective, fee-paying school and held its pupils to high standards – standards that, in the years from his acceptance into the first form through to his departure in the sixth, Nigel Graham had not always met.

Nigel's grasp of trigonometry is tenuous at best, I read. *If Nigel showed as much interest in the official curriculum as he does in his hobby of photography, we might find he has some promise. I find it challenging to find anything to say about a boy who has failed to turn up to a single rugby coaching session all term.*

Only the comments on his music were effusive. Nigel had shown *rare sensitivity, maturity beyond his years, eagerness to learn* that made him *a joy to teach.*

And from his head of year: *Nigel's attendance record continues to be patchy, and his punctuality is nothing short of diabolical.*

But it was the comments from the head teacher – one Bryn Rhys-Gwynn – that interested me the most.

If Nigel is to retain his scholarship place, he had written on not one or two but four reports, *he will need to show the same application to his academic studies as he does to his music.*

So Gray had been granted a free place at an elite private school – presumably on the basis of his musical talent. But he hadn't continued to earn it; in the classroom and on the sports field, he'd been a right slacker – when he bothered turning up at all.

So why hadn't they kicked him out? They'd have been well within their rights to do so. Was his gift for music such that they'd put up with laziness and non-attendance in other areas? Maybe it was – but maybe there was more to it than that.

None of it made sense. None of it seemed to bear any relation to the Gray I had known – a driven, ambitious, focused man. But then the Gray I had known would never have gone near a piano. The Gray I had known bore almost no trace of the Welsh accent the child in the photographs must surely have had.

The Gray I had known had had an affair for almost a year without me finding out, so it should not have come as such a shocking, gut-wrenching surprise to me that I didn't know him anything like as well as I'd thought.

On Gray's computer, I typed the school's name into Google. Its website came up straight away and I clicked twice, first to open the site and then to choose the English- rather than the Welsh-language version.

Mr Rhys-Gwynn, I discovered, had now departed; the current head was the more prosaically named Evan Davies.

Taking another gulp of wine, I picked up my phone and dialled the number, with its unfamiliar 01792 dialling code.

A woman's voice answered after a few rings, giving the name of the school followed by a crisp, 'How may I help you?'

'My name's Anna Graham. My late husband was a pupil at St Gwbert's' – I tried to pronounce it the same way she had, *Goo-bert's* – 'back in the nineties, and I was hoping to find out some more about his time at the school.'

'Your late husband?' The woman's voice was pleasant but without warmth. 'I'm sorry for your loss, Mrs…?'

'Graham,' I repeated. 'My husband's name was Nigel Graham.'

'Nigel Graham,' she repeated. 'And what information was it you were hoping for, Mrs Graham?'

'I… just… I don't know. I suppose some sort of insight from someone who might have known him when he was there, to learn more about what his childhood was like.'

'We're talking about thirty years ago, Mrs Graham. I've worked here twenty myself and I don't think there's anyone on the staff who's been here longer than I have.'

'I know. It's a long time ago. But perhaps written records? Or something on the computer system?'

She clicked her tongue, and I could picture her shaking her head. 'I'm very sorry, but I don't think we'll be able to assist you. If there are any extant records of Mr Graham's time here, which is unlikely, we'd be bound by data protection legislation and unable to release them. We are a school. We take safeguarding seriously.'

Like safeguarding a child who not only hadn't been one for thirty years but had died three months ago was even a thing, I thought with a flash of anger.

'But he's dead. And he was my husband.'

'I'm very sorry for your loss. But we won't be able to help.'

She paused for a second, leaving space for me to thank her. When I didn't do that, she hung up.

Frustrated, I turned back to the photographs. Once again, I turned to the one from 1991, in which the boy I was sure was Gray was standing in front of his taller, dark-haired friend, whose hand on Gray's shoulder looked almost protective. At least he had had one person looking out for him, amid all the skipped lessons and disappointing grades.

But who were you? I asked the photograph, only realising afterwards that I could have been addressing the dark-haired boy or the one in front of him – the one who became my husband.

THIRTY-NINE
LAUREL

'I'm not going to lie, it's a vocation as much as a career,' I said. 'If you want an easy life, or to earn loads of money, then it's probably not for you.'

Lulu nodded, looking intently at me across the hospital coffee-shop table. I could have arranged to meet her somewhere nicer, but I'd figured that if she was serious about becoming a nurse, crap coffee was one of the first things she'd need to get used to. It was a week since I'd last seen her; I'd waited a couple of days after suggesting to Anna that I contact her.

'Is it...' she began, running a finger around the rim of her coffee cup to scrape up the last of the rather scummy froth, 'I mean, how do you cope, when people die and stuff?'

Her brown eyes were full of sadness. Gray's eyes. Gray's death. Gray's daughter.

'There isn't just one answer to that,' I began carefully. 'Different people cope in different ways. As your career progresses, you get – not used to it, but I suppose it balances out better against all the patients you've been able to help. It can be traumatic – of course it can. But there's support for all of us when things start to feel like a lot. And no matter how much you care about your patients, it's not the same as when someone you know personally passes away. It's just not.'

She nodded slowly. I hoped I'd got my answer as right as I could – but her next question took me by surprise.

'Laurel? How did you know my dad?'

Shit. I wished I'd thought to agree some sort of cover story with Anna, but it would have felt too intrusive to ask her what she was happy for me to say, even though our last meeting had been less acrimonious than previous ones.

I didn't want to lie to Lulu, but the truth was obviously impossible to tell, so I settled for half of it.

'We were both into cycling. Your dad helped me out after I had a fall one time, and we got to be friends after that.'

Hopefully, she'd assume that we were members of the same cycling club or something – put two and two together to make five, rather than the correct four. But she didn't seem to be thinking about me; my words had sparked a memory.

'Dad was obsessed with cycling.' She grinned. 'Barney and I used to take the piss out of him about being a middle-aged man in Lycra. He wanted to buy a new bike – an even fancier one – but Mum said she was introducing a "one in, one out" policy, and it turned out he'd got kind of fond of the old one.'

I laughed. It was impossible to imagine the Gray I'd known becoming sentimentally attached to a bicycle. His children must have seen a different version of him – a softer one. The one that was their dad.

'You must miss him terribly,' I said.

Her face dropped and she nodded. 'I do. We all do. Even Augustus. Dad used to play this game where he threw treats and Gus chased them, but he won't do it for any of us.'

'He was a special man. He sounds like an amazing dad. I'm so sad for you all.'

I longed to ask her more about Gray, gather more fragments of treasure to add to the memories I had of him, even though Lulu's memories could never be my own. Instead, though, I turned the conversation back to nursing, offering to send her a list of the universities that offered the most highly regarded BSc degree courses.

But I soon realised she was only half-listening to me. Her eyes had flickered down to her phone, and now she was picking it up, swiping it to life, her face flushing as she read a message.

'Laurel, I – I'm really sorry, but I'm going to have to go.' I could see her struggling, torn between politeness and the urge to be somewhere else – like, *now* – which definitely hadn't been there a moment before.

'That's okay,' I said. 'I reckon we covered a fair bit of ground, didn't we? You're welcome to text me any time if you want to know more.'

'Thanks.' Lulu was already standing up, shoving her phone into her pocket after glancing surreptitiously at her reflection in its blank screen.

'Or,' I added, remembering my promise to Anna, 'if you just want to chat. I know how hard it must have been, losing your dad.'

'Thanks,' she said again, the smile that was so like Gray's lighting up her face. 'I really appreciate it. I'll do that.'

As she hurried away, I found myself hoping that she would. Although I barely knew her, she was Gray's child – a part of him that was still alive and present, more tangible and real by far than the idea of that donated kidney, which somewhere – I hoped – was sustaining the life of a man named Joel who I was increasingly losing hope of ever finding.

I hadn't thought of Orla for several days; she had been kind to me, provided a listening ear when I needed one, but realistically what did she have to offer me other than a few scattered memories from two decades of living near Gray and his family?

I got up from the table, gathered Lulu's mug and mine on to a tray and took it to the counter. It was almost seven – time to head home.

I was emerging from the stairwell on to the ground floor when I almost collided with Harry. Not unusually for him, he was running late for his shift, had given up on waiting for the lift and was about to make a dash up four floors.

'Evening,' I said. 'You've got ninety seconds. You'll make it if you don't have a coronary on the way up.'

'Ha very ha. I certainly don't have time to stand around chit-chatting with you,' he joked. 'I was going to leave this in the office on the ward for you, but since you're here you may as well take it.'

He handed over a plain brown A4 envelope, my name and the address of the hospital written on it in elegant, spidery handwriting. There was no ward number, so it must have sat at the front desk until one of the reception staff saw Harry and asked him to take it up for me. It wasn't unusual for us to receive post, mostly cards and gifts from grateful patients.

But this felt different. I knew it was different.

'Cheers,' I called to Harry's departing back. 'Have a good night.'

I waited until I was home before opening the envelope – waited until I'd made a cup of tea and microwaved a jacket potato for my dinner.

I sat down on the sofa with my tea, stuck a random episode of *A Place in the Sun* on the telly, took the envelope out of my bag and slit the flap open with the back of my teaspoon. There was a card inside, too small for the length of the envelope, and two sheets of printed paper that looked like they had been cut from a magazine, folded into three.

I read the card first.

Dear Laurel,

I'm sorry it has taken a while for me to send this to you. I can only blame my memory, which took its time revealing what I'd hoped to be able to share with you – and my clumsy fingers, which made me leave off a digit when I took your phone number. But here it is. I will not tell you not to get your hopes up, because I think it is likely this is what you were looking for. I do hope, though, that this knowledge will bring you comfort.

With love,
Orla Clifford

I set the card aside and unfolded the pages, noticing that my hands were trembling. The first thing I saw was a full-page advertisement for an insurance company, evidently one that specialised in high-end cars. When I turned the two pages over, there was another ad, this time for package holidays for the over-fifties.

I might not be there yet, but I will be soon enough, I thought gloomily.

Then I opened out the pages so their insides were facing each other and saw why Orla had sent them to me.

It was an article from a specialist music magazine: an interview with a violinist. The left-hand page was a photograph of him with his instrument, the amphitheatre of a concert hall in the background. He was holding the violin so that its neck was alongside his face, his hands wrapped almost tenderly around it, its body resting on his thighs. The man was wearing an open-necked white shirt and faded blue jeans.

He was strikingly good looking with dark hair, slightly threaded with grey, and blue eyes. His features were strong without being sharp. His half-smile revealed a dimple in his left cheek.

Printed over the photograph were the words:

Twenty Questions for Joel Chamberlain

The interview itself was on the other page. My hands were so unsteady that I could hear the fluttering of the paper as I held it up to read. The first few questions were concerned with music, and I skimmed over them, the answers meaning far less to me than I guessed they would to regular readers of *The Strad*, which was the title printed at the bottom of the article alongside the page number.

They revealed that the piece of music Joel most enjoyed playing was 'The Last Rose of Summer' by Heinrich Wilhelm Ernst, a tune and a composer that meant nothing to me. The place where he most enjoyed performing was St David's Hall ('An iconic venue in my home city of Cardiff'), closely followed by his back garden ('My neighbours probably hate me' – a glimmer of humanity that made me smile).

'Yes, but is it you?' I asked aloud, my eyes returning briefly to the photograph before I read on.

The questions after that got more personal and more interesting. Joel had had scrambled eggs on wholemeal toast for breakfast that day, followed by a Pink Lady apple and a cup of builder's tea (*My man!* I thought). When he wasn't working, he enjoyed long bike rides along something called the Taff Trail, which sounded appealing. His favourite indulgence was a glass of red wine in the bath (*Okay, Joel, you do you*).

Clearly, the editor saved the best questions for last.

Have you ever been in love?

Yes, but sadly not for a long time. Unless you count Bertha, my rescue Sealyham Terrier. I love her unconditionally and I hope it's reciprocated.

Tell us about a moment that changed you.

When I was twenty-one, I received a kidney transplant. It saved my life and I will be forever grateful.

I read the words again, so slowly it was as if I was taking in one letter at a time.

I'd found him. Or Orla had. Or he had been there all along. Somewhere inside that man – inside his body when he played his violin in his garden, lay in the bath or cycled on that trail in Wales – was a piece of Gray. This was the man whose life Gray had saved. The man Gray had loved enough to risk his own life for.

My heart hammering, I turned back to the page with the picture on it and studied it closely, as if I would be able to detect some hint of Gray – Gray's body, Gray's DNA, the life force that had been Gray's – in Joel Chamberlain's handsome face.

As I stared at the page, I heard my phone vibrate on the coffee table. It was a WhatsApp message from Lulu, sent to the group I'd created that included her mother.

It was so great to see you just now Laurel! Thank you so much for spending so much time with me – hope you got home safely xx

She'd added a string of flower emojis and a smiley face.

I read her message again, puzzled. It was more than two hours since she'd hurriedly departed the coffee shop. And *so much time?* We'd spent barely thirty minutes together.

Something about her message wasn't right. Where had she gone when that urgent message summoned her away? And why was she trying to deceive her mother about where she'd been for those lost two hours?

FORTY

ANNA

I found the church hall without difficulty, which was just as well because my train to Wales had been delayed, the connecting bus hadn't turned up and I was late. Late and stressed about my decision to leave the children alone, despite Lulu's promise that they would be fine and Orla being next door if they needed anything.

I'd made the decision to come here on a whim. After being knocked back by the school receptionist, I'd managed to locate the former headmaster, Bryn Rhys-Gwynn, on – of all places – LinkedIn.

My late husband was a pupil at St Gwbert's, I'd typed. *Would you be able to share anything you can recall about his time there?*

Then I'd thought, *No*. Far too easy for him to say that wasn't possible. So I'd deleted that and found myself writing, *I wonder if it would be possible to meet you for a chat?* instead.

To my surprise, he had replied within half an hour.

I'm at Bethesda Chapel Hall on Saturdays from five o'clock, he'd written. *You can find me there.*

And now here I was – late, puffing and sweating – at the top of the hill where the unassuming white-painted building stood, recognisable mostly by its proximity to the starkly simple, slate-roofed chapel that stood next to it.

I paused a few metres from the entrance to the hall, recovering my breath and taking a few furtive puffs on my sour-cherry vape. My feet were hurting, and I needed a wee, but those would have to wait – thanks to my late-running train and the irregular bus service, it was almost six o'clock. From within the hall, I could hear men's voices talking – a hum that rose to a shout of laughter and then dropped back to a hum.

I stepped through the doorway and the room immediately fell silent. I blinked in the dim light, feeling blood rush to my cheeks before realising that the silence had nothing to do with me: there were men there, at least a couple of dozen of them, but all of them were gathered at the far end of the room and had their backs to me.

In the stillness, I could hear the buzzing of a fly and the thump of its body against a window.

Then a voice began singing, so softly at first I could barely hear it.

> '*Mine eyes have seen the glory of the coming of the Lord*
> *He is trampling out the vintage where the grapes of wrath are stored.*'

It's a choir practice, I realised – a Welsh male-voice choir.

Then the voice was joined by others, swelling in harmony as they sang the chorus:

> '*Glory, Glory Hallelujah.*'

And I found I could do nothing but stand and listen, the hairs on the back of my neck rising in awe.

By the time the song ended, I was wiping tears from my eyes. There was another moment of total silence, and then the voices broke out again, no longer in close harmony but in chatter and laughter. The men turned and began making their way across the room towards me, some wiping sweat from their faces, others tucking sheet music into their pockets.

They were all ages, from a couple of boys barely older than Barney to elderly men, one leaning on a stick as he shuffled across the wooden floor, a couple of his friends accompanying his slow progress. He was tall with a head of pure white hair, tidily brushed. He was wearing jeans and a yellow-and-black checked shirt.

When he saw me, he raised the hand that wasn't on the cane, and I took a few tentative steps forward, meeting him in the centre of the hall.

'Mr Rhys-Gwynn?' I held out my hand.

'Call me Bryn.' His grip was dry and firm. 'You must be Mrs Graham.'

'Anna.' I smiled.

'I'll see you at the Red Lion shortly, lads.' His voice was deep and full, not at all frail. 'I'll just take a few minutes with this lady.'

'Why does Bryn get all the girls?' joked one of the younger men, but Bryn Rhys-Gwynn directed a silencing glare at him that was pure headmaster, and the young man scurried out with his mates.

'Shall we go outside?' he suggested. 'Since it's such a glorious evening?'

I kept pace with his slow steps as we left the hall, emerging into the daylight, startlingly bright after the gloom of the hall although the sun was already sinking. Bryn led me to a bench overlooking the churchyard, which stretched away down the hill, punctuated by moss-covered gravestones jutting crookedly skywards.

I wondered whether Gray's mother's was one of them.

'So.' He lowered himself carefully on to the bench and turned to face me. 'Your husband was a pupil of mine, back in the day. I can recall several boys named Graham – was this Peter, Daffyd or Nigel? There was also Tomos, but it can't have been him because he was singing the baritone section back there a few minutes ago.'

He might be frail, but his memory was sharp as anything, I realised. 'Nigel.'

'And he's passed away?'

I nodded. 'Earlier this year. Pancreatic cancer. It was very sudden, and it's made me realise... well, made me realise how little I know about his childhood.'

'I'm very sorry to hear that.' He sighed. 'I remember Nigel well. He was a pupil at St Gwbert's from 1990 to 1996.'

'Those were the dates on the reports I found,' I confirmed. 'And he was there on a scholarship?'

Bryn nodded. 'St Gwbert's was – and still is – fortunate in that several of our alumni left generous endowments, which are used to fund places for gifted boys whose families wouldn't otherwise be able to afford our fees. Nigel was one of those.'

'He was good at music, then?' I asked.

'Oh, yes.' Bryn smiled, turning his face up to the sun as if he was hearing rather than seeing it. 'Quite exceptionally able. It surprises me that...'

'That I didn't know?' I felt my cheeks colour. 'I mean, Gray – Nigel – my late husband, he had a good singing voice. I knew that. When we were in the car and a tune he liked came on the radio, or it was one of the kids' birthdays, I'd hear him sing and it was lovely. But he was never into music like some people are. Actually, he said he hated it. Classical music especially.'

Bryn smiled again, raising his eyebrows, and I felt my blush deepen.

'I'm sorry,' I said. 'I'm making it sound like you and your colleagues didn't do a good job. I'm sure you did. He just never talked about school. Not at all. I assumed that – well, that he hadn't been particularly happy.'

He sighed. 'I'm afraid that pastoral care back then wasn't what it is now. The boys in our care – the scholarship boys in particular – came under a lot of pressure to perform musically, academically and on the sports field. Nigel rebelled somewhat against that – against the latter two, at any rate. There were discussions every year about not renewing his scholarship, but he was too gifted for us to let him go. Besides, the impression I had was that his problems were at home, rather than at school. Insofar as we could, we tried to provide stability – a place of refuge for him, as it were.'

'So he was happy at school?'

'I don't remember him as a happy boy generally, I'm afraid. He had one good friend, though. One boy – Joel Chamberlain. As the years went by, Joel's family appeared to take Nigel under their wing. His own mother, you see...'

I pressed my hands between my knees, leaning forward on the bench. 'His mother what?'

'She was... I suppose these days you'd call it neglectful. I got the impression there were mental health issues at play.'

Oh God. Gray's mother – her death when she must have been in her forties, probably the age I was now or perhaps even younger. Could it have been...?

'I believe she passed away,' I said carefully. 'When Gray – Nigel – was at university.'

He shook his head wearily. 'I did not know that. How sad.'

He hadn't known about Gray's mother's death, and I sensed that there was nothing more he did know – nothing he could tell me.

But I asked, 'Joel – Chamberlain, was it? Are you still in touch with him?'

He looked surprised. 'Of course. He's *the* Joel Chamberlain.'

My blank look made him laugh.

'I'm sorry,' I said. 'I'm not...'

'Not a musical person. Of course. He's a world-renowned violinist. One of our most famous alumni. He often returns to the school to play and give talks, and Seren, his mother, is on our board of governors. I'm sure she'll be happy for me to give you her number.'

He scrolled through his phone and found it, and I entered the eleven digits into my own phone.

'There's one other thing,' I said. 'A song – Gray mentioned that it would have been played at his mother's funeral, and I'm sure I remember him singing it to our children when they were babies.'

He smiled. Instead of a conventional answer, he began to sing, his voice low and clear in the golden air. For the second time that day, I felt that prickling sensation on the back of my neck as I was transported back to the bathroom in the house on Damask Square, my breasts leaking milk into the warm water as I heard Gray singing to our baby.

> 'Holl amrantau'r sêr ddywedant
> Ar hyd y nos
> "Dyma'r ffordd i fro gogoniant,"
> Ar hyd y nos.'

'What does it mean?' I asked, my own voice sounding thin and high after his.

'It's a lullaby, and as you say, a funeral song. The original lyrics are somewhat untranslatable. But the title means "All Through the Night".'

I thanked him for his time and watched him make his way painstakingly back down the hill in the direction of the Red Lion. Gray could have been there: could have been singing in the choir like Tomos Graham, joining his friends for a pint, alive and at home in the place where he grew up.

But he wasn't. He'd chosen to leave it all behind, erasing his memories, his past, even the music that had been his comfort. Why? What happened in that neglectful home?

I swiped my phone to life and located Seren Chamberlain's number. If I hurried, I could make the last train back to London – or, if she was able to see me, I could stay overnight. But before I dialled, something made me check my WhatsApp.

There was a new message from Laurel.

Hi Anna, I'm sorry to bother you. Lulu was meant to meet me tonight for a burger and a chat, but she hasn't turned up. I can't get hold of her. I thought you should know.

Shit. Feeling sweat springing out all over my body – but at the same time a creeping coldness – I sprinted down the hill to the bus stop, my fingers fumbling on the screen of my phone. Pressing it to my ear, I listened as first Lulu and then Barney's numbers rang out. The last train back to London was at half past eight. I'd assumed I would make it easily and be home by one as I'd promised the children, but I was cutting it fine.

To my relief, the bus arrived just as I did. I boarded and flopped into a seat, checking my phone again and hammering out texts to Orla and Barney. Then I tapped the Google Maps app, hoping to reassure myself that I'd make it back in time.

My heart plummeted when I saw the little warning icon on my journey plan. The flooding on the line that had caused the earlier delay had had a knock-on effect, and the late train from Swansea back to Paddington was cancelled.

Don't panic, Anna, I urged myself. *You're in Wales, not the Australian outback. You have options.*

But, as it turned out, I didn't. After unsuccessful attempts to order an Uber, I dialled the two minicab office numbers that were displayed next to the closed ticket office, only to be explained to as if I was hard of thinking that the Ospreys were playing Cardiff and no drivers were available. My own driving licence was at home.

I was stuck here overnight, and my daughter was missing.

FORTY-ONE

ORLA

20 *September* 2024

Another morning, and another Graham child turned up at my door last night. I shouldn't joke about it – not even here, in these pages that only I will read – because really it is not a laughing matter. They might both be here now, safely asleep, but Anna will have some difficult questions to ask her daughter – and herself.

When she messaged me yesterday to ask if I would be home, because she needed to go urgently and unexpectedly to Wales, I offered to have them both here, or to go and stay at number eight for the night. But Anna told me that Lulu had promised to be on her best behaviour and begged to be allowed to prove herself responsible by looking after her brother after she got home from meeting Laurel for a burger.

How strange that Gray's daughter and Gray's lover should be meeting up, I thought, but I didn't say that to Anna.

But Lulu did not keep her promise. It wasn't late when I received Anna's call – the first of her calls – telling me that Lulu wasn't where she was supposed to be, and wasn't answering her phone. Shortly after that, Barney knocked on my door, all awkward and embarrassed in his tracksuit bottoms and hoodie, and told me that Lulu had gone out, leaving him alone, and not returned. His mother's train home had been cancelled and Anna, having eventually got hold of him, had ordered him to come round and wait at my house.

He didn't say so, but I could tell her instructions had come as a relief to him. I assured him that I had been about to go and knock on his door and invite him over myself, because I too could do with some company. I invited him in and gave him cocoa and biscuits, because being a boy on the cusp of his teens he is hungry even in an emergency. We found a Spotify playlist of Martha Argerich's piano solos, and settled down to wait. I tried calling Lulu myself, and also received no answer. I thought about calling the police, even though I was certain that wherever Lulu was, she was there of her own volition.

Fortunately, I did not have to do that, because just as Barney was reaching again for the biscuit tin, I heard the same sound I had heard several weeks before – the car screeching into the square, pulling up outside number five, then noisily and unnecessarily revving its engine again.

That'll be her, I said, as Barney's face dissolved into relief.

I hurried to the front door and opened it just as Lulu was stepping out of the car.

You don't have to make so much noise, she was protesting, half annoyed and half laughing.

In the beam of the car's interior light, I could see a young man's face at the wheel, half shadowed by a baseball cap. A young man – but a man significantly older than Lulu. When I was her age, it wasn't uncommon for girls to have older boyfriends – it was seen almost as a badge of honour. But things have changed now, and rightly so. Now, we have different words to describe this kind of relationship. I was appalled, and I know Anna will be too.

See you later, I heard Lulu say, and I could tell that the casualness in her words was forced.

Then she turned and saw me, and her face fell. We both waited for the car to screech out of the square, the fumes of its exhaust hanging in the still night air, then she came over to me, shame-faced, and said she was sorry.

I told her that her mother was stuck overnight in Wales, and she had better come in and stay overnight in one of my spare rooms, and she humbly agreed, then greeted her brother, attempting a casual, nothing-to-see-here tone.

That's not cool, what you did, he said.

What? Lulu demanded. Nothing happened.

But something has and, as Barney said, it's not cool. I could tell they didn't want to be around each other, so not long after that I sent them to bed in separate rooms, before texting Anna to assure her that Lulu was here and safe. How she will deal with this when she gets back later today remains to be seen.

FORTY-TWO

ANNA

I squirmed uncomfortably in the narrow economy-class train seat. The only available spot had been by the window at a table, the other three seats at which were occupied by a harassed-looking woman and her two pre-school children.

I had spent a sleepless night in a cheap hotel near the station, with no change of clothes or even a toothbrush. The news from Orla that Lulu had turned up safely had flooded me with relief, but done little to alleviate my anger – at my daughter, but most of all at myself.

'Sorry,' the mum mouthed at me across the table as her smaller child decided that now was the time to test the volume at which he was capable of screeching.

'It gets easier,' I said, as kindly as I could.

Except *that*, of course, was the biggest load of bollocks ever. I was returning home to deal with the fallout of my own child's actions: my sixteen-year-old daughter, who I'd trusted, or at least prayed, had learned her lesson.

Clearly, I'd been wrong. Wrong on more levels than I could count. Wrong to think it would be okay to leave the kids alone. Wrong to believe Lulu when she said she would be having an early dinner with Laurel and would make sure she and Barney were safely in bed by ten. Wrong to put my own desire to uncover Gray's past above my duties as a mother.

I turned away from the little girl on my right, who was scooping yoghurt out of its pot with her fingers, and gazed out of the window. I couldn't be sure whether the train had passed over the border from Wales to England, but I guessed not – I could still see gently undulating fields, grey stone buildings and, of course, sheep.

I willed the landscape to pass more quickly outside the windows, willed the time to pass – because there was no way I could turn it back. No way I could undo the decision I'd made to leave them alone, even knowing that Lulu's behaviour was erratic, that her grief over the loss of her father was making her act in ways she wouldn't normally.

'Mummy, I need a wee.' The piercing voice of the child next to me interrupted my thoughts. Ten minutes before, it had been her brother who'd needed one, and the mum had had to fight her way through the crowds of people standing in the aisle to the toilet with both her kids, facing a barrage of scowls and tuts.

'You can leave your little boy here,' I offered with a smile. 'I'll make sure he doesn't get up to any mischief.'

She looked at me. Her hair was escaping from its ponytail and there was yoghurt on her jumper. Her kids' toys, books and snack wrappers were scattered all over the table, and I could see she was nearing the end of her tether.

'Thank you,' she said. 'That's very kind, but I'll keep them both with me.'

I felt a stab of guilt. That woman was a better mother than I was – keeping her children close to her, looking after them, protecting them from harm. Of course Lulu shouldn't have gone off on her own – but I should have been there, been with them, being their mother.

By the time I eventually made it back to Damask Square it was mid morning and my guilt hadn't subsided. It gnawed at me, taking turns with surges of panic at what might have happened to Lulu in my absence. I let myself into the house, calling out that I was home, but there was no answer from the kids; only Augustus came padding up the stairs to meet me.

'Barney? Lulu?' I called out anxiously.

'I'm in the kitchen.' Barney's voice drifted up, along with the smell of burned toast.

When I went downstairs, I found him there, surrounded by an empty can of tuna, an open packet of bread and smears of mayonnaise. He gave me a brief recap of the previous night's events, saying that he didn't know where Lulu had been then, but she was in her bedroom now.

'Okay,' I said. 'I'll talk to her. Barney – I'm sorry.'

I pulled him into my arms and held him tight. His head came almost up to my chin – my big boy, but still a child. A child I should have protected, and hadn't.

He looked at me in surprise. 'That's okay.'

'I love you, you know.'

'Love you, Mum,' he said around a mouthful of tuna melt.

Lulu's bedroom door was closed. I tapped and then, when there was no reply, opened it. She was lying face down on her bed and she was crying.

All my anger evaporating, I hurried over and sat down next to her.

'Hi, darling.'

The only response was a fresh outpouring of sobs.

'What happened last night?' I asked. 'You can tell me.'

She cried a bit more and I waited, stroking her hair, feeling sorrow and guilt twisting my insides like a vice. At last she turned over and I took a tissue from next to the bed and wiped her eyes.

'I went to see Callum,' she said, almost wearily.

Cold fear gripped me. 'Right. Who's Callum?'

'He's a boy – a guy. I met him when I was in the park roller-skating with Aisha.'

'Does he go to your school?'

She shook her head. 'He's got a job.'

A job? How old is this Callum? But I didn't ask that. 'Go on.'

'I was with him that other – last time. When you grounded me I couldn't see him but we texted and... stuff. And we were texting yesterday evening.'

I was appalled. I could guess what form that texting had taken. How dare he do that to my daughter? And what had Lulu been thinking? I'd warned her about things like that – about sending photos from her phone. But I'd left her alone – this was on me.

'He asked me to go meet him,' she went on. 'He was, like, begging. He said he missed me so much. So I went, instead of going to meet Laurel.'

'And what happened?'

She put her hands over her face and turned away from me. 'I went to his place. And I – we had sex. Then he brought me home in his car.'

His place? God. My little girl, alone with a man old enough to have a job and a car. Anything could have happened. Anything did happen.

'And now' – she burst into a fresh storm of tears – 'this morning, I went to message him and he's blocked me on everything. He's ghosted me, Mum.'

FORTY-THREE
LAUREL

The last few notes of music fell like raindrops into complete silence, and I realised I was holding my breath. I had been sitting dead still in my seat for the past two and a half hours, not even getting up to queue for the toilet in the interval: from the moment the conductor stepped out to rapturous applause and the lights in the concert hall dimmed, I'd been utterly captivated.

I had never experienced anything like it before. Everything about the evening – the eager buzz of anticipation as the audience filed in, the glow of the instruments beneath the lights, the intent faces of the musicians and the precise movements of their hands – had held me in a kind of spell.

All that, and the music itself. The way it swelled from near silence into something so powerful I felt as if I was being pressed back into my seat. The way some bits made me smile and others brought tears to my eyes. The total precision of it all – like surgery, only using sound.

Since reading the article about Joel Chamberlain, I'd been besieged by doubt: should I contact him? Could I? What possible justification could I have for getting in touch with a man on the basis of such a bizarre and tenuous link? *Hi, you don't know me but you've got my ex-lover's kidney?* He'd think I was mad, and perhaps he'd be right.

And Gray? Was I being horribly disloyal to him?

Perhaps meeting him would prove disappointing. Perhaps all the interviews with him I'd read online over the past couple of weeks had been misleading – suck-up journalists looking to give a good impression of a man who was arrogant or rude or just a diva.

So I'd settled for seeing him – and hearing him, in a context where thousands of other people were doing exactly the same, after googling his name and learning that he was playing in a concert at the Royal Albert Hall. I didn't know what I'd been expecting, but it wasn't this – this power, this magic.

I had no way of knowing whether Gray had been aware, when he had made the sacrifice that had saved Joel Chamberlain's life, that his decision would make this possible.

The silence broke as the hall erupted into ecstatic applause. Around me, the audience rose to their feet in unison, clapping and whooping like they'd been listening to One Direction instead of Mozart. I stood too, almost toppling over in my heels, stiff after sitting motionless for so long. I was in the same black dress I'd worn to dinner with Gray on Valentine's Day, and had realised as soon as I arrived that I was overdressed, but now it felt appropriate to be in something glamorous, the crystals Gray had given me sparkling as brightly as tears in my earlobes.

'Magnificent,' the woman next to me was saying. 'Chamberlain was phenomenal.'

'As always,' her companion said. 'What a talent!'

I realised I had been so busy listening I'd almost forgotten why I had come to the Royal Albert Hall on this Wednesday night, spending what had felt like a crazy sum of money on a last-minute ticket. It had taken me a while to spot Joel Chamberlain on stage, and longer still to identify the sound of his violin among the other instruments, and even once I had, he'd become just a part of the glorious machine of the orchestra.

Now, though, my sense of purpose returned. I let myself be

swept along with the crowd, reluctantly joined the queue for the ladies', then emerged into the chilly, drizzly night. But I didn't follow the stream of people heading towards the Tube station. I made my way around the building, looking for what Google had promised I'd find.

And there it was, a cluster of people waiting there with phones and programmes in their hands, huddled against the cold beneath a sign that said 'Stage Door'. Hanging back slightly, I waited too.

It was more than twenty minutes before the door opened and one of the musicians emerged, her instrument case in one hand and a bouquet of yellow roses in the other. She was a young Black woman, who I remembered seeing on the right of the stage, her fingers moving almost tenderly over the keys of her instrument. My programme had informed me that it was called an oboe, and that she was called Maria Dlamini.

Within seconds, she was mobbed by a cluster of about a dozen people, holding out their programmes for her to sign and posing for selfies with her. She signed and smiled and dished out flowers from her bouquet to the delight of her fans, then thanked everyone and said goodnight. I watched her walk off in the direction of the station, now looking like just another normal woman on her way home, all the stardust that had illuminated her in the footlights dimmed.

The conductor came out next and was similarly surrounded, but his signing and smiling session took a bit longer because there were more people after his autograph, and people seemed to want to ask him questions about his interpretation of the pieces we'd heard. Neither they nor his answers meant anything to me, and I found myself beginning to worry that Joel Chamberlain had already left by another exit, or that he'd somehow slip past me in the crowd.

But just as the conductor was hailing a black cab and getting in, the stage door opened once again and Joel came out.

In the flesh, he was just as good-looking as his photograph. Not as tall as I'd expected, but broad shouldered and lean, and with a quality the camera hadn't been able to capture – a kind of radiance, as if he had been lit somehow from within by the music he'd been playing, and the glow had yet to subside.

Or perhaps it was something more commonplace than that – just the star quality that would have made him a brilliant performer where other people were just brilliant musicians. I had no way of knowing and wasn't inclined to analyse – all I knew was that the people crowding round him for autographs and selfies were mostly women, and they all looked as smitten as if they were teenagers after a James Bay gig.

And I could kind of see where they were coming from.

It felt like a long time before he'd scrawled his signature for the last time and smiled up into a camera lens for a final selfie and there was no one else waiting to speak to him. As I watched, his shoulders seemed to relax, whatever light had been shining from him dimmed and he turned to walk away in the same direction Maria Dlamini had.

It was now or never. I stepped forward, about to call out his name.

But before I could, I heard someone say mine.

'Laurel? What are you doing here?'

It was Anna. Her face was flushed – I wondered fleetingly whether she too had been moved to tears by the music.

But it wasn't the concert she wanted to discuss with me.

'Do you realise what's happened to my daughter?' she demanded. 'If I hadn't agreed to let her meet you – if you hadn't given her the chance to go off with that boy – she'd still be safe. And now you're here. Like what you did with my husband wasn't enough. Like helping my daughter sneak around behind my back wasn't enough – now you're prying into Gray's past, aren't you? He's dead. Lulu's had her heart broken. Isn't that enough for you to finally leave my family alone?'

Out of the corner of my eye, I could see Joel Chamberlain getting into a taxi, apparently oblivious to Anna and me. But I couldn't think about him right now – Anna's fury was overwhelming, and my instinct was only to defend myself.

'What are you talking about?' I heard my own voice rising. 'I was only trying to help with Lulu. I told you when she didn't come and meet me, because I was worried about her. So you could keep her safe. And if you're so concerned about her, why aren't you with her now? You're here for the same reason I am, aren't you?'

I noticed curious eyes turning to watch us as the last of the concertgoers left the hall to make their way home. But Anna, who I imagined would normally be far more conscious of the disapproval of strangers than I was, didn't seem to care.

'You ruined my marriage,' she exploded. 'I can't even mourn my husband properly because of you. You took that away from me. And now – my daughter...'

No one slaps the faces of hysterical women any more, thank God. No one even uses that unscientific, misogynistic word. But if it had been fifty years ago, I had to admit I'd have been sorely tempted to do both.

Instead, I reached out my arms to her. 'Come on, Anna. Calm down. Why don't we have a drink, and you can tell me all about it?'

Then she fell into my arms, sobbing helplessly.

FORTY-FOUR
ANNA

Before I could protest, I found myself sitting at a Formica table in the kind of café where taxi drivers stop for a break during a night shift, a steaming cup of tea in front of me into which Laurel was heaping teaspoons of sugar.

'What's happened to Lulu?' she asked, tearing open a cellophane packet of mass-produced shortbread biscuits and putting one on my saucer. 'Is she hurt?'

I dug in my bag for a tissue, wiped my eyes and blew my nose, then took a sip of tea. It was over-stewed, over-sweet and surprisingly comforting. Across the table from me, Laurel's face was wary and concerned.

Is she going to throw her tea in my face? I imagined her thinking. Well, I wasn't going to do that; I'd embarrassed myself enough already for one night.

'She's okay,' I said coolly. 'She's at Orla's tonight. She sneaked off to see some boy.'

Laurel shook her head. 'That's not great, is it? I'm sorry – if I'd known that was likely to happen, I wouldn't have agreed to meet up with her when you weren't there. But she's okay, at least?'

Her concern disarmed me, and the desire to share what had

happened with another adult – another woman – was strong. I found myself saying, 'They had sex. Then he ghosted her.'

Laurel winced. 'Oh no. Poor Lulu. I suspected she was doing something she didn't want either of us to know about, but I – you know. Like you said just now, it's not really—'

'Your business?' I dunked my biscuit in the tea and took a soggy bite. 'No. It's not. But you're involved now, so you might as well know.'

'I thought it was okay to arrange to see her,' she fretted. 'I never expected her not to turn up. I can see why you—'

I shook my head. 'This isn't your fault. I'm sorry about how I behaved back there. I just...'

'Went off on one?' She smiled, and I felt a stab of the familiar jealousy – there was something about that smile, its warmth, its openness, its promise of fun, that reminded me afresh why Gray could have fallen in love with this woman. 'Hey, it's totally understandable. When you're worried about someone and you can't lash out at them, you lash out at whoever else is nearest. And it's not like I've done nothing to deserve being lashed out at.'

'I'm sorry, anyway,' I said.

Laurel sipped her tea, looking at me cautiously. 'Will Lulu – I mean, physically...? She'll be okay?'

'She's taken the morning-after pill, if that's what you mean. I suppose we'll have a conversation about STI checks when she's ready to talk about that.'

'Poor girl,' Laurel sighed. 'I mean, we've all been there, haven't we? But it must be so different when it's your daughter.'

'Oh God. When I was that age I was sneaking off to clubs with fake ID and getting up to all sorts.'

'It was underground raves for me.' Laurel flashed that smile at me again. 'I put myself in so many dodgy situations. My parents would've hit the roof if they'd known.'

'But they didn't know, did they? God, mobile phones have a lot to answer for.'

'It certainly makes it a lot harder for young people to do the stuff young people do,' she agreed.

'I just wanted to keep her safe.' I blew my nose again. 'That was always Gray's thing. He never wanted anything bad to happen to our kids. I didn't either, of course – I don't. But he was always the more protective of us. And now that he's gone...'

'It's all on you,' she said. 'I get that. It's a lot.'

'And with her father not being here,' I went on, 'I mean, an older boy – not that this Callum is any kind of father figure, the miserable shit – but she's so much more vulnerable. So much more likely to fall for whatever male attention she can get. I should've known that.'

'You're grieving too, Anna,' Laurel said gently. 'Don't be too hard on yourself. You can't be everywhere at once – physically or emotionally.'

'I wasn't there, though. Physically or emotionally. I was off in Wales, trying to find out about Gray.'

'You were?' Curiosity sparked in Laurel's eyes. 'Did you... I mean, is that why you were at the concert tonight?'

'I wanted to hear Joel Chamberlain play,' I explained. 'It turns out – I found out, when I was in Wales – that he was at school with Gray. An elite school for boys with a talent for music.'

'Really? They were at school together? So that's how...'

'How what?'

'How they met. I thought it might have been later, at university or something.'

'Wait.' A thought formed in my mind as I drank the last tepid dregs of my tea, avoiding the soggy biscuit crumbs in the bottom of the cup. 'How did you find out that Joel knew Gray? Gray didn't tell you, did he?'

She shook her head. 'He just mentioned his name. I tracked him down myself, because I wanted to meet the person Gray donated his kidney to. But you knew that already, of course.'

If I had wanted to pretend her revelation wasn't news to me, I would have failed. Her words hit me with such force that I felt my eyes widen and heard myself gasp. I had recognised Joel as the boy in the school photograph when I saw him on stage, but it had never crossed my mind that he and Gray could have had this other, even deeper connection.

'No. No, I didn't,' I said. 'I had no idea.'

'I...' She flushed, and went on hastily, 'I tried to find out. I was curious, because there was – you know. Some part of Gray that was still alive. Apart from your children, obviously. Gray never said much to me about it, only his name. And then I saw an interview with him in a magazine where it said he'd had a kidney transplant, and I realised I'd found him.'

Suddenly, I remembered the card – the twenty-fifth anniversary card that had arrived after Gray's death, signed with a J. That must have been the occasion it was marking. Not a woman; not a lover. A friend with a debt of gratitude.

'What did you find out, in Wales?' Laurel was asking.

My meeting with Bryn suddenly seemed like a long time ago. I tried to transport myself back to the sunny bench, the old man next to me, the voices of the choir still fresh and sweet in my memory.

'Gray was unhappy at school,' I said, sadness weighing heavy in my stomach. 'There was something about his home life – his mother. She was neglectful, troubled maybe. But she's dead now – she's been dead for years, since before I met him. So I'll never know what went on.'

'Joel would know, though,' Laurel said.

'Joel and Joel's mother.' I took my phone out of my bag. The number was still there in my list of contacts where I'd saved it. Seren Chamberlain, mother of the boy who had grown up to be a world-class violinist, whose best friend had been a gifted pianist, but left all of that behind him. Might she know why? Could she answer the questions I had about Gray, which seemed to be multiplying rather than reducing the more I found out?

And did I want to find out? It didn't matter whether I wanted to, I realised – I *needed* to.

'I'm going to talk to her,' I said. 'To Seren Chamberlain. I'm going to call her tomorrow.'

Laurel spoke as if she hadn't heard me, her fingers twisting her teaspoon where it rested on her saucer. 'I'm going to see Joel. At least, I'm going to message him and ask if he'll meet me. If he doesn't mind.'

Then she looked up, like she'd just remembered I was there. 'If you don't mind,' she added.

FORTY-FIVE
ORLA

28 *September 2024*

Anna asked me to babysit the children last night – if babysitting is even the word, given that Barney is barely a child any more and Lulu is practically an adult. She suggested I have them round at my place – a sort of double lock, I suppose: not only insurance that Lulu wouldn't be able to sneak off anywhere again, if indeed she was minded to do so, but also a form of punishment, because being minded by me is nowhere near as interesting a prospect as being at home alone or round at a friend's house.

For Barney, though, it didn't seem like much of a hardship at all. As soon as we'd eaten our takeaway pizzas, paid for by Anna, he asked if it was okay for him to play the piano, and I gladly agreed.

Must you? grumbled his sister, plugging her headphones into her ears. It'll be more cringe than Katy Perry singing Woman's World.

Mum's gone to see Joel Chamberlain at the Royal Albert Hall, Barney said. I'm proper salty about it. At least here I can have some music.

You might be pleasantly surprised, I told Lulu. Your brother's been working hard.

So Lulu took her headphones out. She and I and the cats sat together on the sofa and Barney began to play – hesitantly at first, because he's not used to having an audience, but then with growing confidence, even showing off a bit as he got to what I guessed was a particularly complex point in the piece, speeding up and then bursting into giggles as he hit a succession of wrong notes.

Hey, Lulu said. You're actually not shit.

I am quite shit, her brother countered modestly. But I'm getting better.

Lulu looked at him almost as if she was seeing him for the first time. Since when's this been a thing?

Barney explained that he has been coming round here a few times a week for the past few months to practise, since before his father's death, and looked at me slightly doubtfully as he told his sister that I hadn't minded – I'd encouraged it. I reassured him that I didn't mind at all.

Lulu said, Wow. You know, if you'd started when you were younger, you could've been, like, a prodigy or something. Like Mozart. Only not deaf.

That was Beethoven, Barney said. Don't you know anything?

Then I offered them some of the strawberry ice cream I have in the freezer, and they followed me eagerly to the kitchen. While we ate, a sudden connection leaped into my mind. Joel Chamberlain. The musician Anna had gone to see play; the man whose photograph I cut from Beatrice's magazine and sent to Laurel. The man who must have been the recipient of Gray's kidney donation all those years ago.

It was the taste of the ice cream that reminded me of it. When I'm ill, it's one of the few foods I can face. My grandmother always used to tempt me with it when I was a child, and I suppose the comfort it gives me is associated with that, rather than with any physical benefit.

When I'd been laid in bed with a cold, all those years ago, and the strange man came to knock at the door of number eight, only to be told by Gray never to come again, I'd eventually made my way downstairs and ice cream was the first thing I ate. That man – that stranger – was Joel Chamberlain.

I am as certain of it as I can be. What was he doing here, and why did Gray not want to reconnect with an old friend?

FORTY-SIX
LAUREL

I stepped through the glass doors into the hotel lobby, the red carpet soft beneath my feet. Two liveried doormen stood on either side of the entrance, politely welcoming expressions on their faces; I returned their smiles but didn't speak to them. I was feeling as out of place as I had arriving at the luxury country hotel where I'd spent Valentine's night with Gray – more so, because this time I wasn't sure of the welcome I'd receive from the person I'd come to meet.

I'd made my approach to Joel Chamberlain cautiously and formally, using the email address I had found online for his agent and explaining that I'd known Nigel Graham, a former school friend of Joel's, and would appreciate it if he could meet me to talk about him. I hadn't known what I'd do if my email was ignored or my request refused – but to my surprise I had woken to an email in response to mine, sent late the previous night.

Laurel,

My agent forwarded your message to me. I'd be glad to speak to you, but I am only in London until late morning tomorrow. Perhaps you could come to the hotel where I'm staying?

And he'd provided the address of this plushy, yet somehow generic, five-star hotel on Kensington High Street. It was the sort of place where well-heeled tourists might base themselves for a long weekend, or visitors from the Middle East planning a shopping spree at Harrods and Harvey Nichols.

It wasn't the sort of place that had a computerised check-in system, like the Premier Inn where Gray and I had spent that handful of nights. But that was just as well, because I wasn't checking in.

I approached the reception desk where more smiling, uniformed staff were greeting guests, and porters with trolleys were whisking vast suitcases off in the direction of the lifts.

'How may I help you, Madam?' asked a heavily made-up blonde woman.

I swallowed. 'I'm here to see someone who's staying here. Joel Chamberlain. My name's Laurel Norton.'

'One moment please.'

She lifted a telephone from its cradle, spoke briefly into it, then said, 'Please take a seat.'

I took one – a red velvet armchair next to a varnished wood table holding an arrangement of lilies and copies of that day's newspapers. The papers were too unspoiled and crisp for me to dare to pick one up, so I sat empty handed, my bag on my lap, watching the lift doors.

After a few minutes, Joel Chamberlain emerged. He was recognisable from the photo I'd seen in the magazine and recognisable as the musician who'd captivated me on stage at the Royal Albert Hall a few days before – but also not. The charisma that had illuminated him then was dimmed now – he was just a rangy, graceful man in jeans and a faded sweatshirt.

He approached the reception desk and said something to the blonde woman, who gestured. Then he turned and approached me, and I stood up, extending my hand to him.

'Thank you for meeting me,' I said. 'I know this is kind of

weird. I'm not a stalker, I promise. Although I saw you play the other night. It was wonderful.'

He looked down at me, his expression somewhere between curious and puzzled. 'Thank you. I'm delighted you enjoyed it.'

'I did. I... I've never heard anything like it before. I was only there because I hoped to talk to you about Nigel Graham.'

'Nigel.' He said the name slowly, as if he'd forgotten how to pronounce it and was remembering. 'Of course. Are you... Is he here?'

His eyes left my face, glancing involuntarily around.

'No,' I said. Then I added gently, 'He passed away four months ago. We were close. I wanted to find the person who he... To find you.'

The smile left his face, and he turned pale.

'We should sit down,' he said, and it looked to me as if he needed to sit. 'Would you like something? A coffee?'

The cadence of his voice was familiar, and I realised it was a stronger version of the accent that had been almost imperceptible in Gray's voice.

I shook my head. He led me through the lobby, away from the crowds to a sofa that faced away from the room, another glossy table holding newspapers in front of it. I sat down, and he joined me, close enough to touch.

'This is totally weird,' I said. 'I'm so sorry to accost you like this. You must think I'm—'

'Some kind of nutter?' He smiled, and I felt immediately more at ease. 'Maybe, at first, when I got your message. But you knew Nigel. It's been a long time. I'm sorry to hear he passed away. What happened?'

I told him. It had been long enough, now, that I could talk about Gray without crying, but I still heard my breath catch when I said that his cancer had not been treatable.

When Joel heard that, his face became still.

'I see,' he said. 'Because of what he did for me.'

I shook my head. 'It's not just that. Gray – Nigel – he told me that, before he met me, his health wasn't the best. He didn't look after himself. He was pre-diabetic. The damage that he did to his body wasn't just because he had only one kidney.'

'It can't have helped, though.'

'Well, perhaps not. But neither of you could have known.'

'Still. I'm alive now and he's not.' He spoke with a kind of hesitancy, as if he was learning a foreign language. 'If it wasn't for what he did, it would likely be the other way around.'

Gently, I asked, 'Are you able to tell me what led to it?'

He nodded. 'I have a condition called Fabry disease. It's—'

'Alpha-galactosidase A deficiency,' I said.

'Nigel told you?'

'No. He never really talked about it. But after – after his death, I wanted to find out more about... well, about you. I looked into it. I'm a nurse – I'm interested in stuff like that.'

'Then you know it presents with a range of symptoms. I'm receiving chaperone therapy now – I'm perfectly well. Treatment has advanced hugely. But twenty-five years ago, I wasn't. I was diagnosed relatively late, in my late teens. By the time I was in my third year at university my kidneys were failing. I thought it was a death sentence – that, or I'd need dialysis all my life.'

'Which wouldn't exactly have been compatible with being a professional musician,' I guessed.

'Exactly. Hospital visits three times a week and spending months on tour internationally kind of don't go well together. And that was what I always wanted. My dream.'

I could imagine it. Actually, I didn't need to, because I'd seen it far too often: footballers' careers shattered before they'd properly got started by injury. Young women on the cusp of starting families having their lives derailed by a cancer diagnosis. Little children surviving road accidents with life-changing injuries.

But that hadn't happened to Joel. Joel was right here, living his dream.

'And so Gray offered...?' I hazarded.

'He did. We'd lost touch, after we left school. He made it pretty clear that he wanted to put that part of his life behind him, and that meant putting me behind him too. It was – it hurt me. It came as a shock, because we had been the sort of friends you think you'll be forever. But at that time of life – leaving school, starting university – people move on and friendships change. So I accepted that.'

'But you didn't lose touch?'

He smiled, as if the memory brought him happiness. 'We both went to London for uni, and although it's a pretty big place, it wasn't vanishingly improbable that we'd run into each other. And we did – one morning on the Tube.'

'That's quite a coincidence. What happened?'

'It was – it was a dark time for me. Deafness is a symptom of Fabry disease, and I'd escaped that – I thought I was in the clear. Then I found out my kidneys were failing. I thought that would be it – thought there was no hope of me becoming a professional musician any more. So I played every chance I got. I used to busk, down in the Underground. Nigel was on his way somewhere and he recognised the sound of my fiddle.'

'So he came and spoke to you?' I tried to imagine what that must have been like for Joel – meeting an old friend, what should have been a happy coincidence soured by the news he had to break.

He nodded. 'We went for a coffee. I told him what was happening, and he made the offer to be a transplant donor, if we were compatible. Straight away.'

I smiled, thinking how like Gray that was. The impulsiveness, the generosity. Not thinking what consequences his actions might have.

'And you were compatible.'

'We were. Now that was vanishingly improbable, but it happened.' He looked down at his hands – the long, elegant fingers – as if realising how lucky he was to have them. 'I was grateful at the time, of course. But it all happened pretty fast. It's only really since then – every birthday, every Christmas, every time I step on stage – that I realise how much I owe him. And now I can never tell him.'

Oh, Gray. You knew, didn't you? Surely you knew what a wonderful, selfless thing you did?

'He must have known how you felt.' I could feel a lump building in my throat. 'Surely. He said… I remember him saying something about it being payment of a debt. For a while I thought that might mean – you know. Something negative. But it obviously wasn't.'

'It wasn't.' Joel met my eyes, and I saw the clear blue I remembered from the photograph, before he looked back down at his hands. 'It was the other kind of debt, I suppose. A debt of gratitude.'

'What did you – I mean, you must have done something absolutely amazing for him to have felt that way. To have literally saved your life.'

'It wasn't so much me. I was just there – just a mate, when I guess he really needed a friend. It was more my mother he was grateful to. My dad too, I guess. We were a kind of second family to him, and I think that meant far more than I realised at the time.'

'So what… I mean, Gray never talked to me about his family. Apart from' – I felt colour rush to my cheeks – 'his family here. His wife and his kids.'

He met my eyes again. 'How did you know him, Laurel? Not that it's any of my business. But you were close to him.'

I wanted to drop my eyes, but I didn't. His clear, deep blue gaze held me almost mesmerised. He'd been so honest with me; it was the least I could do to reciprocate.

'I met him quite randomly,' I said. 'Even more randomly than you busking, because we hadn't known each other before. I knew he was married, right from the beginning. But it was just…'

I shrugged helplessly.

Joel smiled. There was something in his smile I couldn't quite read – disappointment, maybe?

'The heart wants what it wants,' he said. 'Nigel was always charming. People loved him.'

'Yes.' Now I felt the tears I'd been holding back begin to flow. 'I loved him. I didn't mean for that to happen, but it did.'

He reached out and took my hand, sandwiching it between his two warm palms. 'I'm sorry. It must be hard to grieve in that situation.'

'I guess that was partly why I wanted to find you,' I said softly. 'Not that I knew who you were, but to find the person who Gray had done that thing for – made that sacrifice for. To know there was a part of him that's still here, and that it was worth it.'

Now he laughed – not a proper laugh, but a sad, almost bitter one. 'And was it?'

I said, 'Oh. Yes. I mean – hearing you play. Knowing that it's because of Gray that you can do that. I'm sure it would have been worth it to him, and it is for me too.'

'He was a good person,' Joel said. 'A damaged one, but good.'

I said, 'I know. I've always known that.'

When I got up to leave, he stood too. We reached out to shake hands, but then, making the decision at the exact same time, we took a step closer and extended our arms, moving into a close embrace.

It felt like it lasted a long time. I could feel his breath on my hair and the steady beating of his heart through our clothes. I almost expected to feel some sense of Gray in his body, as if Joel could spiritually channel him like Whoopi Goldberg in that scene from *Ghost*. But there was nothing of Gray there at all – only Joel.

Joel and me, together in a bland hotel lobby, holding each other like lovers before a long parting – or maybe like two people whose relationship was just beginning.

FORTY-SEVEN
ANNA

'And your son is a musician?' I asked Seren Chamberlain politely. 'I heard him play a few days ago. I was curious – and I was impressed.'

I took a sip of my cappuccino to settle my nerves.

'First violinist with the National Orchestra of Wales,' she told me proudly. 'He's overcome so many challenges to achieve what he has. I travel to see him perform whenever I can, and today seemed like the perfect opportunity to meet you too.'

'I do appreciate it.' I meant it – but still my tone was polite and stilted.

'And I'm very sorry for your loss, Anna.' Her formality matched mine, but I wondered whether she was remembering the boy she had known – Nigel.

'Thank you.'

We fell into an awkward silence, filled by the roar of the coffee machine behind us.

Seren leaned towards me and cleared her throat. 'Bryn – the former head teacher at St Gwbert's – told me you were interested in finding out more about your late husband's schooldays.'

'That's right. It feels as if – well, it's always felt like that's something he never shared much with me. Now that he's gone, I find myself wanting to know more. Particularly for our children, because they'll never be able to ask him about that part of his life now.'

I thought of the bequest Gray had asked to make to the charity he seemed to have no connection with, his affair with Laurel, the dire place our marriage had been in before his diagnosis. But that was too much information – there was no need to share any of it with this prim-looking woman, with her neat, tailored dress, her pot of tea and the beige hearing aids clearly visible behind her ears.

'He was a very gifted pianist, your Nigel,' she observed. 'But you must know that.'

'I didn't,' I said, more bitterly than I intended. 'Until recently, I had no idea... It was something he never talked about.'

She shook her head, pouring more tea into her cup. 'Such a shame. But understandable, I suppose. His home life was... well, it was troubled.'

'Can you tell me more about that? I know his father wasn't really around. That must have been hard for him.'

'Hard, perhaps, yes. Certainly it might have been easier if Nigel had had a father who was more present. Because it was his mother who... I don't like to say she was the problem.'

'But she *was* the problem?'

Seren finished her tea. 'I rather think, Anna, that I would like a glass of wine. Would you?'

'Yes.' Probably too eagerly, I stood up. 'I'll get them.'

I grabbed some tiny bottles of white from the café fridge, paid for them and returned to our table.

'Maybe you could start at the beginning,' I suggested, taking a sip and feeling it hit my bloodstream almost immediately.

I realised I hadn't eaten all day, but that didn't matter.

She sighed. 'I only knew Nigel when he was a boy. Joel had been accepted into St Gwbert's, and we were delighted – it wasn't just that it's a good school, although it is, it was because of the advantages it would give him when it came to his music. And we knew – he'd had some health problems. He wasn't a well child.'

Which is why he ended up needing a kidney transplant, I thought. But I didn't want to talk about Joel now – not least because I got the sense that, given half a chance, Seren Chamberlain would talk about nothing else for hours on end.

'Gray – Nigel's mum must have been proud too.'

'That was the funny thing,' she said. 'I never got the impression she was. Bryn mentioned once that his primary school headmistress had helped Nigel with the application and all Louisa Graham did was sign the forms.'

Louisa Graham – it was the first time she had mentioned Gray's mother's name. I leaned across the table, opening the second of my miniature bottles of wine. I felt as if I was getting closer, now, to what I'd come there to discover.

'She must have known he had a gift for music, though,' I said.

'I believe so.' Seren's eyes were distant, as if she was struggling to recall details of a time far in the past. 'I think Gray may have sung in the church choir as a child, long before I knew him. Louisa herself used to play an instrument – it may have been the flute. But that was before... Before I knew him.'

'Tell me about that?' I urged. 'About how you got to know him.'

'I remember the first time I met Nigel,' she went on. 'He came home after school with Joel. They would both have been thirteen at the time, and I offered them sandwiches. You know what boys are like at that age – bottomless pits for food. Nigel ate his sandwich, and then he looked at me, all hopeful, like Oliver Twist. But he didn't say anything. It was Joel who said, "Is there any more, Mum? Nigel only gets bananas in his packed lunch."'

No wonder he hated them, I thought, my heart twisting with sadness for the timid boy who was to become the confident man I fell in love with.

'You must have thought that was strange.'

'I certainly did. Joel explained afterwards that he'd been sharing his lunch with Nigel – it wasn't just that he was a bottomless pit. And then I noticed other things – his school uniform didn't fit properly. It was way too small, and it was none too clean, either. And he – well, there's no other way to put it. The boy was grubby.'

I thought of Barney, who was grubby too sometimes and had to be nagged to shower. No one had nagged Gray.

Now that Seren had started talking, she seemed to be finding it easier to carry on – the memories flowing almost too fast for her words to keep up. Perhaps the wine was helping.

'I started looking out for him after that, and Joel did too. I'd send in extra food. I passed Joel's old uniform on to Nigel – Joel was taller and growing faster. I told Joel Nigel was welcome to come over to ours after school whenever he wanted. But that wasn't always possible, because he said his mother needed him.'

Feeling as if a piece of a puzzle was falling into place, I asked, 'So his mother was ill?'

'That's what I assumed at first. I tried asking Nigel about it, but you've got to be careful, you know, with boys that age. They don't always understand, or parents try to shield them from things, or they get embarrassed. He wouldn't open up to me about what was going on at home. They didn't live very close to us – their house was in Merthyr Adwen, a village about twelve miles from the school. Nigel was meant to get the bus in, but sometimes he missed it and then he'd be late because he walked to school. And sometimes he didn't make it in at all. If I asked what happened, he'd just say, "I had to be with Mam." So I decided to make some enquiries. It's a small community, you know – people talk.'

'And what did people say?'

'I felt grubby myself, listening to gossip.' She took a sip of wine and gave a little shudder. 'I tried to find out whether she was receiving treatment at the hospital for something. But she wasn't. People would say, "Ah, Louisa Graham." And they'd look at you funny, or they'd laugh. There was a stigma, even then.'

'So it was...' I guessed. 'It was mental illness, rather than something physical?'

She sighed, a sound full of regret and self-reproach. 'I can see that now. But at the time, people just thought she was a bit of an odd one. She'd have arguments with strangers in shops. She'd be in the pub until closing time on her own. Someone said they saw her in the GP surgery with Nigel the once, with cuts all over her face. Sometimes she wouldn't leave the house for weeks at a time. And other times...'

I waited, my hands clenched tightly between my thighs.

'Other times she would go out. And some of those times' – she lowered her voice – 'she'd bring men home, after she'd been to the pub. Not always nice men, but never the same one twice. Like I said, people talked.'

I tried to imagine how Barney would feel if people talked about me like that, but I couldn't.

'And with Nigel...' she went on. 'You have to remember, this went on for six years. It was a long time I had to observe what was going on, to see how things changed. I found out details gradually, a few words here, a bit of information there. From Nigel, from Joel, from other people. She was erratic. She'd neglect him and then she'd smother him with love. She'd keep him off school because she said she wasn't well and needed him, and then she'd leave him alone while she went off with some fellow. I suppose he never knew what to expect from one day to the next.'

'Thank goodness he had you,' I said.

'And Joel,' she reminded me, that note of pride in her voice again. 'We did what we could. I even suggested Nigel speak to someone – a counsellor or his head of year at school. But he wouldn't. He was fiercely protective of her. I even found a charity – Merthyr Adwen Young Carers – and I put him in touch with them.'

'Merthyr Adwen Young Carers?' I repeated. 'MAYC?'

'That's right. I believe they tried to help, but Louisa Graham didn't want a respite carer – she wanted Nigel.'

Not YMCA. MAYC. The charity Gray had wanted to make a donation to.

'And he was growing up,' I said.

'He was. And that was when matters came to a head, I

suppose. They were doing A-levels, him and Joel. They were applying for colleges and all that. And one night Nigel came round to our house, late. He asked if he could stay, and I said of course he could. He wouldn't tell me what was happening, but he told Joel. She'd thrown him out.'

'What? Why?'

'Because he wanted to go away to university, off to London. Same as Joel was. She'd said, "If you do that, don't ever bother coming back."'

'So he went,' I said slowly. 'And then she died.'

'Oh, no.' Seren looked at me in surprise. 'She didn't die. She's still alive. I see her every Sunday at chapel. She's quite well now.'

FORTY-EIGHT
LAUREL

Joel and I said goodbye, with a promise to stay in touch and possibly meet the next time he was in London. But, instead of making my own way home, I found myself heading in the direction of Damask Square.

Although I was uncertain of the reception I'd get there, I felt the need to share what I'd learned with Anna. Gray had been hers long before I had known him. What Joel had told me was important for her to know and to share with her children, to help them understand their father better in the same way I now did.

If my dad had done something like that for a friend, how would I feel, I wondered. Pretty damn proud. But then, if it had contributed to his early death, pretty damn shit also. It was for Anna to decide how much she wanted to tell Lulu and Barney – if anything at all – and when.

For now, I'd tell her what I knew.

But when I tapped hesitantly on the door, it wasn't Anna who opened it, but Lulu.

She blushed absolutely scarlet when she saw me. 'Hi, Laurel.'

'Hey, Lulu. How's it going?'

'I've been meaning to text you, but I didn't know what to say. I feel really bad about not showing up when I said I would. I was...'

Now wasn't the time to let her know her mother had already told me why she hadn't turned up.

'That's okay,' I reassured her. 'Please don't worry about it. We can do it another time. Is your mum around?'

She shook her head. 'She's out. But she said she'd be back this afternoon. Why don't you come in? I made a cherry cake. It's a bit flat but it tastes good.'

I realised I hadn't had lunch. 'That would be amazing. If you don't mind?'

By way of an answer, she turned and led the way downstairs. The familiar kitchen was less tidy than usual – two empty wine bottles stood on the floor by the island, the sink was full of cloudy water and crumbs scattered the worktop. But the air was sweet with the fragrance of baking.

Lulu flicked the coffee machine on and set about making cappuccinos, cutting two slabs of cake and putting them on plates.

'So, like I said,' she mumbled a few minutes later, her mouth full, 'I feel really bad. I messed up. I feel like I owe you an explanation.'

'You don't,' I said, 'but I'm happy for you to tell me, if you want.'

She nodded. 'I was seeing this guy. Callum. Kind of behind Mum's back. Well, totally behind Mum's back, if I'm honest.'

'Would she not want you to have boyfriends?' I asked.

Lulu grimaced. 'Not ones like Callum. He's a bit older than me and he's... well, he's not the kind of person I usually hang out with. Mum wouldn't like him. Dad wouldn't have, either.'

'But you did?'

She pushed cake crumbs around her plate with a fingertip. 'I don't even know if I did. He paid attention to me. He seemed like he liked me, and I guess I felt like I needed to be liked.'

'I get that,' I said. 'After all, how are you to know who the right person for you is if you don't try some wrong ones first?'

She laughed. 'He was wrong. I get that. But he's... I don't know. I still check my phone the whole time in case it's him. He blocked me, you see. After the night I was meant to be seeing you, when we...'

'Oh no.' Hearing the story from Anna had shocked me, but hearing it from Lulu was heartbreaking. 'You poor thing. What a bastard. You don't deserve to be treated like that, you know. You're worth so much more.'

'I know that, really. But I...' The she fell silent, her head on one side and her eyes wide. 'Fuck. Laurel. I think that's his car.'

'What?' Through the windows at the front of the house, I could hear the roar of a dysfunctional engine and the squeal of tyres. *Of course he drives like a dick if he treats women like one*, I thought.

Lulu's face was frozen. Together, we listened to the thump of a car door closing and, seconds later, the crash of the door knocker.

'I can't open it,' she said. 'I can't see him.'

'He doesn't know we're here. We could just hide and hope he goes away. Or I could answer the door.'

'Will you?'

I grinned. 'You bet I will.'

Leaving Lulu immobile on her stool at the kitchen counter, I hurried upstairs and flung open the front door. A boy stood there – maybe twenty years old, shaven-headed, his jaw pitted with acne scars. He was wearing low-slung jeans and a grey hoodie, and he had the kind of swagger I'd seen all too often in Accident & Emergency on Saturday nights.

I gave him a hard stare. 'Can I help you?'

'I'm looking for Lulu.' His tone was belligerent. 'You her mum?'

I said, 'No. And if you're Callum, I don't think she wants to see you.'

'She can tell me that herself, can't she?'

'She's got better things to do with her time than talk to you,' I told him coldly.

Then I heard the sound of Lulu's trainers on the stairs behind me.

'Actually' – she appeared behind me, slightly out of breath, and I stepped aside – 'I don't have anything better to do right now.'

What? I thought. *Don't weaken now, girl.*

But Lulu said, 'Laurel's right. I don't want to see you, Callum. Not today or any other day.'

'That's not what you said the other night,' he sneered.

'Well, I'm saying it now. You're a horrible person. You treated me like shit, and I deserve better. You might have unblocked me but I'm blocking you, and you're staying blocked. And your car's leaking oil all over the road, so I suggest you move it before I get it clamped.'

'I...' Callum began. Lulu and I stared at him in silence. Then he said, 'Fine. Your loss.'

He turned and strutted back to his car, but slipped on some fallen leaves and would have fallen if he hadn't clutched the wing mirror. Then he slammed into the driver's seat and pulled away with a squeal of tyres which I hoped wasn't loud enough to drown out the sound of Lulu's and my laughter.

I was trembling slightly from adrenaline, but giddy with triumph – not because I'd stood up to some pathetic wannabe roadman, but because I'd stood up for Lulu.

'God,' she said, 'what was I thinking? What a loser.'

'I mean, I don't like to say it,' I said. 'I'm sure he has good qualities. But he does look like a gerbil.'

We were still giggling when Anna arrived home twenty minutes later. She looked at us with curiosity but – I was relieved to notice – without actual hostility.

Lulu didn't hang around long, though. It was like the strange closeness that had sprung up between her and me embarrassed her, because she waited until her mother had eaten a piece of cake and praised it, then drifted off upstairs to her room, saying, 'Thanks, Laurel. Good chat. See you.'

'What are you doing here?' Anna asked, once the sound of her daughter's footsteps had receded.

'I came to see you. You weren't here, so Lulu let me in.' I

debated filling Anna in on our encounter with Callum, but decided against it – it was up to Lulu whether to tell her mother. 'We were just chatting.'

'What were you chatting about?' Almost automatically, Anna went to the fridge, opened a bottle of white wine and splashed it into two glasses. I hadn't planned on drinking, but there seemed no way to refuse. The cold rims of our glasses brushed against each other.

'Nothing much,' I said. 'I was just waiting for you to get back. How are you doing?'

'I don't know if you heard' – her voice was full of weary sarcasm – 'but my husband had an affair, and then he was diagnosed with cancer and died. My daughter's been shagging some creep with a souped-up Vauxhall Corsa, and my son appears to have forgotten I exist. Today I found out that my late husband's mother, who he told me had been dead twenty-seven years, isn't. Apart from that, brilliant.'

The news I had been about to break to her about Joel felt almost insignificant in comparison to that. But even if I'd wanted to interrupt her to share it, I couldn't have, because she carried on speaking as if I wasn't there.

'I thought,' she said, 'before Gray died, there was a change he wanted to make to his will. I thought it was something to do with you. I thought he was leaving you money, some cash to go with those rocks you were wearing in your ears the other night.'

'What?' My fingers moved involuntarily to brush one of my earlobes, although the crystal earrings were safe in their box at home. 'They're... I mean, they're pretty. They were a gift from Gray – that's the only reason they're valuable. And if he'd left me money I'd have—'

'Those are one-carat D flawless diamonds, Laurel,' she said. 'They're worth over four grand.'

'What?' My finger sprung away from my earlobe as if it was red hot. 'He – Gray never said.'

Anna's face crumpled. 'Well, mind you don't keep them gathering dust in their box now you know. He wouldn't have wanted that.'

That was exactly what I'd been thinking I would do. But I said, 'I won't. But you were saying – about his will.'

'Yes. He wanted to make a bequest to a charity, it turned out, not to you. To something called the MAYC. I thought it was the YMCA at first, but it's not. I just found out now – Seren Chamberlain told me. It's a charity based in Wales for young carers.'

'But Gray wasn't... was he?'

'His mother had a personality disorder. His childhood was awful. Seren told me all about it. Apparently his mother – Louisa – has undergone treatment and recovered well. But I can't... I'm still trying to process it all.'

'I understand,' I said. 'That's why I wanted to find out who Joel was. Or at least, find out who the friend who Gray had donated a kidney to was. I didn't know it was Joel then. And I'm still trying to process that.'

'Well, look at us,' Anna said mockingly. 'Nancy Drew One and Two. And how do you feel now that your investigation has concluded?'

'I don't know. I suppose I would have understood it better if I'd come at it from the other end, like you did. By finding out more about Gray's relationship with Joel. Because as far as I could tell it was just a way for him to – I don't know. Finally remove the last thing tying him to his past. Joel described it as a debt of gratitude.'

Anna nodded, then gestured to me with her empty glass. 'Another?'

'I'm all right, thanks.'

She poured wine into her own glass, carrying on the thread of our conversation as if it hadn't been broken.

'A debt of gratitude. That makes sense. They – Joel and Seren, and I suppose Joel's father, although he died a couple of years ago, she says – were like a second family to Gray when he was at school. Or like a first family, because his mother was never really there.'

'Because of her mental illness?'

Anna nodded, then briefly explained what Seren had told her about Gray's relationship with his mother: the erratic, dangerous behaviour; the self-harm with alcohol, prescription drugs and sharp objects; the men she'd bring home late at night. And the way she had behaved to Gray, veering unpredictably from cold anger to suffocating love.

'No wonder he wanted to get away from that,' I said when she had finished, my throat constricting so it was hard to get the words out.

'And no wonder he felt grateful to Joel. I used to think... Gray had a self-destructive streak too, you know. He never took care of his health until quite recently. Until it was too late, I suppose.'

'Did he know his mother was still alive?' I asked.

Anna looked down at her glass for a long time. 'He did. Joel came to see him, years ago, when he was visiting London. Seren told me. It was just after Lulu was born. Louisa had... She'd tried to take her own life, and that was when she finally got help.'

'And Joel told Gray this?'

She nodded. 'Gray said he wasn't interested. He said he couldn't risk our children being damaged by her the way he was. He said she'd told him she never wanted to see him again and that was what was going to happen.'

I was silenced, shocked that Gray could have been capable of such cruelty – but at the same time, understanding the deep trauma that lay behind his decision.

'Perhaps she hoped he would change his mind eventually,' I said at last.

'Maybe. But now... I don't know whether I should contact her. She's the children's grandmother, after all. I don't know what Gray would have wanted.'

'He would have wanted you and the children to be happy,' I said.

'I know. But I don't see how we ever can be.'

Anna put her face in her hands and started to cry. After hesitating only a moment, I put my arms around her and held her close.

FORTY-NINE
ANNA

Gray was alive. I saw him in the garden, the low autumn sun shining behind him so that at first I wasn't sure it was really him. But, from the upstairs window, I could clearly see a figure below me, sweeping the ground. I could hear the swish of the broom over the flagstones and the rustle of the leaves as they piled up against the base of the silver birch tree.

There was another sound too – music. I could hear it only faintly, and when I tried to open the window to be sure I found that the sash was stuck. Frustrated, I turned and hurried downstairs. But when I reached the kitchen, it was chaos – unwashed glasses and leftover food everywhere, the aftermath of a party.

I'd have to clear up before I could go outside. I began gathering up plates and glasses, but realised that there was no dishwasher where it should have been, nor any sink. I was going to have to stack everything in a washing-up bowl and carry it upstairs to do in the bath, the way I had for months during the house renovations, when we'd had no kitchen.

Why had we thrown a party in a building site? It seemed we had. Perhaps our guests were still there, outside, and that was why music was playing.

I could hear it more clearly now: the notes of a piano drifting in like feathers carried by a breeze. And there *were* feathers too – thousands of them, as if it was snowing indoors. Augustus must have caught a bird. I would have to find its body and clear that away too, in case one of the children saw it, before I could trace the source of the music.

But the call of the sound was too strong. Abandoning the messy kitchen, I pushed open the glass doors leading to the garden (how were they there, when they had been installed after the rest of the kitchen?) and stepped outside.

Somehow, it was no longer autumn but full summer. The climbing roses Gray had planted along the fence were in full bloom – perhaps it was their petals I had seen drifting in the air, and not feathers after all? But I didn't look at them, because there, in the centre of the garden where the birch tree should have been, was a grand piano.

The sun glinted off its polished top, making it almost too bright to look at, as if it was topped by a mirror instead of a piece of mahogany. But, despite the glare, I could see Gray sitting there, smiling, his hands floating over the keys, the music everywhere.

I sat next to him on the stool. I could smell his cologne – violet and sandalwood – and feel the warmth of his body next to mine.

'I've forgotten how to play,' he said. 'I'm out of practice.'

I said, 'Let me help.'

I reached my hands out and placed my fingers on the keys. I didn't know how to play – I'd never got past 'Chopsticks' as a child. But now the notes came easily from under my hands, my fingers moving in sequence like ballerinas on stage. I played faster and faster, but I couldn't keep up with the tune alone until Gray's hands joined mine, his fingers slotting into the spaces between my own.

The music surged, louder and louder, faster and faster. We couldn't sustain this pace – the notes were becoming discordant and jumbled.

'We'll wake the children,' Gray said, and I remembered him

saying that once before, when we'd had sex out in the garden on a summer night after too much champagne.

I said, 'They're fast asleep. It's after midnight.'

But our rhythm was broken now.

'Stop,' I said. 'This isn't working.'

Gray didn't stop, even though I asked him to over and over, struggling to hear my own voice above the crashing chords. Somehow he was still playing even though I could feel his hand on my shoulder, shaking me almost roughly.

'Mum.' I heard Barney's voice; we'd woken the children after all. 'Mum? Are you all right?'

Now I could recognise the tune we had been playing – it was the alarm going off on my phone. The piano stool became the sofa in the front room – the ground floor space that we seldom used. Why was I there? I must have fallen asleep there after Laurel had left.

I opened my eyes and my hangover hit me like a brick.

'You were having a nightmare,' Barney said.

He was squatting down next to me, his face full of confusion and concern.

With difficulty, I sat up. I was fully dressed except for my shoes, which I must have kicked off before I fell asleep. I must have set an alarm too, but I had no idea why.

'What time is it?'

'It's six o'clock. It's nearly dinnertime.' Barney's tone was almost accusatory. 'You were saying, "Stop, stop." Was someone hurting you in your dream?'

'No.' I wiped my face with my hand. I'd been drooling – how, when my mouth was as dry as sawdust? 'I was having a dream about Dad. He was still alive.'

'I have that dream too,' he said. 'Lulu does as well.'

'I suppose it's a thing.'

'Mum. You don't usually sleep on the sofa. Were you...?'

'I'd had too much to drink, when Laurel was here earlier.' And more after she left. In fact, come to think of it, I'd been drinking solidly since meeting Seren that morning. 'I'm sorry.'

'Would you like a cup of tea?'

'That would be lovely. Thank you, darling.' Then my memory began to snap into focus, and I asked urgently, 'Is Lulu here?'

He was already halfway down the stairs. 'She's been in her room all afternoon. She's watching YouTube videos about nurse training. I'm keeping out of her way in case she tries to practise first aid on me.'

Thank God for that. Perhaps only Barney would realise the state I was in.

I struggled to my feet and made it to the ground floor loo, where to my relief I didn't throw up.

Then I went downstairs to find Barney. The kitchen was tidy – a surprise, because the shadow of my dream was still hanging over me. There were a few crumbs of food in Augustus's bowl. Barney was fishing a teabag out of a mug.

'You're an angel,' I told him. 'You cleaned the kitchen and everything. Thank you.'

'That's all right.' But his face was wary, and he couldn't quite meet my eyes.

I sat down and he brought me my tea. It was stewed dark, with just a splash of milk, exactly the way I liked it.

'Barney,' I said. 'About all this – this afternoon. You seeing me like that – I'm sorry.'

'That's okay,' he muttered. Then he added, 'You know what Dad said, before he – you know.'

'What was that?'

'He said, "Take care of your mum." And me and Lulu promised.'

Jesus. I felt my face burn with shame. At the time, I hadn't understood what lay behind Gray's words, but now I did. Now I knew, because of what Seren Chamberlain had told me, what taking care of his mum had meant to Gray.

Those years of looking after the person who should have

looked after him. The chaos, the uncertainty. And I knew what it had led to: the decision to leave it all behind – to erase his childhood entirely. To reject his mother completely, even after she had tried to take her own life.

If I carried on like this, I'd be doing that to Barney. I'd be replaying the teenage years his father had endured. And I'd be risking my son – my precious boy – hating me and leaving me behind forever like Gray had left Louisa.

And I mustn't – I couldn't. This would have to change. I would have to change.

But first, there was something I needed to do to chase away the last of Gray's demons.

FIFTY
LAUREL

I looked around my flat with satisfaction. It was no larger or more luxurious than it had been when I moved in, but it looked and felt like home – it *was* home. I'd printed and framed a selfie of me and Gray and put it by my bed. On my tiny dining table was a vase of bronze-and-gold chrysanthemums. The smell of roasting chicken made my mouth water, same as it used to when my mum cooked Sunday lunch, and there was champagne chilling in the fridge.

The doorbell chimed, and I opened it, expecting only one person but seeing two.

'We were on the same train,' Mel said, 'so we walked over together. How nice is this?'

'Aren't we punctual?' Harry handed over a bottle of wine, and Mel presented me with a box of chocolates. 'We had to be. We knew if we were late, dinner would be cremated instead of just burned.'

'Stop it!' I scolded. 'I'll have you know I can follow a Delia Smith recipe as well as millions of other people. I'd offer you the grand tour, but it'll only take about ninety seconds.'

'Given we've waited months for it, it'll be worth it,' he said.

I showed them around and they exclaimed over everything – how lovely the view of lights and a bit of pond from my balcony was, how clean my bathroom was, how lucky I was to have storage space for a hoover and even an ironing board.

'Not that I actually own an ironing board,' I said. 'I haven't ironed anything for about twenty years.'

'But you certainly hoover,' Mel said. 'It's all spotless.'

'Clearly Laurel's got a secret wife she's not told us about,' Harry teased, 'who's done all of the actual work.'

I opened a bottle of wine, and the three of us squeezed on to the sofa together, eating crisps and exchanging hospital gossip.

Then Mel put her hand on my knee and said, 'Sorry you could only get the B-list, Laurel.'

'Speak for yourself.' Harry did his best outraged face. 'I'm pure A-list, right up there with Lady Gaga.'

I laughed. 'There's no one I'd rather have as my first guests than you two. Honest.'

I expected it to feel like a lie, but I realised it didn't. All these months, I'd put off inviting people round because they couldn't be Gray, and it was Gray who I'd wanted to show around my new home most of all. I'd imagined cooking for him, waking up in the morning and seeing his face on the pillow next to mine, him bringing a razor and a toothbrush to keep in my bathroom.

That would never happen now. But I found myself wondering, as I got up to check on the potatoes, whether it ever would have done. I imagined him checking his watch, saying, 'Pumpkin o'clock, darling,' putting on his clothes and leaving. And if he had ever left Anna, how would he have fitted in here, in my humble little flat, after the spacious luxury of Damask Square? No matter how hard I tried, I couldn't picture it.

The realisation left with me a hollow sense of sadness, like abandoning a long-held dream. But I also felt relieved, because I'd never again have to experience the guilt I'd suffered over what we were doing, the knowledge that by being with me, he was betraying and lying to someone else.

Now, as the initial grief and shock of his death waned, I could more clearly see Gray as he really had been, not just as the man I'd fallen in love with. A complex man, damaged by his past and never fully healed. A man who felt like, having been robbed of a happy childhood, he was entitled to take his happiness where he could find it.

But, thanks to Joel, there was another side of him I had seen. The Gray who had made a huge sacrifice, literally giving away a part of his body, out of gratitude and loyalty. The Gray who had turned his back on his unhappy past and courageously forged a new future – even a new identity – for himself. The forlorn, unhappy, unkempt child who had become a man surrounded by all the riches of love.

'Those spuds aren't going to get any crisper if you stand there staring at them, you know,' Harry said.

Mel appeared at my shoulder. 'They look beautifully crisp to me. Want me to carve the chicken?'

I looked at the bird in its roasting tin, its golden skin freckled with pepper and herbs, and realised I hadn't got that far in Delia's instructions.

'Please,' I said. 'They didn't cover chicken anatomy at nurse school.'

'But they did at basic-life-skills school,' Mel teased. 'Guess you were off sick that day.'

I laughed. 'Still, that beats sustaining-a-healthy-relationship school, which I never enrolled for.'

'Me neither,' sighed Harry. 'Looks like I'm destined to be stuck on the apps forever.'

'There are worse things than being single,' Mel said. 'And anyway, we do have healthy relationships. We just have them with each other.'

While Mel set about dismembering the chicken, I made the gravy, adding flour then white wine to the juices in the roasting tin, stirring furiously until it all thickened and looked reasonably lump-free. Then I poured it out into a jug and put a pan of water on to boil for the broccoli.

'You've got all quiet, Laurel,' Harry remarked.

'I'm just concentrating,' I said defensively.

Mel looked at me over the chicken. 'No you're not. You're thinking about something. Maybe about someone. As soon as we started talking about relationships, you went all quiet. Got something you need to share with the group?'

'Give the woman a break,' Harry protested. 'She's still grieving, poor love.'

'Is that it, Laurel?' Mel put down the knife and laid a hand on my arm. 'Are you feeling sad?'

Her words made tears prick my eyes. I *was* sad – there was no denying that. I'd be sad about Gray for a long time, because I'd loved him, and he had died. But there was something else as well – something I had to admit to myself about my relationship with him, even if I couldn't ever admit it to my friends.

It should never have happened. It had been bad for me and bad for Anna. For all the happiness it had brought me at the time, there had been an equal weight of guilt that tarnished all the memories I had of him. The only person who had really benefitted from it was Gray.

'I am a bit sad.' I pulled off a piece of kitchen roll and blew my nose. 'I guess I feel like I wasted a load of time – over a year – with Gray. He wasn't a bad person, but it shouldn't have happened. If he hadn't died…'

'Do you think he'd have left her?' Mel asked.

I shook my head. 'I wouldn't have wanted him to, even if he'd said he was going to. And if she'd found out – well, she did find out, because he told her, but you know what I mean – and she'd kicked him out and he'd moved in with me, it wouldn't have worked.'

'Because he'd have moved on to someone else?' Harry said, and Mel glared at him. 'Sorry. But I've shagged a few married guys in my time, and I know how it goes.'

'Maybe he would,' I said. 'Maybe he wouldn't. But I don't think I could have ever been happy. Not because I wouldn't have trusted him – I can't know that. But breaking up a family, being the other woman – it's horrible. I mean, it didn't even come to that, and still I'm not proud of what I did.'

'You weren't the one cheating though,' Mel pointed out. 'He was. If it hadn't been you, it would've...'

She stopped herself, so I finished for her. 'Been someone else. Probably.'

Harry said, 'I don't want to lower the tone, but if you don't get that broccoli drained, it'll be like my nan's Christmas sprouts.'

'What? Right. Thanks.' I upended the pan into the colander and added, 'I think we're ready to eat.'

After we'd finished the food, the wine and Mel's chocolates, we slumped on the sofa and soon all began to yawn, and then Mel and Harry said they'd better get moving if they weren't going to miss the last train. It was only after they'd left that I allowed my thoughts to return to Gray – although not entirely to Gray.

I took out my phone and looked at the series of text messages I'd been exchanging over the past few days. They were friendly – nothing more. But reading them again made me smile, especially the last one I'd received, which had been signed off with a kiss.

My reply had been typed several hours before, but not sent. I read it again. It was only a few words – inconsequential words, but they might change everything for me.

So tell me more about cycling on the Taff Trail?

I pressed Send.

Then I lifted the framed photograph up off its place by my bed and stared at it for a long time. That familiar, smiling face – the face I'd seen sparkling with laughter, contorted with sexual pleasure and, ultimately, still in death.

'I loved you, Gray,' I told him.

Then I opened the bedside table drawer, slid the frame inside and closed it again.

FIFTY-ONE
ANNA

The little bus laboured up the hill. So far on the fifteen-minute journey it had made several ascents, but this was the steepest yet. I turned to look out of the window, hoping to see green valleys falling away beneath me, but everything was blanketed in grey mist, visibility reduced to just a few feet so all I could see was the edge of the road and a bit of stone wall with a few blurry shapes beyond it that might or might not have been sheep.

But my phone told me I was nearing my destination and, sure enough, after a final effort the bus jolted to a stop and the driver's voice crackled over the tannoy, 'Merthyr Adwen.'

I'd arrived at my destination – the place where Gray grew up. I wondered how its name might have sounded in his voice – whether the Welsh accent he'd almost totally erased would have re-emerged, and he'd have sounded like the bus driver.

Hoisting my bag over my shoulder, and not forgetting my umbrella, I got out. Wind immediately whipped rain against my face, flattening my jeans against my legs and making me realise that the umbrella would be worse than useless. My hands already turning numb from the cold, I huddled under the bus shelter and checked the map on my phone.

If Gray had been with me, we wouldn't have needed a map. He

would have known the route from memory, perhaps taking my hand and leading me onwards, our arms swinging in unison. He'd have said, 'Come on, slow coach – let's get out of this pissing rain.'

How I wished he was there with me. I felt an almost physical yearning for him: his vitality, his laughter, the warmth of his hand in mine. But if he was alive, I wouldn't be here. It was only his death that had led me to this place, and now I must do what I had to do alone.

Over the sound of the rain hammering on the roof of the bus shelter, I could almost hear his voice. Not the Welsh-accented one I'd speculated about, but his usual, familiar tone: the voice I'd heard almost every day of my life for more than twenty years.

It's okay, Anna. You've got this.

Without hesitating any longer, I stepped out into the rain.

It was only a five-minute walk, but my waterproof jacket was already streaming with moisture by the time I reached the row of modest red-brick houses. There were about a dozen of them, with small, bare gardens in front of them. I could see Christmas lights sparkling in a few of the windows; the curtains were drawn over others, although it had only just begun to get dark. I could hear the yapping of a small dog, a baby crying – and music.

The music surprised me, in this humble, rather forlorn place. It was the notes of a flute, drifting clearly into the thick twilight like a promise of brightness and hope. I followed the sound, and it led me to one of the doors – number seven. I raised a cold hand and pressed the doorbell.

The music stopped immediately, and a few moments later the door opened.

A woman stood there, smiling tentatively. She was about twenty-five years older than me, dressed in leggings and a knitted jumper with a reindeer's face on the front. Her grey hair hung in a plait over one shoulder. Her eyes were the rich brown of espresso coffee.

'Louisa.' I said the name that was also my daughter's.

'Anna.' The smile remained cautious. 'Please, come in.'

The door opened directly into the front room, a small space, but tidy and warm. There was a sofa, a dining table with two chairs, a television and a music stand, the silver flute lying on top of it, incongruously beautiful.

'Would you like a cup of tea?' she asked. 'You must be cold.'

'Thank you.'

She gestured to the sofa, and I took off my coat and sat down, hearing the hum of a kettle and the clink of china from the nearby kitchen.

I tried to imagine Gray living in this house, but failed.

Louisa returned a few minutes later, a mug in each hand. She put them down on the table then hurried out again, coming back with a pint bottle of milk and a sugar bowl. I said yes, please to milk and no, thank you to sugar, and she handed one of the mugs to me.

'Thank you for coming,' she said. 'It's a long way.'

I shrugged. 'Thank you for having me.'

Then we both said together, 'I'm sorry for your loss,' and smiled in unison, the tension seeming to lift a little.

'It's supposed to be the worst thing in the world, losing a child.' Louisa's accent was hard to identify – not the lilting Welsh I'd heard since getting off the train, but something else that could have placed her almost anywhere. 'But really, I lost him years ago.'

I nodded, willing her to go on.

Her shoulders seemed to slacken with something like relief. She looked down at the surface of her tea but didn't drink any of it, and then she began.

'I was a terrible mother. I can see that now, but at the time... I was a mess. I was ill, but I didn't know it then. I thought the world was against me. I was alone, after Dylan left. Nigel was all I had, and I needed him, but at the same time I pushed him away.'

'I know,' I said. 'It wasn't your fault.'

As tactfully as I could, I explained what Seren Chamberlain had told me, leaving out the bit about bringing dodgy men home from the pub.

'I can remember very little of it now,' Louisa told me. 'After

Nigel left – after I cut contact with him – I had a breakdown. It was after that that I was diagnosed with borderline personality disorder, although my therapist prefers to call it emotionally unstable personality disorder... I was lucky – I got help. It took a while, but I did. In the past I'd probably have been locked up in some asylum.'

'But you're – you've recovered now?'

'As much as anyone with this condition can be said to have,' she replied sadly. 'I still have therapy – talking therapies, cognitive behavioural therapy, the lot. It helps. Music helps, and walking in the hills. But not medication. If it did, I'd rattle when I walked.'

'I'm glad,' I told her. 'I'm glad you're well, and here. But you never saw Gray – Nigel – again?'

She shook her head.

'He did think of you, you know. Our daughter is named after you. We call her Lulu.'

Louisa put down her empty mug and brushed away a tear. 'I'm glad of that. After what happened, I thought he would never want to have anything to do with me again. But it turned out that wasn't the case.'

I felt a jolt of shock. 'Really?'

She reached over to the table again and took up a large brown envelope. It was the kind that lawyers use, with a gusset and a loop of string to hold the flap closed, and I could see that it was full to bulging point.

'He wrote to me,' she said. 'For twenty years, he wrote a card on my birthday, and on his birthday and at Christmas. He wrote when he met you, and when you got married and when your children were born. He didn't want to see me, but he was thinking of me, all this time.'

'That must have been...' I began, but I couldn't frame the words for how it would have made Louisa feel.

'I tried, you know,' she said. 'I tried to get in touch with him. Or Seren Chamberlain did. It was after your Louisa was born, after I... I'd been in hospital. We thought then that he might be willing to see me. Seren got her boy, Joel, to look on Nigel's Facebook and he located your house from the posts Nigel had put on there. And Joel went and saw Nigel there.'

'I know,' I said. 'I'm so sorry for how he reacted. That must have hurt.'

She nodded slowly. I could see in her face the pain that rejection had caused.

'Nigel never mentioned it in his letters to me,' she went on. 'But they kept coming. I knew I had to accept that that was all he would give me – all I deserved to have of my son.'

'No one deserves to be rejected by their child like that.' My words surprised me with their fierceness. 'It wasn't your fault. You weren't well.'

'And then I was well again.' She spoke slowly, almost meditatively. 'But fifteen years later, it was Nigel who was sick. He wrote to me then as well. He told me what was happening. But he still didn't want to see me. I never got to say goodbye.'

'I'm sorry, Louisa.' I put my hand over hers. 'So sorry for the loss of your son.'

She looked down, then back up at me, and she smiled.

'There was one last letter, though,' she said. 'Nigel wrote it before he passed away, and I received it afterwards. I think you should read it.'

She lifted her hand from under mine, slowly and carefully as if I was a sleeping child she didn't want to wake. Then she lifted the brown envelope and tipped its contents into her lap. It was packed so tightly she had to shake it to release the envelopes inside, and there were so many of them that they overflowed her lap and cascaded to the floor.

Many of them were worn and smudged with finger marks, I noticed with a stab of pain, as if they had been opened and reread many, many times.

But one was still new and pristine: a plain white DL envelope with the address here in Merthyr Adwen written on it in Gray's familiar hand.

The letter wasn't handwritten, though – it was typed and had been printed out. The single sheet of paper fluttered as Louisa handed it to me, because her hand was trembling.

Dear Mam

By the time you read this, it will all be over. I have asked our neighbour, a friend who I trust, to post it for me once I am gone, and by the time you read it, it will be too late for me to unmake the decision I made all those years ago.

At the time, it felt like it was the only decision I could have made. I didn't want to be Nigel any more: the boy with the chaotic home life, the charity case at school, the one who had only one friend. I wanted to be someone else, and I suppose now I am.

But not for much longer. In a few days I will leave the home I have made with Anna and go to the place where I will die. I'll leave behind everything I wanted when I turned my back on you – my family, my house, my career. It is a long time since I heard anyone call me Nigel, and soon I will hear someone call me Gray, the name I chose, for the final time.

Death has a way of focusing the mind, that's for sure. When I first told Anna I had no mother – that you had died when I was barely out of my teens – it felt like the only way for me to move past my old life. But when I met Joel on the Underground that time and he told me about his illness, I knew that there was something else I could do. I could create an anchor – a link to the past that could be broken only when one of us died. I assumed it would be Joel, but things don't always work out how you expect.

Now, though, I find myself looking back at those decisions and wondering why. What was the point? I could have explained to Anna, when I knew you were recovering, why I had lied to her, and she would have understood. I might have been afraid to let you into my children's lives at first, but that could have changed. I could have played the piano again, shared that with my Barney, who I think will be a fine musician one day.

I could have had a family that wasn't built on a lie.

It's too late now for any of that. If Anna finds you, show her this letter and let her decide what to do: to let our children continue to believe the falsehood I told, or to reveal to them who their father really was and where he came from.

I am sorry. I will always be your son.

Nigel

As I looked down at the page, a tear dropped from my eye, staining and wrinkling the paper.

'I'm sorry.' Hastily, I thrust it back towards Louisa.

But she said, 'I've cried on it enough myself, Anna. A few more tears won't make any difference.'

I sniffed and half-laughed, taking the letter back and gazing again at the lines of type, so hard they blurred before my eyes.

'Take your time,' she went on. 'Have another cup of tea.'

She poured more tea into my mug, then stood up and returned to her music stand. A few moments later, the first notes of music drifted into the humble room, falling as softly and gently into the silence as my tears were dropping down on to the page.

FIFTY-TWO

LAUREL

As we rounded a bend in the trail, a gust of wind caught my bike, and I had to brace my arms to stay on course as I felt the rain buffet the side of my face. It was no longer coming directly into my eyes, though, so at least I could see the view ahead – the trail climbing steeply upwards before it curved again beyond a fairytale stone castle perched on the top of the hill we had been toiling up for the past twenty minutes.

The relative calm of the bay, the Airbnb apartment where I was staying and my faithful little car all felt a long way away – and so they were, about twenty miles by now. But they didn't feel as far away as London, where I knew the streets would be crammed with Christmas shoppers, lights twinkling in windows, everything urban and safe.

There was nothing cosy about this landscape. It was pure wilderness: the granite boulders that studded the sides of the track, the distant glint of a lake like a sheet of stainless steel under the grey sky, the fury of the wind in my ears almost drowning out the cry of a bird.

'What was that?' I called, sure my voice would be carried away before it could be heard.

But at the same moment, next to me, I heard Joel call out,

'Kestrel,' his arm briefly leaving the handlebars of his bike to point skywards.

I raised my streaming eyes and caught a glimpse of the bird, soaring in an effortless arc overhead, its trajectory apparently independent of the wind. Then I looked down again, my thighs burning as I powered on up the hill.

We reached the summit side by side. There'd been no competitiveness between us – no racing to see who could reach the top first. I didn't know the way, and he did, so at first I'd followed him, but later he'd slowed down and gestured for me to come alongside so he could more easily point out the sights as we passed them.

'That's Castell Coch over there.'

'We're just passing Aberfan now.'

'Sometimes I see otters in the river here.'

We hadn't seen any otters today, and before long the steepness of the ascent had made much more conversation than that impossible. But I was captivated by the beauty of the landscape surrounding us and exhilarated by the challenge of this long ride. If anything, the terrible weather created a sense of companionability – camaraderie, even – when a particularly fierce blast of wind brought us almost to a standstill and we fought to keep going up the ever-steepening slopes, catching each other's eyes and laughing as much as our breath would allow us to.

Now, cresting the hill where the ruined castle stood, we stopped, as if this was what we had agreed to do. I got off my bike, my leggings soaked through and my thighs feeling like jelly. The rain had eased but the wind was still fierce: I could see the dark clouds roiling above me, parting briefly to reveal a glimpse of blue then snapping closed again. Below us, the valley stretched away in rough waves like a choppy green sea.

'How far have we come?' I asked, when I'd got my breath back enough to say anything.

'About fifty kilometres.' He grinned. 'It gets harder after this. Coffee?'

'Oh my God, yes please.'

He took a thermos flask out of his bag and poured coffee into two plastic beakers, handing one to me. I stripped off my wet glove, wrapping my fingers around the cup for warmth, and took a sip. It was strong, sweet and scalding hot.

'KitKat?' I offered, rummaging in my own bag.

He grinned. 'My kind of performance nutrition.'

I handed him a bar and took one for myself, and we both stripped off the wrapping, simultaneously dunking the chocolate in our coffee before taking enormous bites.

'Hits the spot, right?' I asked, smiling.

'It does. Thank you.'

'Thank you for being such a great guide,' I said. 'This is spectacular.'

'I'd say December isn't the best time of year to experience it – but then again...'

'I can imagine it on a sunny day,' I mused. 'Blue sky, no wind...'

'You're in Wales,' he reminded me. 'Nothing's guaranteed.'

'True.' I laughed. 'But still – today... this – it's magical.'

'It's pretty special,' he agreed. 'When I come up here, it's like nothing else exists. Just me and the mountains.'

'I get that. It makes you feel—'

'Alive,' he said, at the same moment I did. Then he asked, 'What else makes you feel like this?'

'I guess,' I replied around the last of my KitKat, 'work. When I've had a long, knackering day but I know I've really made a difference. Seeing my friends – when we laugh so much we almost puke. You?'

'Music, obviously. Bertha, my dog.' He looked at me sideways and smiled. 'Sex.'

I laughed. 'Same. Can't knock it. But when you feel like this – I guess it must make you think of Gray.'

'It does.' His face turned sombre. 'Every time something happens and I think, God, this is wonderful, I know I've got him to thank for it.'

'Is it...' I began, then I tried again. 'Does it feel like a burden?'

He looked surprised. 'God, no. Not ever. There are a lot of people like me out there who've had a second chance of life, but not so many that it's common, you know? So when I think about it, I think how fucking lucky I am to be one of them. It's cheesy, but it makes me feel blessed.'

He held out his hand and I passed him my empty coffee cup, our cold fingers just touching.

'Do you want to go on, or go back?' he asked. 'It's almost two.'

'Maybe best to go back. Not sure I fancy this in the dark.'

'And besides' – he smiled – 'there's a great pub I know that has an open fire and does killer shepherd's pie.'

'Sold.'

We shouldered our bags again and mounted our bikes, turning back the way we had come. The wind was mostly behind us now, and the trail mostly downhill, so it took way less time to return than it had going out. Still, getting into a hot shower and then into clean, dry clothes in my Airbnb felt like heaven.

I met Joel just before seven at the pub, as we'd arranged. He'd showered and changed too; his dark hair was still damp, and he was wearing a navy-blue wool jumper the same colour as his eyes. He'd bought a bottle of wine and found a table right by the blazing fire. I joined him there, feeling the heat of the flames soak into me from the outside and the warmth of the wine from the inside.

There was another kind of warmth too. I looked at him, wondering if he was feeling it as well.

Then he said, 'You know, there's another thing I'm grateful to Nigel – to Gray – for.'

'What's that?'

'Meeting you,' he said.

FIFTY-THREE
ANNA

'This one's string's broken, Mum.' Barney held out a sparkly gold bauble for me to inspect. It was one of the cheap ones that Gray and I had bought at Woolworths the first year we were in the house, when it was a building site and we had no money, but we were so happy and in love we were determined to make Christmas magical in spite of those things.

Alongside the decorations we had accumulated since – the fancy glass ones, the artisan ones bought on various holidays abroad, even the ones hand-crafted by the children – it looked mass-produced and shabby. But it was part of our history, and it deserved its place on the magnificent Norwegian spruce tree that Barney had carried from the market and wrestled down the stairs, which was already in its place by the window, festooned with lights and laden with the contents of the boxes Lulu had brought down from the loft.

'There's some ribbon in my sewing kit,' I told him. 'We'll tie a bit on. It'll be fine. Run and fetch it.'

'Okay.' He headed for the stairs, then stopped halfway up. 'Where's your sewing kit?'

'Honestly.' I rolled my eyes in mock exasperation. 'Sometimes you behave like a weekend guest who arrived two hours ago, not someone who's lived in this house for thirteen years. It's in the bottom of the chest of drawers in my bedroom.'

'Sorry, Mum. I just wasn't sure...'

I smiled. 'Don't worry, darling. I understand.'

And I did. In the past year, the bedroom had been transformed into a hospital room and back again to a bedroom. For a while, 'my bedroom' hadn't been the room I'd shared with Gray but the spare room down the landing. And just recently, half of the things that had lived in the drawers and wardrobes had been sorted through and removed. Where Gray's stuff had been before, there was now empty space.

When I'd told Orla that it was about time I tackled the task, she offered to come and help.

'In case you need a hand. Or just some moral support. It won't be easy.'

I accepted gratefully. 'And I thought... This might sound weird, but I thought I might ask Laurel if she wants to come too. Just in case there's anything of Gray's she'd like to keep for herself.'

'I think that would be a kind thing to do.' Orla smiled approvingly.

So, on a Saturday morning when Lulu was at cheerleading and Barney was at football, the three of us had gone into the bedroom and tackled the job. The first part had been easy – there were rows of shirts from what Gray had called his 'fat period', which he'd kept as a kind of insurance policy, together with suits and jeans in the same sizes, and those went straight into a pile for the charity shop.

'It's so weird to think of Gray wearing these,' Laurel had said, holding up a shirt with a size-eighteen collar. 'I only ever knew him as... well, you know.'

She'd trailed off, as if worried that she had overstepped.

'Hey, it's okay.' I touched her arm. 'There are things here from before I knew him too. Like this.'

I pulled a tie out from the extensive collection Gray had amassed over the years – even though it was ages since he'd needed to wear one regularly. This wasn't silk like most of the others, but polyester, with wide maroon and narrow gold stripes against a navy-blue background. I'd never noticed it before – and certainly never seen him wear it. I peered at it more closely. On the wide end was a crest I recognised.

'Oh my God,' I said. 'It's his old school tie. From St Gwbert's.'

Laurel leaned in to look. 'I wonder if Joel still has his too.'

'He must have had some happy memories of that place.' I ran the tie through my fingers. 'Or he wouldn't have kept it.'

'The rest of them can go to charity, can't they?' Orla said. 'They're in perfect condition. Someone might want to buy the lot for an upcycling project – a cushion, or even a woman's skirt.'

I handed her the heavy bundle of rainbow-coloured silk, then sat down on the bed, still holding the old, cheap tie.

'I should send it to Louisa,' I decided. 'But I feel... I'd feel almost like I was fobbing her off, when I still haven't decided what to do about introducing her to the kids.'

'It's a big decision.' Laurel sat down next to me.

After our separate visits to Wales – she to see Joel, I to meet Louisa – we'd had a debrief over coffee. I'd told her about the letters Gray had written to his mother, all the cards and notes sent over the years, as well as the final one, which Orla had admitted posting after Gray's death as he'd asked. Laurel had told me about cycling on the Taff Trail with Joel, and said how much Gray would have loved it – but I sensed that there might be something else about that visit that she wasn't ready to confide in me.

I nodded. 'I think, if Gray was able to make the choice now, he'd probably want her to be in their lives somehow. They're older now and she lives far away. And her mental health is quite stable now. She won't damage them like she damaged Gray. And that wasn't even her fault, really. Poor woman.'

'Have you told them about her?' Laurel asked. 'I mean – that she wasn't dead after all?'

'I haven't. I know that if I did, they'd want to meet her – of course they would. She's their grandmother. They'd be curious, apart from anything else, and – well, it's a link to their father. It's an important thing.'

'Family and identity.' Orla removed a stack of suits from the wardrobe. 'Would you want to keep one of these for Barney, Anna? He'll grow into it in a couple of years.'

'Maybe the grey one. That was his favourite. What were you going to say – about family and identity?'

Orla sighed, laying the suits on the bed and turning back to the wardrobe. 'Just that they're important. And they're tied so closely to each other – especially for teenagers, who are just figuring out who they are. It was around then that Beatrice became so determined to track down her birth mother – me. If people don't know the full truth about their background, it makes it harder for them to grow into themselves. And secrets are harmful.'

Her back was to me, but I saw her shoulders rise and fall in another long sigh. I knew that she was thinking not only about Barney and Lulu and the secret I was considering keeping from them, but also about something else – something closer to her own heart.

'Which of these need doing?' Laurel moved over to the chest of drawers and opened the top one – the one where Gray's socks lived. I remembered with a flash of sadness how I had found the earrings Gray bought for her in there, all those months ago. I would never tell her how that had made me feel – although I was fairly sure she could guess.

'They wouldn't have to meet her if they didn't want to,' she went on. 'Or if they met and didn't get on, it could kind of run its natural course, if you know what I mean.'

'You're right.' I pulled out a bundle of socks and pants. 'These may as well all go straight into the textile recycling. After all, older kids don't see their grandparents that often. They only spend a few days a year with my mum and dad.'

'It's not really about what Gray would have wanted any more,' Orla pointed out, turning back to the wardrobe and lifting out a sheaf of casual shirts on their hangers. 'He made his choice. And from what you've said, he regretted it – but he couldn't go back on it until it was too late. It's about what *you* want, Anna, and what you think is best for those children.'

I removed a pale pink linen shirt from her arms. 'I'll keep this for Lulu. She used to nick it and wear it as a beach cover-up when we were on holiday. It's – for me, anyway, being in touch with Louisa is also about having another part of Gray in my life. I know it sounds selfish, but—'

'It's not selfish at all, Anna,' Laurel assured me.

'And speaking of which,' I said, 'you're not just here to work. If there's anything of his you'd like to keep, you must say.'

She shook her head. 'I don't think so. Thanks, Anna. I'm so grateful you asked. Except, maybe...'

While she was speaking, I'd opened the next drawer down, which held Gray's cycling clothes – the endless pairs of padded-seat leggings and Lycra jumpers that always used to make the kids say, 'Oh look, it's Bradley Wiggins,' when Gray came downstairs dressed for a ride.

'Maybe what?' I asked.

Tentatively, she reached out and took one of the cycling tops from the pile. It wasn't even a particularly nice one – just a regular long-sleeved red jersey in technical fabric, with a half-zip down the front.

'Maybe this?'

I looked doubtfully at the top, then at Laurel's narrow shoulders and slim waist. It had been tight on Gray, but it would be ridiculously baggy on her.

'Are you sure? Of course, you're welcome to it. But isn't there something else you'd like? A watch or something?'

She shook her head. 'It wouldn't actually be for me. It would be for Joel.'

Understanding dawning, I'd handed over the top, and Laurel had blushed like a teenager.

'Mum,' Lulu said now. 'Come on. Are we going to finish decorating this tree or are you going to stand there staring into space?'

'Sorry, darling. I was miles away.'

I heard the thump of Barney's trainers on the stairs as he returned with a scrap of ribbon, which I secured to the bauble.

'Just the star now,' I said. 'Which of you wants to do that?'

They looked at each other. When the kids were small, Gray used to lift one of them up – first Lulu, then each in turn for a few years, then Barney when Lulu got too big – and hold them up high while they secured the sparkling gold star to the top of the tree. Then they'd both got too big for that, and Gray had done it himself.

'I reckon this'll be the last year I'm taller than you,' Lulu said.

'You go for it, then.' Barney grinned. 'Just don't mess it up.'

Lulu didn't. She stood on a chair and reached up high and secured the star to the topmost branch of the tree, and then we switched on the lights.

'Good job.' I pulled them both close to me and held them for as long as they'd let me, the lights flickering softly on their faces.

Then Barney pulled away from me and said, 'Mum.'

'What is it, sweetheart?'

'Are we still going to leave a mince pie and a glass of sherry out for Santa on Christmas Eve?'

I thought for a moment. That had been another of Gray's tasks – last thing before the children went to bed, the plate and glass would be carefully arranged on the kitchen table. They hadn't believed properly in Father Christmas for years now, but the ritual had continued.

'Of course we are,' I told them. 'Last thing we want is a pissed-off Santa, right? We'll do it together.'

They both laughed, hiding their relief that this memory of their father would be kept alive for as long as they needed it.

Then I said, 'Come on, let's put the kettle on and make some hot chocolate. There's something I want to talk to you both about.'

'Is it about Dad?' Lulu asked doubtfully, at the same time as her brother asked, 'Can we have marshmallows?'

'Of course we can. And yes, it's kind of about your dad. But mostly it's about your grandmother – your dad's mam.'

FIFTY-FOUR

ORLA

24 December 2024

It is early morning on Christmas Eve, and I am sitting here alone in my kitchen with the cats. The sun will not be up for another half an hour, and Damask Square is dark and silent. When I opened the front door earlier to put food out for the birds, I stood there for a moment in the stillness of a winter wonderland, frost glinting on the railings of the square and the branches of the trees, a few lights twinkling bravely in the darkness, the distant sound of traffic on the main road still barely a hum.

Then a robin trilled its first, urgent call and the day had begun.

Last night, Anna held the pre-Christmas drinks party that has been hosted at number eight for the past fifteen years. The house was as full of people as ever: our neighbours, Anna's sisters and their families, friends of Anna's and of Gray's – all the faces I have seen there over the years, all gathered there to give the Graham family their love and support.

It was brave of her, without Gray – I know she and the children will be feeling his absence more keenly than ever at this time of year, when we are constantly reminded of what families are and what they mean.

But she and the children seem to be finding their way in their new unit of three. Barney showed me the piano his mother had bought him for an early Christmas present, in pride of place at the centre of the room, Augustus the cat asleep on its lid. Lulu was passing round the sausage rolls she'd made using her father's recipe. Anna offered me a taste of her cranberry mocktail.

It's not so bad, she said with a half-laugh. Fifty-nine days off the booze and I'm getting used to it now.

I had arrived with Laurel, who told me she was shy about turning up on her own.

She said to Anna, Actually, I'd love one of those. I'm not drinking either.

We looked at her, Anna and I, with curiosity and then dawning understanding.

I know. She laughed nervously. It's mad. I'm forty-three.

And it all came spilling out. She hasn't told him yet – Joel Chamberlain, the man she would never have met were it not for her relationship with Gray and his death. The man with the genetic condition that necessitated a kidney transplant; the condition which if Laurel has a son he will be safe from, and if she has a daughter she will carry.

I don't know what Joel's going to say, Laurel told us. The excitement shone out of her and I feel optimistic for her. Laurel is a resilient woman – alone or in a partnership with this man I hope will fall in love with her as she is falling in love with him, she will make the best of it.

The way she feels, the way I can see Anna feels – resolutely carrying on, greeting each day without the man they loved, coming to terms with his flaws and his secrets and his death – fills me with awe at the strength of women. I feel confident too that when Anna introduces Gray's mother to the family, her own strength will add to Anna's and help her and her children understand what made Gray the man he was.

I am filled with hope as I meet this new day, thinking of Gray's reinvention of himself and the family it allowed him to create, of the grandmother Barney and Lulu will soon meet, of Laurel's excitement as she moves into a new and unknown phase of her life, of my own daughter, Beatrice, who will be arriving here later today – even of that robin singing its heart out in the darkness of Damask Square.

There was singing last night too. Barney took his seat at the piano, glowing with pride, and Lulu stood by his side. The room fell silent as his hands alighted on the keys and he began to play.

Gray used to sing this to them when they were babies, Laurel whispered to me. Joel sent me an English translation of the lyrics. It's a lullaby and a funeral song, but also a Christmas song.

Every star in heaven is singing
All through the night,
Hear the glorious music ringing
All through the night.

Barney's voice was pure and true, Lulu's less so, but she did her best.

Look, my love, the stars are smiling
All through the night.

FIFTY-FIVE
LAUREL

Leaning over my handlebars, I felt my thighs begin to burn as the gradient got steeper. It was six months since I'd last cycled this route but, despite that, it felt familiar. Already, I could see the castle ahead. My muscle memory seemed to recall the series of bends in the path, like a child's drawing of a snake; I even instinctively altered course to avoid a rough area on the surface of the track.

In terms of conditions, it should have felt much easier than last time. The day was clear – glancing over my shoulder, I was able to appreciate the panorama of valleys and peaks, illuminated by warm sunshine in a blue sky. The wind was gentle, so staying on course was easy. It was warm, but not so hot as to present a challenge.

But my body had other ideas. My balance as I stood in the pedals was awkward, my centre of mass not where I expected it to be. My lung capacity felt reduced. A few miles back, I'd had to stop because the toes in my left foot had suddenly been seized by cramp.

Now that the summit was in reach, though, I felt freshly energised. I could feel the blood surging through me, being taken by my pounding heart to the muscles that needed it. The balmy air flowed smoothly into my lungs. My hands felt relaxed and agile, not like frozen lumps of meat as they had last time.

I reached the summit easily, swung out of the saddle and stood taking in the view. Seconds later, Joel joined me. He was wearing the red Lycra top that had been Gray's.

'What's with the burst of speed, Victoria Pendleton? Aren't you meant to be taking it easy?'

'Taking what easy?' I laughed, pulling off my helmet to feel the breeze in my sweaty hair. 'I'm pregnant, not incapacitated.'

'There I was thinking you'd want to spend your visit resting up, being brought cups of tea and having your feet massaged,' he grumbled, unclipping his water bottle and handing it to me.

'I mean, now you mention it, I wouldn't say no to a cup of tea and a foot massage. Maybe tomorrow.'

He slipped his arm round my waist, and I leaned into him, the damp heat of his body meeting mine. Just the same as before, I knew that in the distance, out of sight, my little car was waiting, ready to take me back to London. But this time – as it had been the past few times I'd visited – it was parked outside Joel's house, not at an Airbnb. Just as when he came to London, he now stayed with me, not at the fancy hotels where he'd told me he'd always felt uncomfortable.

It was on the first of those visits, in January, that I'd told him I was pregnant.

'This is just as weird for me as it's going to be for you,' I'd said, sitting across from him at a coffee shop in the Barbican Centre. 'Whatever you want to do is fine with me. But I felt I should let you know right away.'

He looked at me, puzzled at first and then with dawning understanding. 'You're not...?'

I nodded. 'Sorry. It really wasn't meant to happen. To be honest, I feel like a right chump. But also...'

His face lit up in a smile. 'Delighted? Because I am. Or I think I will be, once this has had a chance to sink in.'

'I mean, you can be as involved as you want to be,' I gabbled.

'And if you want a relationship with the baby, that doesn't mean you have to have one with me. I'll completely understand if you don't. It was just the one night – we hardly know each other.'

'I can think of a really good way to fix that.' He reached across the table and took my hand. 'I want to get to know you better, Laurel. I want to be in your life and this child's life. I think we can try and figure this out.'

And so we'd tried – we were still trying. Between my work and Joel's, between my commitments in London and his in Cardiff and abroad, we couldn't spend much time together. But what we could was precious, and it made me happy in ways I thought I'd never experience again after Gray's death.

I didn't know whether our relationship would work out. It was still too new; we were still only beginning to get to know each other. But I knew that even if it didn't, I wanted my child to have the things that Joel would be able to give him or her – music, these mountains and valleys, his own intense appreciation of the life he had because Gray had given it to him.

He reached out a hand and caressed my cheek. 'Shall we go on, or go back?'

'Oh, let's go on, this time.' I smiled up at him, loving the way his eyes mirrored the intense blue of the sky.

Except suddenly, the sky wasn't blue any more. As if from nowhere, a heavy black cloud had blotted out the sun. A gust of wind felt chilly against my damp skin. Almost immediately, heavy drops of rain began to fall.

'What the hell is this?' I asked, laughing.

'Welcome to Wales,' he said. 'When you can see the mountains, it's going to rain. When you can't see them, it's raining.'

'But I didn't bring a jacket. It looked glorious when we set off this morning.'

'Just as well I brought a spare one for you.'

'You did?'

'Sure. I'd have told you to bring your own, but then it wouldn't have rained, and you'd have said…'

'I'm only pregnant, I'm not going to dissolve.'

'Exactly.' We laughed and kissed, the falling rain beginning to soak through my clothes before he enveloped me in a too-large waterproof jacket.

'Still want to carry on?' he asked.

'For sure. KitKat first?'

I offered him one and we ate quickly and hungrily. Then we swung on to our bikes and set off, slowly at first and then faster as the track levelled off, heading onwards and upwards instead of down and back.

FIFTY-SIX
ANNA

The final notes of 'You and I' swelled into the stillness of the auditorium, the black-and-white chequered stage set seeming to glow under the lights. Then the hall erupted into rapturous applause, whoops and wolf whistles threatening to send the roof soaring up into the balmy June night.

The cast and chorus tumbled on to the stage, tired and jubilant, looking like secondary school pupils again instead of the passionate performers they'd been for the past two hours. But I wasn't looking at them. I was looking at my son, his hands still suspended over the piano keys, his hair damp with sweat, a grin of disbelieving delight beginning to spread over his face.

Then the girl who'd played Svetlana hopped off the stage, seized his hand and pulled him up to join the others as they basked in applause.

It was only a school adaptation of an old West End musical, but – if I said so myself – the kids had done *Chess* proud. All Barney's late-night rehearsals, all my fretting about whether he was neglecting his studies in favour of this, all the times I'd come down to find the kitchen in carnage thanks to his midnight scrambled-egg making, were worth it to see the glow of pride and achievement on his face now.

'That was glorious.' Next to me, Louisa was still dabbing her eyes. 'I can't believe that was my grandson up there.'

Since before Christmas, when I first told the children they had another grandmother, we'd navigated this new relationship with caution. Lulu and Barney were old enough to understand about mental health struggles, although Gray's denial of his mother's existence had been harder for them to get their heads around.

'Why would he do that, Mum?' Barney had asked. 'I can't imagine deciding I didn't want to see *you* again – not ever.'

I snuggled him closer to me. 'I hope you never do. It must have been an incredibly painful decision for Dad to make. But he was only young, remember – only a couple of years older than Lulu. And he wanted to name you after her, didn't he, sweetheart? That meant a lot to him.'

'I wish we could ask him about it,' Lulu had said. 'There's so much we didn't know about him.'

'I know,' I said. 'But there's also so much we've found out.'

When I took the children to Wales to meet Louisa over the Easter break, we'd all felt awkward and nervous. Louisa made tea and showed the children the cards and letters Gray had sent her over the years, and they had marvelled over the news of Gray's graduation, our wedding and their own births, told in their father's words.

'I felt almost as if I knew you,' Louisa had said sadly. 'But I never thought I would get to meet you properly.'

Tentatively, she suggested that they might like to attend the Easter church service at the chapel, and to my surprise they had agreed. The choir had sung 'Guide Me, O Thou Great Redeemer', and although the tune was familiar to us, the Welsh lyrics had made it feel less religious and more... spiritual, somehow.

I'd found myself moved to tears then, as I had been earlier tonight when I'd had to stifle a sob during 'I Know Him So Well', and Lulu had passed me a tissue before gripping my hand and not letting it go until the song finished.

'My baby brother,' she said now. 'Not bad for a smelly little kid.'

'He did so well.' I blew my nose. 'He was so nervous earlier, I was terrified for him.'

On Louisa's other side, I saw Orla smile. 'Sometimes you've just got to let them take the leap and watch them fly.'

Then Louisa whispered something to her, and she said, 'We'll see you outside. We're just going to...'

The two of them edged their way along the row of seats, presumably heading off to find the ladies' before the queue got too bad.

'Mum.' Lulu leaned in close to me. 'You know the guy who was playing Freddie?'

'Wasn't he amazing? One of the mums said on the WhatsApp group he's going to RADA next year.'

'He asked me out.' She smiled shyly.

'He did? What did you say?'

'I said I'd think about it. But if he asks again I might say yes. He's hot, right? And nice. Not up himself at all.'

I smiled down at her glowing, excited face. 'I'm not sure being in a relationship with an actor would be the easiest thing, you know.'

'Mum! Steady on. We're talking a movie and a pizza, not marriage.'

I laughed. 'Just as well. I don't want you marrying anyone any time soon.'

'Good, because I'm not going to.'

The third curtain call was coming to an end. The audience was still on its feet, but the clapping was dying down, everyone's hands presumably smarting as much as my own were. The drama teacher, who'd joined the pupils on stage to share in the applause, had presented bouquets to the lead performers and one to Barney, who was holding it clumsily as if he'd never seen flowers before.

Lulu and I joined the stream of people making their way to the exit. Parents who I couldn't recall ever speaking to before approached me to congratulate me on my son's achievement, and I saw Lulu bask in reflected glory, selflessly happy for her brother.

Several said, 'Your husband would have been so proud.'

I said, 'Thank you. Yes, he would.'

Would he? Of course. Surely seeing his son excel, finding a gift that everyone seemed to think had come out of nowhere, would have delighted Gray. Perhaps it would even have helped him rediscover the talent he had turned his back on.

But then, if Gray had still been alive, perhaps Barney would never have found music at all.

At last, we emerged from the stuffy hall into the cool night. The crowd seemed to be making its way in the direction of the white-clothed table laden with bottles, where the PTA was doing a roaring trade in Pimm's and Prosecco.

I was relieved to notice that I didn't want a drink – not one bit.

Lulu and I took our water bottles out of our bags and drank, moving together away from the crowds, finding a bench on the edge of the playing field where we sat to wait for Orla and Louisa.

'Mum.' Her voice was hesitant. 'Can I ask you something?'

'Of course.' I steeled myself for her question: would she find her calling in life like Barney had found his? I was sure she would – she already had a summer internship arranged at the hospital where Laurel worked, and was confident that she'd smashed her mock A-levels. Did I still miss Gray? Yes, I did, and I always would. Was Jordan – the boy who'd played Freddie – as right for her as Callum had been wrong? I had no idea – that, she would have to discover for herself.

But I hadn't prepared myself for the question she did ask.

'Mum. Were Dad and Laurel sleeping together?'

Six months earlier, I might have lied. The loss of her father would have been too recent to tarnish his memory; my own anger too fresh to prevent me exposing it to my daughter; my jealousy of Laurel too intense to admit anything that might push my daughter further away from me.

Then, I might still have believed that some truths were better kept hidden.

Now, I felt differently. The secrets that had clouded Gray's entire adult life, the lies he had told me, the damage done to him in childhood that had made him the man he had been, had caused enough harm. It was time to break their power.

'Yes,' I said. 'Yes, they were.'

'Was Dad in love with her?'

'I think so. Or I think he thought so.'

'Would he have left us?'

I sighed. 'I don't know, darling. I think probably not. I think he loved us all too much for that. And I don't think Laurel would have wanted it either.'

'Would you have kicked him out?'

I managed a trembly laugh. 'That's what you're supposed to do, isn't it? Get your ducks in a row, leave the bastard. But I'm not sure about that, either. And we'll never know, will we?'

'Being an adult is shit, isn't it?' Her mouth was drooping at the corners like a sad-face emoji.

I reached for her hand and gripped it fiercely. 'No. It's complicated, that's for sure. But it's wonderful. Look at everything I've got – you, Barney, Augustus, the house, your nanna – all of that is thanks to your dad.'

'So you don't mind any more?'

'About Laurel? No, I don't. She's a good person, and your dad was too. And Louisa. But sometimes good people do bad things, and it's how you deal with them that really matters.'

'You mind about Dad dying, though, don't you?' she asked.

'Oh, yes. I'll always mind about that.'

I put my arm around her and pulled her close to me, feeling her hair tickle my lips as I kissed her silken head.

Then we got to our feet and walked slowly away together to find Barney, Orla and Louisa and make our way back to Damask Square.

A LETTER FROM THE AUTHOR

Huge thanks for reading *All the Things We Never Knew*. If you'd like to be kept up to date on my future releases, please take a moment to sign up to my author newsletter.

www.stormpublishing.co/sophie-ranald

As always, please take a moment to leave a review on Amazon and connect with me on social media – I'd love to hear from you.

I do hope you have enjoyed reading *All the Things We Never Knew*. Writing it has been a process full of ups and downs, early starts and late nights as I faced up to the challenge of taking my characters on their fraught and complex emotional journeys.

If you would like to read more about Orla and how she came to live on Damask Square, do check out *All Our Missing Pieces*.

And, as always, thank you from the bottom of my heart for giving your time to read this novel.

Much love,

Sophie

www.sophieranald.com

instagram.com/sophieranald
facebook.com/SophieRanald

ACKNOWLEDGEMENTS

There are some books that glide almost effortlessly out of my keyboard, leaving me with a sense of happy accomplishment at the end of each day. It's fair to say that this book was not one of those. The journey from initial concept to final draft has been tortuous and at times I felt like giving up and hurling my laptop out of the nearest window!

Fortunately, I was able to turn to my wonderful editor at Storm, Claire Bord, when it all got too much. Claire's support during the process of writing and editing *All the Things We Never Knew* has been invaluable, from listening to me moan to offering ideas that rescued me from sticky plot holes to relentlessly scrutinising every line of every draft to make it as good as it could possibly be. Thank you, Claire, from the bottom of my heart.

Also at Storm, I have had the support of a brilliant team: Founder Oliver Rhodes, Editorial Operations Director Alexandra Begley, Publicity Manager Anna McKerrow, Head of Digital Marketing Elke Desanghere, Digital Operations Director Chris Lucraft and Assistant Editor Naomi Knox. Copyeditor Andy Richards and proofreader Becca Allen ironed out any remaining wrinkles in the manuscript, Rose Cooper designed the gorgeous cover and Sarah Durham's audio narration has brought my characters to life. Thank you all.

The nature of this story has meant including a certain amount of medical detail. While I didn't want to bog readers down in what can be a depressing subject, I did want to ensure that this element of the novel was as accurate as possible. So I am hugely grateful to my friends Rache and Carole for generously sharing their expertise in this field – any errors are of course my own.

Thanks as always go to the amazing Alice Saunders and her colleagues at The Soho Agency and to my beloved crew at home – my partner, Hopi, and cats, Purrs and Hither.

Made in United States
North Haven, CT
08 October 2025

80552023R00176